'Heartwarming and mysterious with great atmosphere'
Katie Fforde

'Beautifully written and atmospheric'
The Sun

Readers love

Daniela SACERDOTI

'Beautifully written. A great book'

'Emotional.
It made me thin
put it down'

Praise for

Daniela SACERDOTI

'Heartwarming and intriguing' Dani Atkins

'I fell in love with this book' *Prima* magazine

'Beautifully written. A great book' Lesley Pearse

'I was hooked from the beginning' Alice Peterson

'Emotional. Mysterious. It made me think and I couldn't put it down' *Daily Mail*

'Heartwarming and mysterious with great atmosphere'
Katie Fforde

'Beautifully written and atmospheric' *The Sun*

'Will satisfy even the most hopeless romantics. Her descriptions of the idyllic, wild isle are evocative and vivid' *Daily Express*

'A poignant read' *Woman's Own*

'Sacerdoti writes beautiful fiction that feeds the soul'
Shari Low, *Daily Record*

'Such a beautifully written book. Fills you with hope'
Rea's Book Reviews

Daniela Sacerdoti is a phenomenon.

Over one million copies of her novels have been sold in ebook, her debut novel *Watch Over Me* was the eighth bestselling Kindle book of all time in 2015 and she was also ranked as the eleventh top-selling Kindle author. Daniela writes fiction for adults (the Glen Avich series), young adults (the Sarah Midnight trilogy) and children. Her novels have been translated into twelve languages.

Daniela was born and raised in Italy. She studied Classics, then lived in Scotland for fourteen years, where she married and taught in a primary school. Daniela's children's book *Really Weird Removals.com* was shortlisted for the Scottish Children's Book Awards. She has also written for the BBC. Daniela, her husband and their two sons make their home in a tiny village in the Alps.

To discover more about Daniela and her world, visit www.danielasacerdoti.com or find her on Twitter @danisacerdoti.

By Daniela Sacerdoti and available from Headline

Seal Island Series
Keep Me Safe
I Will Find You
Come Back to Me

E-Shorts
Your Hand In Mine
Calling You Home

Also by Daniela Sacerdoti

Glen Avich Quartet
Watch Over Me
Take Me Home
Set Me Free
Don't Be Afraid

Sarah Midnight Trilogy
Dreams
Tide
Spirit

Really Weird Removals.com

Daniela
SACERDOTI

Come Back to Me

First published in Great Britain in 2019 by
HEADLINE REVIEW
An imprint of HEADLINE PUBLISHING GROUP

1

Cataloguing in Publication Data is available from the British Library

ISBN 978 1 4722 3511 4

Map illustration by Laura Hall

Typeset in Baskerville MT Std 12.5/15.5 by Jouve (UK), Milton Keynes

Printed and bound in Great Britain by Clays Ltd, Elcograf S.p.A.

Headline's policy is to use papers that are natural, renewable and recyclable products and made from wood grown in well-managed forests and other controlled sources. The logging and manufacturing processes are expected to conform to the environmental regulations of the country of origin.

HEADLINE PUBLISHING GROUP
An Hachette UK Company
Carmelite House
50 Victoria Embankment
London EC4Y 0DZ

www.headline.co.uk
www.hachette.co.uk

To Sorley, my dreamer – magical, clever, kind.
To Luca, my musician – deep, loyal, loving.
I didn't just make you, you made me.

Seal Island
Grace's Cottage
Fergus's Cottage
Molleson Cottage
Seal Distillery
N
W
E
S
CORRYWRECKAN
Whirlpool
OLLABERRY
MAINLAND
this way
INIS ROAN
Island of the Seals
Sorren's Cottage
Sea Rescue
Catriona's Cottage
Stella Maris

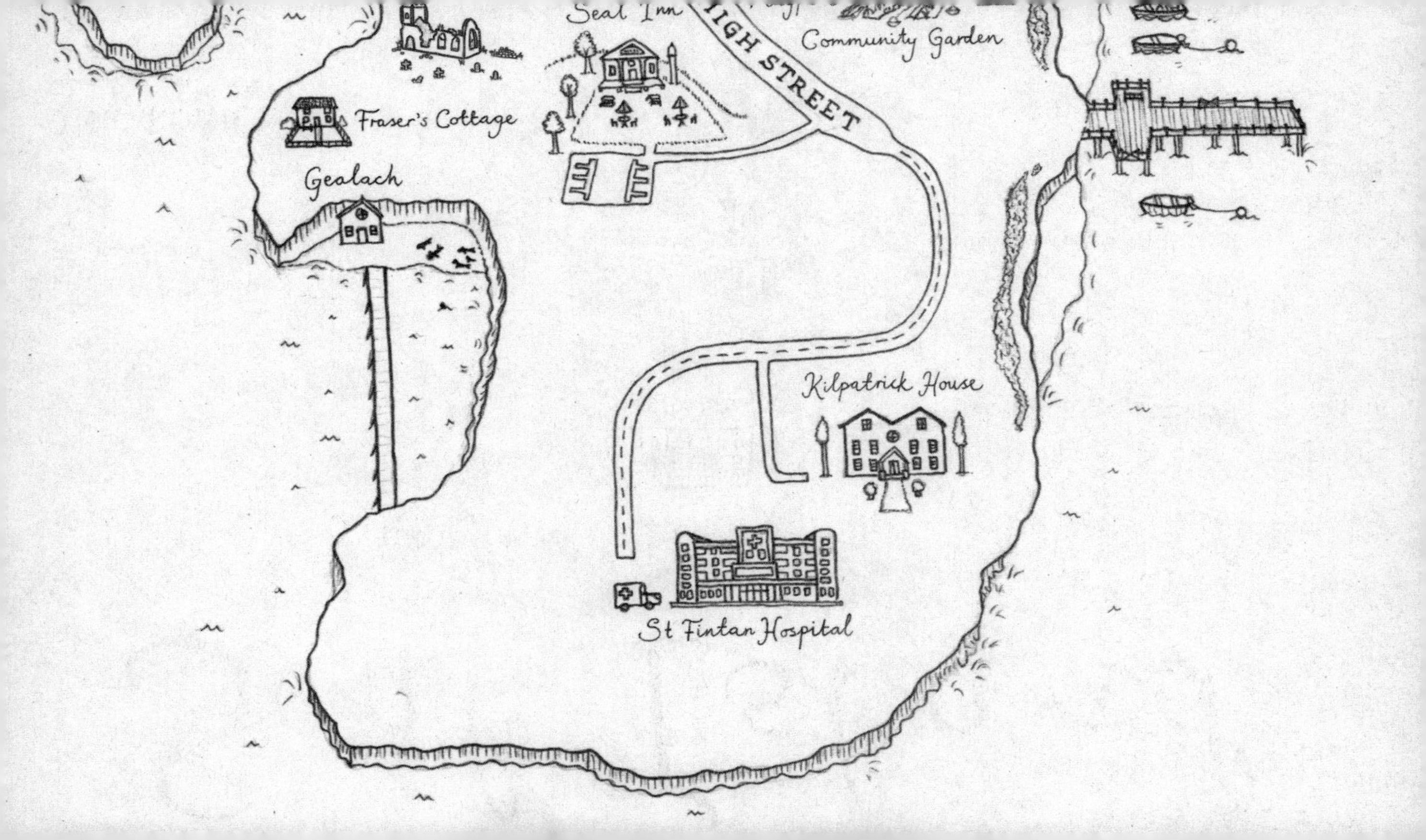
Seal Inn
IGH STREET
Community Garden
Fraser's Cottage
Gealach
Kilpatrick House
St Fintan Hospital

I have cooled the flames of summer,
Her red fires soothed in ice.
Light's anvil now sleeps in silence,
A foundry of dark and brittle dreams.

I have whispered songs in autumn's ear,
Berried notes of frosted airs.
She sits by the hearth now, sewing.
Her blanket of leaves, unfinished.

Solemn and still are watchful stars.
All is as should be, a cold, wordless peace.
My bones ache now *child*, having carried you far
I must rest awhile on white sands, adrift on the wind.

Sleep now Mother, dream in night's dark ocean
The hum of works stirs within, a waking heartbeat.
For you I will weave a dress of bluebells and violets,
A wren's nest, a crown for your silver hair.

Ross Walker, 'Winter and Spring'

Prologue

Rose

Where am I?

What do I remember? I list my memories, like an inventory of all things me. White hands resting on jeans-clad legs. Swings moving in the wind. Rain. Freezing rain. Boots in a puddle, step after step, a place full of mirrors and music. Running down the street, cold air all around me. Branches in the wind, buttered toast, warmth, something pink and gossamer-thin hanging in my room, like a cloud . . . Little girl asleep, little girl lost. Somewhere in this blackness there's a path, a path that leads back to me. I must find the way. I must take the first step. The first step is a memory . . .

My room. Dolls on a shelf, dancing lights. A magic lantern.

But where am I now? I toss and turn, there are sounds and pain, and something cold is poured inside me. Calm returns. Slowly, slowly. Don't get upset, remember, it will come.

Dark walls, the floating images of my magic lantern,

the warmth of blankets, and a soft voice. My brother's voice. I can see his face, and every feature of it makes my child's heart sing with contentment. With him, I am safe. My eyelids fall, and his voice seems to come from far away as sleep claims me slowly, slowly. His words take shape in my memory –

dark,
danger,
lost,
monster,
thread,
safe,
daylight,
girl.

The words fall onto me like rain, and I piece them together. Jacob is telling me a story, one he's told me many times before, because I couldn't have enough of it. Yes, I remember the familiar words cradling me like a lullaby . . . A girl, a labyrinth, a monster. She searches for the right path and leaves the red thread behind her, like a spider spins her silk. The monster is after her and she runs, she runs. The story has an ancient flavour, it fascinates me, and I want to hear it every night, which is why the book sits on my bedside table, the image on the front cover vivid in my memory: a goddess running, a white deer beside her, the full moon in the sky and a little moon on her forehead. Artemis, the goddess of hunting. It's a book of Greek myths and we love it, Jacob and I.

My brother's voice is clear in my memory and this moment is limpid, as if it happened yesterday, while the rest of my life is blurry and vague and tangled up like unspun wool. A thin red thread in my mind, rootless and flickering, for a girl with no body and no identity. I grab the thread and follow my brother's voice. Maybe I'll find my way out of here . . .

There is a light, a blinding light that interrupts my thoughts. I cry inside, I try to squirm and move, but my body doesn't comply. I don't want this light hurting my eyes, I don't want these black shadows over me. I want to go back to where I was, I want to go back to Jacob. Please, *go away* . . . and they do, and I can start my work again at last – my work of casting the red thread that will lead me out of the labyrinth, like the girl in the myth.

Here we go.

I remember . . . I was a child listening to a story, lying in a warm bed. I open my eyes and again I find my brother's face, dark and sweet with his hazelnut eyes and his dark curly hair, and beyond him a magic lantern dancing on the walls, turning, turning; a golden light in the far corner, shaded with cream fabric; the dark window with a smattering of raindrops on the glass; a small, fluffy pink thing that seems to be floating in front of the wardrobe. This is my room, white furniture and light blue walls and a duvet decorated with butterflies. My parents gave me the room of my dreams, exactly like I wanted it. This was back when we were all together, my parents, Jacob and I, and I was still the centre of their world. And there, hanging from the wardrobe door, is my tutu – so that's what the pink fluffy cloud was! Yes. That seems like an important recollection – my *tutu*. The happiness I felt when I wore it . . .

The red thread of memory flickers in the darkness, and I follow. The little girl I used to be loved dancing, and I went to a special place to do it, somewhere full of mirrors, where piano music played. I'd just graduated from the white leotard the younger children wore to the pink one with a tulle skirt – a milestone for me. Here comes another memory – oh please, don't interrupt me now, no lights, no voices! I can see myself on a stage with many other girls, and a boy, I think. I am a slight, small girl with hair in a bun, dressed in white. We're like a line of angels. A young woman plays the piano, and we dance. The sound of applause, and I know my family are there, in the audience, though the lights shine in my eyes and I can't see them. We bow, and then the lights come on.

On the piano there is a pile of medals painted gold, with red ribbons. The young woman – the teacher – calls us one by one to receive them. Finally it is my turn. She must have spoken my name, but I can only see her lips moving. I run towards her with a smile. She slips the medal around my neck, and a wave of happiness washes over me – then, and now too, as I remember. A golden sphere of light shines inside my brain so lost, so lost. I remember what it's like to be happy. Happiness, joy, comfort, *shelter* – yes, that is who I was, that is how my life was. I was a girl enchanted, a girl who had nothing to cry about, nothing to fear.

And then I turn towards the audience, and I see him standing alone. My brother Jacob. My mum and dad are nowhere to be seen, I don't know why. Jacob is standing against the wall, away from the others. And when we are finally released and run to our families, I run to him. I show him the medal, the red ribbon threaded in his fingers . . .

All of a sudden, behind my closed eyes, things happen. People move, shadows dance, lights appear and move, then disappear again. I hear voices and noises, and from the left of me come words of alarm, together with a beeping voice. And I'm not there any more – for a moment, all is black and I don't exist. Am I dead? Is this the end of everything? I soar over land and sea, in a sky full of stars. And then one of the stars comes circling me, circling me, and I see her face. I hear her voice.

The star has a face – she's a woman, long blond hair and blue eyes, just a little older than me. She speaks to me. *Please find him. Find him and tell him.*

I try to listen, I gather all the words she says in my hands, like grains of sand. She tells me her name, and it burns itself in my memory. And then she says *my* name – but I'm wrenched away, and the words I gathered so carefully and kept close to my breast slip through my fingers – and as I return to the grey, silent place that is my home now, gasping for breath and half dead, all I can remember are two words: her name, my name. The message is lost, but I know I will find it again, I will recall every word, find the man she spoke of and deliver the message she whispered.

I know my name is Rose, and I have a message for him.

1

Matthew

'Best of luck,' the guard in a blue uniform said, signing me off, not really looking at me as I walked out, into the *outside.*

I blinked, and again, and again. No, the prison wasn't dark, and the light was not that strong that English summer morning. But I had to blink after three years of not setting foot in the outside world. Everything threw itself at me, the noise, the sights, the smells, and I swayed and trembled. An image flashed in my mind – the boys and girls I'd helped during my years at the shelter, the community where young men and women with addictions worked hard to heal themselves and their relationships, began projects and courses, restarted their lives. I coordinated the various aspects of their care, from doctors to psychologists to sports coaches to their bosses at work, and I thought I *knew.* I thought that sheer empathy and dedication and my studies would be enough to make me understand what they were going through.

I didn't, not by miles.

Only now did I truly realise what it was like to be thrust from a prison cell back into the world, alone and weighed down by guilt and self-loathing. Only now did I fully understand the irony of it all: that the terrible experiences those men and women described would one day be mine – me, the man who'd always played by the rules.

My sentence had come to an end. I was free. Apparently I'd paid my debt to society. The three years I'd spent in a cell had expiated the moment of distraction that led to my wife, my Mia, being killed on a frosty afternoon just before Christmas, as we drove to her parents' house with a boot full of presents. Other people were involved in the accident; I'd destroyed them too.

Society said I'd atoned. Except, of course, I hadn't. I never could. This remorse I carried with me would weigh on my shoulders forever.

The man who walked out of prison wasn't me, but half of me. I'd been broken in two, the best part of me taken away, the person I'd never been without since we were four years old gone. And all that went with it – I could never go back to the job I'd given my heart and soul to, my family had rejected me, my face had been in the papers as that of a killer, and people would not forget. Not that those things truly mattered, given that my Mia was gone. Nothing mattered without her.

Her absence meant the end of my life anyway; nothing else was of any importance.

There was nobody waiting for me outside the square grey building, with bars at the windows and barbed wire on the walls; nobody across the street. No family or friends waiting for me as I stepped out of the system and into the world.

I hadn't told anyone that I was coming out of prison. All the blood family I had left were an aunt and uncle with whom I was never close – I was an only child, my parents had me late in life and they'd both passed away before I even got married. Mia's parents had passed on the message that I was dead to them, that they never wanted to see me or speak to me again. Only Mia's sister, Hannah, had offered me words of forgiveness since the accident, and she'd tried to be there for me while I served my sentence – but I couldn't let myself accept her help, I couldn't face her, I couldn't cope with the shame and guilt. The thought that maybe she needed me too to help her work through Mia's death just wasn't enough to shake me out of my voluntary isolation. I had nothing left to give; I was empty but for self-loathing.

I had to be alone as I stepped out of my cage and into another, self-imposed one. I wasn't supposed to be held and comforted, I wasn't supposed to get into a comfortable car and be given a bed somewhere safe and warm, or provided with meals and support until

I got back on my feet. No. I didn't deserve any of that. Three years hadn't really paid my debt, and nothing ever could. I was out of the damp, claustrophobic cell I'd shared with three other disowned, cast-off men like me, but I would continue to make amends as long as I lived.

I inhaled the tepid air, the smell of petrol fumes and fried food, and felt hollow. Invisible. The first step of my life outside would be purgatory, my own private place of punishment . . . my old home, the home I'd shared with my Mia.

I wandered for a bit, overwhelmed by the noise, by the crowded streets, my backpack over my shoulder, until I found the right bus to take me where I wanted to go, where I'd longed to go since I'd been locked up. As I looked out of the window – shops and people and cars and vans and the landscape running, moving, making me feel slightly seasick, after such a long time without going anywhere but the prison courtyard – I finally saw an estate of new houses, red bricks and tidy gardens, nothing special, nothing unique.

But one of those houses was mine, mine and Mia's.

That house had held all of our dreams.

I'd been advised to sell it, of course, but I'd refused. That was my family home. And during my thirty-six months – one hundred and fifty-six weeks, one thousand and ninety-two days – in prison, I dreamt of going back. Every time my rational mind whispered,

She's not there, there's nothing left, nothing left, I blocked it out.

I wanted to go home. And I would go home.

I stepped off the bus before the right stop, the Acacias visible on top of the gentle hill I'd walked hundreds of times. When I finally saw the house that was mine – simple and inconspicuous, a house like many others and yet unique – my steps became faster and faster until I couldn't contain myself, and I ran. I was nearly there, nearly there. Nearly home. Oh, how I'd dreamt of this moment . . .

Finally I stood in front of the empty driveway and I looked. I looked at the building.

Because that was what it was, a building.

Not a home, not any more.

This place, this empty, forlorn, house-shaped construction used to be the Shearers'. This was where Matthew and Mia lived; *MatthewandMia,* one entity, like we'd been since we were teenagers. A part of me, the part that had refused to acknowledge reality, believed I would somehow find them there – my Mia, and the Matthew I used to be. Or a part of them at least, a scent, a memory, anything that would bring them back to me even for a second.

The second window on the left – there, behind that window – was Mia's studio, with the white walls and the screens, the lighting equipment and reflection boards, the tripods and cameras and even a small darkroom, tucked away from any source of light. And all around, Mia's beautiful, beautiful work, some framed, some pinned up to create a wall-wide collage. All the things I couldn't see and she could – the hidden, the secret, dug out and revealed in her photographs.

Oh God. The house looked dead. The house *was* dead. And still I had to see for myself. I had to make sure Mia wasn't waiting for me, as absurd as it might sound.

It took a few attempts to open the door, after three years of being untouched. The noise of the key and the door scraping on the floor broke the silence, an ugly sound, the sound of something long forsaken. A moment, just a moment where I thought I would call, *I'm home*, and she would come to me barefoot and smiling, and once again it would be Matthew and Mia, as always, for as long as I could remember.

But in the house that was ours, now there was only silence.

What was I expecting? How absurd can the human mind be, denying the evidence, denying reality in order to survive? I could have fallen to my knees – I felt them giving way – but there would be no such dramatics. Just a soul dying, after all. No big deal.

Souls died all the time, whether the body was alive or not.

I was a dead man, still standing, still breathing.

The house was half empty. Mia's half. My things were still there – T-shirts in the drawers, books on the shelves, and anything Mia's family hadn't been interested in taking back, like plates and the toaster and the umbrella stand and all those everyday things that meant nothing to anybody now. Hannah had sent me messages while I was in prison, asking me what I wanted done with my belongings; her generosity, her love towards me astounded me. I could not find it in myself to even reply. What belongings? Who cared? The real work was inhaling and exhaling air in and out of my lungs – that in itself required all my effort.

And anyway, I was in denial.

Everything of mine lay untouched. My work bag in the hall where I'd left it that day, the Chinese menu we'd taken out the day before on the kitchen counter. It was like one of those abandoned places you see after a natural disaster, the dinner still on the table, a child's bike in the garden, post on the doormat, everything stilled in time. I could smell Mia's fresh, flowery scent in the air – but that was an illusion, of course, my mind playing tricks on me. I wandered around like a ghost – somewhere between dumb and desperate – and then I saw something that broke through the dumbness and made the first tears fall. Our toothbrushes – still there, one beside the other, one green, one red. I was hypnotised by those toothbrushes, sitting there like nothing had happened. They'd survived the house sweep, forgotten.

I forced myself to move, meandered in and out of the rooms, opened and closed cupboards and drawers, sat on the carpeted floor, my head between my knees. I cried and reasoned with God, with the person I was before, with Mia. I stood looking out of the window into our garden – and there she was, perched on the back of our little bench, taking photographs of lady-birds, wearing an old pair of my jeans rolled up on her slender ankles, and a T-shirt that was too big for her. There she was, standing on our bed and hammering a nail in the wall to hang a framed photograph of our wedding – there she was, brushing her hair slowly, hypnotically, in that calm way of hers – drinking coffee by the window, dancing with earphones on, sitting on the floor among wires and cameras and laptops, empty cups lined up on the windowsill behind her, engrossed in her work . . .

Part of me wanted to run from the house, part of me wanted to never leave, to live there with a beloved ghost that only I could see. What if I extended my hand to touch her, what if I spoke to her? Would she answer, would she feel real under my touch? A web of memories and longing was being spun around me, too intoxicating to leave, too painful to bear, and all of a sudden, fear was stronger than longing.

I had to get out. Down the stairs and through the door and away from all that ruin, all that loss. I was about to step out into the fresh air, away from the honey and poison of all that had been taken away from me, when I remembered. There might be a piece of her left behind, something only I knew about. A little habit of hers . . .

I turned back and opened the white laminate cupboard above the dishwasher. I blinked and blinked, hoping but not quite believing . . . There was a splash of green leaning against the side of the cupboard. Mia's bag, the one she kept ready to go. It was there. They had forgotten it, they hadn't taken it away – her 'emergency kit', a small Canon she carried whenever she didn't need her proper equipment. For a moment I was frozen, my heart beating hard and painful.

I touched the fabric, light and soft and without dust, and for a second I thought I would meet her fingers, soft and warm as they used to be. I took the bag and ran, ran like a thief from my own house.

I loved you so much, and I cut your life short. You can't possibly hate me more than I hate myself already.

'I hoped you'd never come back,' a voice behind me called as I locked the front door, my own backpack on one shoulder, Mia's precious bag on the other. I turned around to see a short-haired woman in a denim shirt standing on the road a few yards from me. Paula, my former neighbour – she'd come to check who was sneaking in next door. She was a good friend of Mia. They used to go running together, and I'd find them in the living room chatting over a glass of wine when I came home late from work. 'You're not coming back to live here.' It was a statement, not a question. I looked at her evenly. Her chest was rising and falling in a mixture of rage and remembered pain.

Keep it coming, I thought. It's what I deserve.

She had this thing, Mia – she never sat on a chair, or the sofa, or anyway where she was supposed to sit. She sat on the floor, or on the windowsill, or on the armrest. It wasn't restlessness, the reason why she always seemed to be out of line with everyone else, inhabiting the space around her in a different way – on the contrary, she was the calmest, most serene person I knew.

Once, as she perched on the kitchen counter reading a magazine, her legs dangling like a child's – and we were so young, just turned seventeen, really not much more than children – I laid my hands theatrically on the back of a chair.

'Let me introduce you to this great invention, the *chair*,' I said with a smile.

She laughed. 'How boring,' she replied, shrugging her shoulders.

Everything she did, her mannerisms, from the way she brushed her hair to the way she frowned over a grocery list, was irresistible to me. She was my first girlfriend, the girl I loved. And every day I thought, this sunny, shiny woman chose me, an awkward boy who looks at life from the outside in, who's most at ease with people at the edge of things, even at the edge of society, like the kids I worked with. Everybody wanted Mia. But she'd chosen me.

We'd just moved into our first home, the attic of a Victorian house with meter electricity and the relic of a coin phone on the landing, with Irish students living on the first floor and a colony of cats in the unkempt garden. We loved it, because it was ours. I remember that moment, when the sun was setting behind her and playing in her hair, and she was reading an interior design magazine even though our budget was more Argos than Habitat. Is it a cliché to say that with her in art college and me in a social work job at the bottom of the ladder, we had no money to speak of, but we were happy?

Yes. We were happy.

Sitting on that counter, she'd shrugged and threaded one of her braids around her finger – she wore her hair in two braids for a while, and with a fabric flower behind her ear, and long skirts, she was like a modern-day flower child. 'I like a different point of view,' she told me. 'I like seeing things from every angle. It changes your thinking, you know. Everyday things become special if you look at them from above or below . . . or the side.' She tilted her head and closed one eye, an imaginary camera in her hands. 'It's what I want my photographs to do. See the world from a different angle.' I took the magazine gently from her hands then, and began to kiss her the way we did, slow and sweet and for a long, long time.

Mia and I went to school together, all the way from nursery to high school. And all that time, I'd been in love with her. The funny thing is, I can remember exactly when I fell for her.

We were on a nursery trip, and we were playing a game called Bluebird, Bluebird, out in a green grassy field. We played that game all the time – our teachers were obsessed with it. It was so boring. A boy called Seb fell and began to scream – Seb *always* fell, even off his own feet, and usually it was me running to him, the way I always did when someone needed help, but not that time. While all the attention was on Seb, Mia had found a way to escape the teachers' watchful eyes. I saw her crouching under a bush, making herself tiny, in a small tent made of twigs. I was a shy, insecure child who always did what he was told, and her escape was to me the height of rebellion. I was scared and yet in awe of someone who would defy the teachers this way and set herself up for a row, just for a moment of solitude and freedom from the noise and the instructions and the endless organised games that left no time for mischief. Or individual thinking.

To this day, I can't believe I did it, because it was so unlike me, a boy who mainly aimed at being invisible, but I went and hid with her, running as fast as I could so they wouldn't see me. She didn't look up when I joined her and crouched beside her, my face on fire, half elated, half horrified by what I'd done.

'We'll get into trouble,' I whispered.

She shrugged. She kept tracing lines in the dirt and making minuscule mounds, then she snapped a twig into little pieces and positioned them here and there, following a pattern in her head. Outside our leafy refuge, voices were beginning to rise. 'Mia! Mia!' The teachers and helping mums had noticed she was gone. Soon they'd realise I'd disappeared too. My heart was pounding, thinking of the trouble we were in, but I didn't move. She seemed oblivious to the calls.

'What are you doing?'

'I'm making a play park for bugs.' She had a smudge of mud on her cheek and her hands were brown with soil. Her hair was all tangled up.

When a pair of big feet appeared through the small thicket and we were dragged out by the hand, I was so ashamed to be in trouble, but Mia was . . . no, not defiant: indifferent. We were made to sit on a bench while everyone else played, and she leaned back, nose to the sky, like a sunflower facing the sun. 'Dinosaur. Truck. Cat,' she murmured.

I was staring at the other children still stuck playing Bluebird, Bluebird and trying to cope with the entirely new feeling of being a rebel, savouring it and fearing it at the same time, my heart beating like crazy in my little chest.

'Biscuit. Baby. Shoe . . .' Mia turned her head from side to side, still gazing up at the sky.

'What are you doing?' I asked.

'Finding shapes.'

I looked up, but saw only straggly white clouds, immobile in the blue expanse.

Mia saw things from another point of view. And yes, in an innocent four-year-old way I fell for her that day, with her muddy hands and her tangled hair and her eyes that saw the infinitely small and the infinitely big while the rest of us seemed to focus midway, on things that didn't really matter.

'Are you hungry? Can I make you anything? What about toasted cheese? Nice and light.' Jasmin touched my back for a moment, gently. I stiffened, melted a little, toughened up again. Nobody had touched me for three years, except to push or shove me.

'No thanks. You're being kind enough letting me stay.'

'You know it's not a problem. You must stay as long as you need to.' Greg's hair was nearly all grey now, and he was a bit heavier around the middle, but he was still Greg, polished, forceful, groomed. 'We tried to contact you while you were in prison, Matthew. We didn't just desert you, you know . . .' There was a hint of reproach in his words. It was me who'd chosen not to speak to Greg and Jasmin, not to see them. I couldn't bear to see anyone. I was too ashamed. But loneliness seemed to have trumped shame now.

In despair, half regretting my refusal to have anything to do with Hannah – I couldn't bear to hear her voice, so similar to Mia's, or remember the way she'd looked at me in court, with an absence of hate that destroyed me more than blame could – I'd dialled

Greg Briers, the only person I could face at that moment. Someone who'd seen such weakness, such self-destruction in his only son that I knew he would understand how lost I was now.

Simon Briers was one of the first boys I'd worked with in the Neuss Shelter. He was different from everybody else: no broken home, no violent childhood, just an extreme rejection of everything he was, a hollowness inside that had no explanation, or none that we could find. He was a talented musician whose family had the means to help him with his career, an eighteen-year-old who'd always been at the top of the class, a boy any parents would want to have as a son. Drugs had come to him like thieves in the night, until he'd become a ghost of who he used to be. Prison, a therapeutic community, another fall into addiction and then a slow, painful recovery. A year with us, and the return to the surface. The last thing I heard before I entered prison was that he was back at university, studying music.

For some reason, Greg and Jasmin seemed to think I was the one to thank for their son's rebirth, but truth was, it had been a combination of efforts from him, the whole staff and his parents too. When I phoned Greg after three years of silence – struggling to get the words out, confused, clutching Mia's camera bag – he simply asked me where I was, came to fetch me and brought me back to his house. That was it.

I'll never forget that, never.

'How's Simon?' I asked.

'Great, actually.' Greg opened his hands. 'Studying, working, girlfriend, the lot.' He spoke casually, as if he were making small talk. As if they hadn't sweated blood to help their son back from the brink – giving him money for drugs when they were terrified he'd do something stupid, then denying him money, taking him in, then throwing him out, and all the while Greg's hair had turned grey and Jasmin's eyes were dry from too much crying. But it was all behind them now. Studying, working, girlfriend. Three words to signify salvation.

'Look,' Jasmin said, and handed me a photograph they kept on the fridge. It was Simon at his piano, taken from the back, his head turned enough to see his profile, his long nose, his young forehead, the slight, uncoordinated figure of someone very young.

I smiled.

'You did so much good, Matthew. You really did,' Jasmin said.

'Yeah.'

'Your job at the Neuss Shelter . . .' Greg shook his head, as if asking me a question.

'I can never go back. Criminal record,' I said drily. There was a pause.

'So. What's the plan?' he said, perched high at his breakfast bar. He couldn't help it, it was his very way of being – looking forward all the time, to the future. What's gone is gone, surely now we must *succeed*, surely we know it will all go well. That was how he'd built his considerable success – stubbornness and optimism in the face of anything that life threw at him. That was how he'd helped his only son out of darkness.

'Greg, leave him alone. He needs to recuperate. He just came out . . . you know, *out* today . . .' Jasmin was too diplomatic to say the word *prison.*

'Of course. Sorry.'

'No, no, it's okay.' I ran my hand through my damp hair. I'd just had the longest shower in my life, trying to wash away the years of imprisonment and the humiliations that came with them. I suppose water can't wash away memories, the stains of the soul. But it had relaxed me somehow, and I was exhausted, tired to my bones. I couldn't remember a night of uninterrupted sleep in three years. My eyes were closing, but I was afraid that once in bed, insomnia would ambush me once again.

'Well, Matthew always has a plan, don't you?' Greg smiled, determined to lighten the mood. I could see the pity in their eyes, and I hated it. But hey, I couldn't blame them. In their shoes I would have pitied myself.

'Not this time, no,' I said simply. 'Apart from *keep breathing.* That's as far as it goes for now.'

'Well, like Jasmin said, you need to recuperate . . .'

'I just want to get away from Bennington. As far as I can go. You know, somewhere nobody knows me . . . where nobody knows what happened, and blames me or feels sorry for me. Somewhere I don't see ghosts at every corner.'

There was a moment of silence. I hadn't spoken so much in a long time and I had surprised myself, almost cringing at the sound of my own voice.

'Your toasted cheese,' Jasmin said to break the moment, and under the LED spotlights I saw that her eyes were glistening.

'Hey, hey . . . I'll be fine. Don't be sad.'

She laughed through her tears. 'You haven't changed, Matthew. Always thinking of other people.'

I smiled back. Oh yes, I had changed. The old Matthew had disappeared, and all that was left was an empty, Mia-less shell.

'Hey, Matthew. Can I bother you for a moment?' A wedge of light shone through the doorway, and Greg's grey head appeared in the gap. I was in one of his guest rooms, lying uncomfortably in a very comfortable bed – if that makes sense. I'd grown accustomed to a narrow, hard bunk bed with rough sheets and the perennial feeling of being too warm; the grunts and moans of troubled, fretful men all around me. I didn't know how to deal with luxury, or even just comfort.

I didn't know how to sleep without Mia at my side.

I still felt the space beside me sometimes, thinking I'd feel her slumbering form, her hair, her warmth – but there was only emptiness.

How do you live if half of you is gone?

'You couldn't come to my study, could you? I'd like to discuss something with you.'

Maybe he was going to offer me a job, a chance to rebuild my life.

A life I didn't want any more.

'Sure,' I answered, out of politeness really. I didn't think Greg could offer me anything that would help me, except for tonight's comfort and kindness; anything that could help me breathe again.

I followed him into his study – exactly how you'd imagine a lawyer's office would be; all dark wood and leather and expensive furniture. Greg and I were two people who had nothing in common, who would never have become friends, or probably even met, had it not been for Simon. I would never have imagined that our unlikely friendship would one day lead me here, to his study, in the middle of the night. That it would lead to me sleeping in his guest room, carrying all I had with me in one small rucksack.

Suddenly I realised that he was gazing down at my hand. My wedding ring, a simple silver band with an M carved inside. I would not take it off. Never. I hid my left hand in the other and looked away.

'Sit down. Drink?'

'Go ahead.'

'There. A nice Scottish whisky. Lagavulin. You still like Scottish whisky, don't you? Because really it's the best in the world.'

'Yes, of course,' I said half-heartedly.

'Me too. Which leads me to . . . this.' He handed me a heavy glossy brochure.

'What is it?'

'Have a look,' he said, thrusting out his chin. *Molleson Cottage*, it said on the cover, above a photograph that immediately captured my attention. It was a strange shot to be on an agency's brochure. Usually they shoot houses in bright daylight, possibly in the sunshine, to make them look as appealing as possible. But this was a photograph taken in half-light, lilac sky and black land, and the brightly illuminated cube of the house shining golden in the gloom. Its walls were all glass, and the roof, strangely enough, was covered in grass, like a suspended garden.

'Open it. Keep going,' Greg encouraged me.

On the stunning island of Seal, Repetto Luxury Estates in collaboration with Eilean and Seal Estate Agents offers this unique property and the surrounding grounds to an equally unique buyer. Designed by New York architect L. J. Molleson, Molleson Cottage stands on one of Seal's most stunning beaches, famed for their white sands . . .

'Wow. It's beautiful,' I said, and I felt a strange stirring in me. Something not quite like life reawakening – that would have been too much. But loosely related to that. Yes. Loosely related to life.

'It is, isn't it? Two hours' ferry ride from anywhere.'

I turned the pages slowly. The island of Seal, in the Outer Hebrides, sat like a baby island underneath a bigger one, Eilean. A few hundred people lived on it, the brochure said. *A strong sense of community, but also total privacy; superb facilities for golf and surfing, and . . .*

'Why are you showing me this?' I asked.

'Because I bought this place. Last year.'

'Congratulations,' I said without irony. I really didn't see where he was going with this, which, looking back, was probably a bit dim of me.

'Thanks, but . . . well, it wasn't the best of ideas. I thought I'd love it, but turns out I really don't. As for Jasmin, she positively hates it, and you know the way she is . . . compromise isn't exactly her middle name.' He smiled as he talked about his wife. A thousand little pinpricks in my heart.

'How can she hate this?' I said, pointing to the undeniable beauty of the photographs.

'Because it's in the middle of nowhere. She loathes golf, and as for surfing, the water's bloody freezing. She can't even dip a toe in! Nah. Simon went up there to study for a while, though he took his girlfriend with him, so I don't know how much studying got done . . . You know, it's just amazing the way I can let him go now without worrying constantly about what he's up to.'

I smiled. 'I can imagine.'

'He came back with lots of material to submit – you know he wants to write scores for films, documentaries? He said it was a great place to concentrate, but just too isolated for him. And Rowan, his girlfriend, she's an actress. She said she'd go mad if she had to spend time there again.'

'Oh well, you're really selling it!'

Laughter again. 'Well, you're not a nineteen-year-old aspiring actress who wants to be somewhere she can be seen.'

'True. So, the place is like an albatross around your neck?'

'Yes. We rented it out for a bit, and that was okay, but . . . I don't need the money, I don't need the extra work either. So, well, Jasmin and I talked about it earlier, about what you said about wanting to get away. A break from everything. And we thought Molleson would be ideal for you. You can have it.'

'You're offering me a cottage worth . . . let me see . . . *Sale price reserved* . . .'

'Not much short of a million pounds.'

'Right. And you're giving it to me.'

He laughed. 'Not as a present! I'm not that generous. To live in for as long as you like. You want to go to the middle of nowhere. I have a house there. Fate, isn't it? Or maybe karma.' He looked down. 'For all you did for Simon. For us.'

I was silent for a moment. If karma really was a thing, better not think about what would happen to me after what I'd done.

'Greg . . .'

'Look, you don't have to give me an answer right now.'

'Thank you.'

He raised his eyebrows. 'But no thank you?'

'Just thank you. I accept your offer. I . . . Really, I'm grateful.' I lowered my eyes to the brochure and took in a windswept beach, waves lapping the shore, the profile of the hills, soft under the white sky.

Somewhere inside me, the stirring was still there. If anything, it was because a friend was offering me something from the heart. Something I desperately needed – a getaway. Somewhere to hide, at least for a bit. To try and recover what was left of myself.

'You know I can't pay you any rent yet . . .'

'Do I look like I need rent?' Greg said, and I saw in him the hint of arrogance that was part of him, always largely compensated for by his fundamental kindness. That arrogance that had once, unwittingly, nearly destroyed his vulnerable son.

'No. But I will pay my way, as soon as I can.'

'Well, it's not a problem for me. You're coming to work with me as soon as you recover anyway.'

I smiled and looked down. I couldn't think about that. I couldn't think of anything.

'Look. You'll love it there. I promise you. It's a very Matthew and Mia . . . Oh. Oh my God. Sorry. I'm so sorry.'

'It doesn't matter,' I said, and I asked myself what did.

Alone in Greg and Jasmin's guest room, I sat on the bed with the glossy brochure and Mia's bag in front of me.

The future I didn't want to come, and the past I didn't want to let go.

And yet the idea of being far away, alone, anywhere but here – it seemed the only way to keep living. I studied the pictures again – the building itself, and the sea and sky so beautiful that they took my breath away.

I opened Mia's bag slowly, afraid of the pain it would cause me and at the same time longing for that feeling. Her Canon, some lenses, a charger. What photographs were in there? Was I just about to see her face again, to see the life we used to have? I tried to switch the camera on, but after its long sleep while I was in prison, the battery was dead, probably for good. I was both disappointed and relieved.

Her fingers had touched this bag, she had carried it across her body and on her lovely rounded hip. So many times I'd seen her with this camera around her neck, or fishing it out from her bag, sitting on her lap as we drove. It had been an extension of her, something she took with her whenever she didn't need the big heavy equipment she used for events. I couldn't believe her family had left it behind, among the kitchen things nobody was interested in.

She'd left it tucked away, somewhere nobody would look.

She'd left it tucked away for me.

Out there in the night, there was a sea of people grieving for someone – wives, husbands, parents, friends – asking *why why why*. But I had caused my wife's death. I couldn't grieve with a clear heart. I couldn't remember my life with Mia with the sweet relief of memories treasured. Because on that winter morning, looking down at my phone instead of looking at the road, I had swerved, and crashed, and it was all over.

I'm sorry, Mia.

I'm so sorry, so sorry.

2

Grace

October wrapped itself around me like a blanket, and I loved every moment of it. Darkness falling earlier and earlier after the long summer nights, the turning leaves and their symphony of reds, yellows and browns, the chill in the air, the sweet wind and rain and mist and how they softened the island, how they made it look like a dream risen out of the sea – autumn was truly my season.

I was in a good mood. The surgery had been full earlier on, but I was nearly finished, as long as nothing else cropped up. I entertained the hope of being able to work on the music Rosalind and I were arranging for the Christmas concert. The sheets were folded in my bag, reminding me how much I wanted this concert to be perfect . . . no, not perfect: happy. I wanted it to be a moment for us islanders to be together in joy, to celebrate our community. Yes, it was only the beginning of October and there was plenty of time for rehearsals, but believe me, with the kind of singers we had – me included – we needed all the practice we could get. Apart from Rosalind, of course, whose truly magical voice kept everything together.

I opened my door and peeked out.

'Who's next? Oh, hello, Kenny. Come in. How can I help you?'

Kenny McFadyen, a sheep farmer who owned a small flock in the southern part of the island, was – how to put this – an old-fashioned man. He could have gone on the cover of *Shepherd* magazine, if such a thing existed. He had it all, the woollen hat, the thick jumper, the ruddy complexion and the big calloused hands. In the ten years I'd been on the island, he'd been to the surgery only once, and that was because he'd broken his arm after falling while repairing a stone wall. Even then, he was so reluctant to see a doctor, it had taken him two weeks before he'd decided to come. Two weeks with a broken arm, medicating with whisky.

'I have a terrible pain in my foot.'

'Okay. Take your shoe and sock off and I'll have a look.' Kenny took off a heavy boot and a sock that had seen better times and I examined his foot. 'Right. It seems fine to me, no broken bones, I don't think. Only a bit red.'

I wondered if maybe it could be his joints acting up, after so many years outside in the damp fields and a house where the only source of heating was a peat fire, but I wanted to make sure. 'Can you show me your other foot? I want to compare, to see if this one is swollen.'

'My other foot?' Kenny looked panicked.

'Yes. You have two, don't you?' I smiled. We'd known each other for a long time, and I knew he wouldn't feel demeaned by my little joke.

'I can't show you my other foot.'

'Why not?'

'It's this one that hurts.'

'Yes, I understand, but I need to see the other one to decide if the one that hurts is actually swollen. Don't worry, it's nothing bad, I think it might be rheumatism or a bit of arthritis. I can give you some anti-inflammatories to get the edge off the pain, and—'

'I can't, Doctor,' Kenny interrupted me. 'I can't.' He spoke in a *that's it, no more discussion* kind of voice and began slipping his sock back on, avoiding my eye.

I couldn't let this go. 'But why? It won't take a second . . .'

'Because I only washed *this* foot! The sore one. I haven't washed this one . . .' he pointed to his shod foot, 'in a . . . while now. A long while.' He was bright red.

'It doesn't matter, really . . .' I began, but he was already making for the door, hopping with his shoe in his hand like the devil was at his heels – which it probably was, given his allergy to washing them. I ran after him, trying not to laugh.

'Kenny! Come back! I don't mind, honestly.'

Three pairs of eyes – Lorna, our receptionist, Mrs Gibson and Mrs Taggart – followed Kenny as he leapt through the tiny waiting room and outside, and then turned to me as I gave up the chase, my hair in disarray. 'Everything okay, Doctor?' Mrs Gibson said cheerfully. Lorna and I called Mrs Gibson and Mrs Taggart 'G and T'; they came to see me at least once a week, not because there was anything wrong with them usually, just as a recreational activity.

'Everything is fine,' I said with a sigh.

'He's always been allergic to soap, that one,' Mrs Taggart said.

My jaw dropped and my eyes met Lorna's. Yes, we all knew that the wall between my room and the waiting area was so thin that any ailment discussed was everybody's business; not to mention the way our tiny chemist shared premises with the Spar, so you could buy bread and milk while standing side by side with Nuala Hutchison discussing her psoriasis and Malcolm Laird describing the terrible things that eating cheese did to him. But everybody pretended they didn't know, to keep up appearances.

'If he had a bath, there'd be nothing left of him!' said Mrs Gibson, and the pair of them cackled like the witches in *Macbeth*, their knitted berets bobbing in unison.

'Now, now,' Lorna reproached them gently. Lorna was like a human tea cosy, in both looks and personality. She wore her blond hair in a bun on top of her head and clad herself in pastel-coloured cardigans and woollen skirts. She was the island's soft-spoken, understanding mother. She worried for everyone, including me – fretting over my skipped meals and home visits in the middle of the night. She also helped me with the house a couple of times a week, and with all those errands I struggled to do because of my time-consuming job.

Being a doctor on Seal wasn't like being a doctor in Edinburgh. Now I lived and practised in a place where everyone knew me and I knew everyone, where I got to treat three generations of the same family. I knew who was going out with whom: who was getting drunk in the pub every night and who was doing it secretly at home, who took the ferry to Oban to see someone they weren't supposed to see, who'd started taking the pill though her parents knew nothing about it, who was trying for a baby and who had just conceived, who came to the surgery every week for a chat just to know they were not alone, who was forgetting things a bit too often and was too scared to tell their offspring in case they forced them to move off the island to somewhere they could be looked after, who'd just been given terribly bad news and his family had no idea, and so you met them at the Saturday-night ceilidh and had to smile, pretending you didn't know that their husband and father and grandfather would be gone soon. And then there were the surprises, like when you delivered a baby at home, a little boy who'd decided to come too soon; and then marvelled all over again when the same baby turned into the toddler who launched into *Ba ba back ship, have you any woo* in church, while everyone else was intoning 'Abide with Me'.

I was a newcomer, and yet I was embedded in this community. My predecessor was an American doctor who had lasted only a couple of years, and before her the legendary Dr Innes, whose shoes were incredibly hard to fill – and now here I was, Grace Chatto from Edinburgh, unmarried, no children, choosing to live somewhere remote instead of Roan or Ollaberry, the only two villages on the island. Alone in a cottage in the middle of nowhere.

When I'd first arrived, some were unconvinced, especially after the infamous Dr Green from Arizona, who had declared that if she had to spend another winter on this island she would jump off a cliff. People were dismayed, as she told all and sundry how much she hated the island and how she could not leave fast enough, and then went away without looking back, carrying with her all the history the community had entrusted to her, as if it didn't matter. I'd never forget our first and only meeting, where she warned me how I would get depressed here for sure; that she'd come looking for wilderness and a life close to nature, and all she'd found were barren hills and black mornings and endless rain. I nearly felt sorry for her. And I admit I did feel a hint of apprehension at the decision I'd made, as it had been so sudden, and not well received by my family. But I was going to make it work. I was going to do right by the people I'd come to look after.

Yet even after the trauma of Dr Green, most people welcomed me with open arms and a lot of useful advice, such as to keep candles and matches in at all times, no, you won't be able to get everywhere by bike and whatever you do, don't get too close to the edge of the beautiful cliffs behind your home, because bits of them drop into the sea of their own accord. This last being the most useful tip I ever received, because only this month past a small piece of the island had fallen off, and we'd ended up on the national news.

I'd been very happy in Edinburgh. I had my work, I had my family – especially my two beloved nephews. But here on this island I had discovered a new way of life and a new me – no, not a new me: a *freer* me. Seal suited me like a made-to-measure dress – the hills weren't barren to me, they were a symphony of earthy colours; the weather fronts coming in from the Atlantic invigorated me; and the small appointments of island life – the choir, the ceilidhs, the community garden, the travelling library, the fund-raisers for the school and for the Sea Rescue, the yearly celebration of the Blessing of the Boats – were the punctuation of my weeks, my months, my years, setting the rhythm to my existence.

And then there was Fergus, my neighbour.

My friend, my best friend.

More than a friend, really.

Fergus, who'd disappeared almost completely in the last month or so, apart from a few harried texts . . .

'Mrs Taggart, your turn, I think?' I said, gesturing towards my room.

'Ah no, I'm good, thanks, Doctor.'

'Mrs Gibson?' I asked, knowing the answer.

'I'm all right too. In perfect health!'

'Just here for a chat, then?' My eyes went from one to the other. Sure, who needs a coffee shop when there's a nice warm surgery where you get plenty of gossip, a free cup of tea and a complimentary blood pressure check?

'You know me, I love a blether!' said Mrs Gibson. Yes, and a funeral, another much-enjoyed social event. Behind her, unseen, Lorna rolled her eyes.

'Here we are!' said a soft sing-song voice behind me. A gust of chilly breeze filled the surgery and I turned to see Carla, my friend and patient, back from the hospital with her brand-new baby girl in tow, her huge bump now turned into a soft little belly. There were black shadows under her eyes, but her smile was something to behold, and the happiness on her face warmed my heart. The baby slept, a little fist beside her face, snug in a white blanket and pink hat.

A chorus of *aaaws* erupted from the ladies. 'This is Emma,' Carla said, beaming with pride – and no, it's not a cliché, she really was beaming. Oh, what a lovely name she'd chosen.

The joy I felt for her overflowed, and I hugged her. 'Congratulations!' Her third pregnancy – there was a little boy in between – had been long to come and hard to get through, so Emma's arrival was even more of a gift.

As we cooed over her, the baby woke up and looked at me with her huge trusting eyes, and again I felt that wrench, that strange pain I'd had to live with for a few years now. But as always, I hid it behind a smile.

'Are you well?' I asked Carla, so that nobody would notice my upset.

Carla took her gaze away from Emma to look at me. It seemed nearly a physical effort for her – I'd seen it in so many new mothers, this instinct to keep their eyes on their babies all the time. 'Never been better. I hope to be back at rehearsals soon.'

'I think we'll forgive you if you miss a couple. Oh Carla, she's beautiful. I'm so happy for you.'

'Thank you. I brought her here to show you.'

'How thoughtful, thank you. I was going to come up with Sharon anyway.' Sharon was our nurse, and went to visit all new mothers back from the hospital on the mainland.

'It's an easy day today, Doctor, isn't it?' Mrs Gibson said, contemplating Emma's perfection. 'We're here for a chat, Carla is showing off her wee one . . .'

'Well, Kenny had something up with him but he didn't wash his feet,' Mrs Taggart reminded her.

Silence fell in the room. Carla looked at me, and I fought to remain expressionless.

'Anyone for tea and a wee cake?' Lorna said at last,

waving a box of teacakes in the air with a sweet smile. Bless her.

'Oh, why not, might as well!' The ladies were of one mind, and there was a flurry of activity while mugs were taken out and the kettle filled.

I softly stroked the baby's cheek with my finger. 'Ah, sure. Not that I need a break. Here I am, doing nothing!'

'Hardly doing nothing. You're keeping an eye on all of us, Doctor,' Mrs Gibson said, unexpectedly.

'So you are,' Carla agreed, and held her baby to her chest in a way that stabbed me a little once again. She noticed my expression and gave me a curious look. Patients never saw me as a human being with a life and a story of my own, and that was good – I was the instrument for their healing, and that was all. But in a place so small, many of my patients were also my friends; and Carla, I often thought, could see through people in a way that was sometimes startling. Both she and her sister Catriona had this gift. And yes, I felt that Carla had just guessed the regrets of a fifty-year-old woman who had never married, never had children, who lived in a house full of pictures of her nephews.

'You go home now, try and catch up on some sleep,' I said, to put an end to the moment.

'Yeah, I am a little bit tired all right. She's been feeding every two hours and I'm still sore – you know, *the forceps* . . .' she mouthed. The three mothers present gave each other a knowing look. Childbirth: don't ask, don't tell.

I knew how it was as a doctor; I didn't know how it was as a woman.

That sting again. More and more painful as the years passed. I stroked Emma's soft cheek once more, and looked deep into the eyes of what I'd lost.

At the end of the day, after a couple of home visits, I made my way to the community centre for choir rehearsals. My good mood had morphed into something more pensive; I was still reeling from the feelings that baby Emma had stirred in me. I took a breath – I had to get a hold of myself. I'd made choices in my life and I'd lived with them for a long time. Things could not change now, not at my age. Even thinking of it or dreaming of it would be toxic.

No. I was a woman who stood by her decisions, no matter what.

The community centre was a whitewashed building not too far from the centre of Roan, but tucked slightly away nonetheless. As I took out my keys and opened the door, the smell of damp and moss filled my nostrils, always present no matter how often we lit the peat stove. There was nobody there yet, which was a first. Usually I rushed in late, when Rosalind had already started. I made my way inside, switched the light on and put down the bags of fresh scones and jam I'd bought earlier. Then I sat at the piano, rubbing my hands together to warm them. I was about to start a tune when a stunning woman with long red-gold hair walked through the door. Catriona, Carla's little sister.

'You're back!' I said. She was smiling, and her cornflower eyes were framed by black glasses that made her look even prettier. She gave me a hug and I breathed in her usual scent of salt water, like she'd just come in from a dip in the sea.

'I am. And happy to be. Though Japan was amazing. Honestly, *amazing* – I can't find any other words. But I can't believe my sister just went and gave birth a month earlier than scheduled!'

'I know! You nearly missed it. Isn't Emma wonderful?'

'She is. My second niece . . . I'm so lucky.' She put her hands up. 'Please don't say it.'

'Say what?'

' "It's your turn next." Because I'm nowhere near ready.'

I understand, but don't leave it too long . . . you might find you change your mind when it's too late. I was dying to tell her that, the wisdom of my fifty years to the relative youth of her thirty, but I didn't. She wouldn't have wanted to hear it. And although she was engaged, I had a feeling that all was not well between her and her fiancé. You pick things up when three hundred-odd people tell you their business day in, day out.

'So, Japan was amazing,' I said instead.

'Oh yes. Tokyo was incredible, a crazy place. The lights, the shops . . . oh Grace, the amount of people! And everything keeps going at night, twenty-four hours a day. You can do your grocery shopping or go for noodles at four in the morning. I'm not sure if it's a futuristic dream or a nightmare. Bit of both, I suppose,' she said, looking at the scones. 'Do you mind if I . . . ?'

'Sure, help yourself. You know, I'm not surprised you enjoyed Japan. I loved living in Tokyo.'

'You lived in Tokyo? Seriously? How many things do we not know about you?'

I laughed. 'Did I not tell you? We were there for about three years. We moved around a lot, you know . . . my dad taught at various universities. Hong Kong, Switzerland, Norway, Japan . . . Actually, Tokyo was the place where I was happiest. I loved my school and had a little best friend . . . Tetsuko was her name.' I smiled at the recollection. 'I was devastated when we left and resumed wandering after my dad.' I played a few notes on the piano to warm my hands.

'Until you ended up in Seal.' She looked at me thoughtfully.

'Until I ended up here. A stroke of luck,' I said honestly.

I still remembered the first time I heard of Seal. I was in the small staffroom in my old surgery in Edinburgh. One of the young doctors, Andrew, was reading the *Herald.* 'Oh wow. Look at this,' he said.

'They're advertising for a doctor on this tiny island . . . Look at the pictures!'

'Would you go?' I asked, only half listening.

'Nah. My girlfriend would leave me. She needs shops and theatres and museums or she'll implode. Would *you*?'

'Ach, no. My family are here. And I've done enough travelling,' I said, laughing.

But truth was, my younger nephew had joined the older one at university in England, and in the last few years I'd lost both my parents. I loved my brothers dearly, but with my nephews' departure I felt a void in my life. Something in me was beginning to stir, a sense of restlessness, but I had no idea where it would lead me.

That night, the universe had once again showed me its mysterious ways – though my grandmother, devout as she was, would certainly have said it was some sort of divine intervention. Jumping channels here and there while cooking my dinner, I stopped at the sight of the most incredible aqua waters. I thought it had to be a travel programme on the Caribbean, or some southern hemisphere island, but a soft-sounding Scottish voice told me it was the Hebrides. I stood there with an oven glove in one hand and a wooden spoon in the other, as if I'd never seen such a place before, as if that wasn't my own country. On cue, the voiceover announced scenes from Seal, and I saw impossible cliffs, dolphins jumping and basking sharks making their slow way through azure waters; an ancient bridge covered in foxgloves, stags locking horns, a foaming whirlpool, misty hills, and soft white clouds covering a thousand shades of brown and purple and green . . .

It wasn't a slow, pondered decision. It was a moment of madness, because I decided that night. I had fallen for a place I'd never visited before.

I got the job – partly I think because not many people had applied in the first place. Working in such an isolated place meant being available at all hours, seven days a week. Only when I'd accepted did it all sink in. I was going to move to a Hebridean island two hours away from the mainland, on my own. I didn't know whether I should be terrified or elated. A bit of both, probably. But my brothers weren't happy at all, especially James, to whom I was closest.

'You're running away,' he said.

'James, come on. Running away from what?' I laughed.

'From what happened twenty years ago.'

I was silent for a moment. I could speak about it now without bursting into tears; I'd been able to do that for a long time. But it still hurt. I gazed at my brother and once again I was struck by the resemblance between us – the same dark blond hair, wavy and unruly, the same grey eyes, slight build and small stature. People mistook us for twins. 'What happened happened,' I said. 'It's finished.'

'But it's not really. I mean . . . I don't want to upset

you, but I think a piece of you is still back there in the past, still trying to deal with the whole thing.'

'That's unfair. And it's also untrue. I've moved on. I have a life . . . I have you, and Charlie, and my nephews, and my sisters-in-law. I have a job I love and plenty of friends. I didn't get stuck. I'm not there. I'm *here*.'

'Then why are you dropping everything and going away, if you have so much?'

'Because . . .'

'Because?'

I smiled and made light of it. 'Because I'm having a mid-life crisis, and I really don't feel like getting a tattoo or buying a motorbike.'

I don't remember what he replied, but my argument didn't leave much room for discussion. Ten years later, I couldn't even imagine living anywhere else but on my little island in the Atlantic.

'A scone for your thoughts?' Catriona smiled, and I realised I'd been lost in a reverie.

'Oh, sorry. Just . . . pensive. Now,' I said, rising from the piano and lining up a few chairs. 'Tell me more about Japan.'

'Well, being an island girl, the place I loved the most was Hokkaido.'

'Oh . . . I never made it there. It must be wonderful.'

'It is. It's wild – mountains, lakes, woods. We did a trek on a forest road, and once in a while you find these sanctuaries . . . like little shrines. When we got to the Shintoist temple, I met a girl there, one of the priestesses. We all made a bit of conversation with her – the interpreter was there, of course – and she singled me out.'

I wasn't surprised. Catriona always got singled out, either because of her looks or because of the aura she had around her. There was something magnetic about her – Carla had it too, though to a lesser degree, and Angela as well. Had I not been a rational person, I would have said there was something magical about the McCrimmon women.

'She asked me where I was from,' Catriona continued. 'I said Seal, and she said something to me but I didn't understand it, and our interpreter had gone ahead. Then she disappeared inside the temple. I was about to go too, but she called me back and gave me this.' She dug into her jacket and took out a little blue fabric pendant hanging on a short thread. It was silky and soft, shaped like a rectangle, embroidered in white and darker blue. 'And that's why I'm here. I mean, I'm here for the rehearsal, of course, but I also had to give you this.'

'Oh, that's lovely. How nice of you to think of me!'

'I didn't really think of you.' She laughed. 'No, that came out wrong! I mean, it wasn't me who thought of you. It was the priestess.'

'You mean the Shintoist priestess?'

'Yes, she explained to me what this amulet is, but

she did it in Japanese, so obviously I didn't have a clue. She repeated the word *gureisu* over and over again, with a little bow. I was about to call our interpreter, but we had to rush off to a theatre thing in Kyoto. On the bus I asked the interpreter what *gureisu* meant, and he said "grace". Then he said that this is called a . . . Wait . . .' She looked up. 'An *omamori*. Yes, *omamori*. They have different purposes, but this one is used to make a wish. You go to the temple and ask your ancestors to make it come true. He said, "This is for grace, for grace," with a bow of the head. So I thought . . . well, it's for you. For Grace.'

I laughed. 'That's not what he meant!'

'Well, I know, but this grace thing made me think of you, so here you are.'

'Can I make a wish without going to a temple?'

Catriona shrugged and smiled. 'It's worth a try.'

'How do you know there's something I wish for?'

'We all have something to wish for . . . Hello!' The choristers had started to arrive, and the blue door kept opening and closing on its old and not-so-solid hinges. Our conversation came to an end in a flurry of greetings and various baked goods being placed on our refreshments table. I slipped the pendant into my pocket.

'Oh, hi, Rosalind!' I called to the brown-haired girl who'd just come in. Rosalind was the director of the choir and a beautiful singer. The first time I'd heard her, in the Seal Inn, I'd ended up in floods of tears – and crying is a rare occurrence for me. There was something about her voice that was kind of miraculous; she could have been world famous, I was sure of that.

'Hey. Just back from Frankfurt. In bits.' She gazed at me with sleepy eyes.

'Let me know if the wish comes true,' Catriona whispered with a smile, and went to sit down, leaving behind a final whiff of salt and seaweed. I nestled the little charm carefully in my palm and then in my pocket.

'Okay, settle down, everyone,' Rosalind said in her gentle way. We were starting. I surveyed the choir from my vantage point at the piano, and saw that once again, Fergus wasn't there.

I was worried.

And not just that. I missed him.

A little more than I thought I would.

I forgot all about Catriona's pendant until I got home and slipped my hand into my pocket, looking for my house keys. I placed it carefully on the kitchen table, waiting to find a suitable place for it, then had a quick dinner and a sleepy shower and went to bed. My eyes closed immediately after another long, long day, knowing I could be woken any time and called out.

I woke with a jolt as my rescue cat, Hyde – found wandering on the dunes a few years ago, pathetically thin, with a swollen eye and matted fur – jumped on my chest. I groaned. He began to sting me lightly with his claws, lifting the thin fabric of my pyjamas and purring loudly. Hyde lived in a state of perpetual rage and was always ready for a fight – as his missing ear proved. I was one of the two creatures he was nice to. The other was Fergus.

'What *is* up with you? It's . . .' I looked at the alarm clock. 'Three in the morning!' I didn't know why I was whispering. It wasn't as if there was anyone else in the house.

Or was there? My heart skipped a beat as the thought of an intruder entered my mind. I couldn't help being alarmed. Usually Hyde went hunting at night and didn't come back until dawn, to rest and sleep after his campaign. To stay in the house and look for my company at night was completely out of character.

'Are you playing the guard cat?' I said, and then my own joke freaked me out. A guard against what? Against *whom*?

I froze. Did I have something to fend off an intruder with? I didn't even own a rolling pin. Maybe a shovel? But it was in the shed, and the intruder would have plenty of time to get to me before I grabbed it, not to mention the fact that I couldn't lift it over my head . . . *Grace! Get a grip.*

Hyde began to meow and dig his claws deeper, albeit still gently. Then he jumped down and began pacing up and down in front of the door. Of course.

He was hungry. The night hunt had been unsuccessful, so he'd come in for a snack. He'd never done it before, but there was always a first time.

'Okay, cat, maybe you're hungry, but let's not make a habit of this. I'm not getting up to feed you at three in the morning again.'

I flicked the light switch, but nothing happened: a blackout. I grabbed the little torch I kept on my bedside table – on Seal, blackouts were frequent – and reluctantly slipped out of the duvet and onto the cold floor. As I walked downstairs by the feeble light of the torch, Hyde danced between my feet. 'You'll make me fall, silly cat!' I hissed.

I walked briskly – or as briskly as I could after being woken up from deep sleep – to convince myself that I wasn't scared. Oh. I'd never noticed before that there were so many dark corners in my kitchen. I swallowed, my mouth dry, and opened the cupboard. But Hyde didn't even give me time to pour food into his bowl before he began meowing in front of the back door.

'You have a flap! Get out!' I said, and the sound of my voice in the solitude of the night was startling. A strange feeling was blossoming inside me, a feeling of deep disquiet, deeper than the fear of an intruder. There was something uncanny about the cat's behaviour, and something strange in the air . . .

Suddenly I realised how warm it was; it was three in the morning on Seal and I was standing in my pyjamas and not even shivering, nor were there goose bumps on my arms. I stepped towards the kitchen window. The breeze outside seemed to be whispering, the black branches of the ash tree gently tapping on the glass.

But if it was whispering, what was it trying to say?

On impulse, I opened the door, and a gust of wind hit me – it was mild, as if it came from some southern country. There were no lights as far as the eye could see. Warm wind from the Atlantic?

Hyde kept circling my feet as I stood in front of the door, but didn't dart out. I closed my eyes for a moment to feel the strange balmy breeze against my skin, listening to the beating drum of my heart. Hyde was rubbing himself against my legs, as if pushing me outside. I wasn't exactly afraid – or not that I would admit to – but it was all too uncanny for my liking.

The warm wind caressed my face. It was gentle, but there was something to it, like an underlying electric charge, that made the hair on the back of my neck stand up. I opened my eyes again in the black night – and that was when I saw it, hanging from a lower branch of the ash tree, moving slowly in the breeze. A tiny rectangle hanging from a thread, a flash of blue as the light of my torch illuminated it. The *omamori*.

I felt like I was swallowing my own heart as I stepped forward, feet bare on the grass, and disentangled it from the branch. How had it got there? I'd put it on the kitchen table when I came back from the rehearsal, I was sure. The cat? It couldn't be. The amulet had been neatly tied with a small knot.

Beyond weird. Too weird to look for an explanation, the least unlikely among a host of unlikely ones being an insomniac magpie getting into the house and stealing it. I shook my head silently in the semi-darkness, illuminated by a young moon and a smattering of pulsing stars. I'd always been comfortably led by logic, by reason. And the Japanese talisman a friend had given me flying of its own accord and materialising on a tree wasn't in the normal order of things.

But the night was so warm, the darkness so full, and the talisman was swaying gently from the branch in a near-hypnotic way. There was no other choice but to open my mind, to let myself go a little.

What I did next, I did it by instinct. I stood on my toes and freed the *omamori* from its knot. Then, holding it tight in my hand, I closed my eyes again and did what Catriona had told me to do.

Warm, salty wind.

Soft sea in the distance.

Vast, vast night all around me.

Silk against my skin . . .

I made a wish.

The wind blew cold again, and I shivered. When I opened my eyes, everything was in its place again – the soft noise of the sea, the deserted beach, the silently growing moon. It was as if I'd been somewhere strange, somewhere alien, and now I was back home. Hyde darted past me, towards the dunes, and I stood for a second with the *omamori* still in my hand, my eyes wide, wondering what had just happened.

3

Matthew

Had it not been for the estate agent driving in front of me, guiding me from the harbour to the house, I would have missed it. With the gloaming starting, and no lights yet on in the scattered buildings around it, Molleson Cottage seemed to disappear into the little hill it leaned on. I stopped the car and sat back in the seat for a moment. A hobbit house, a fox's den, a rabbit's burrow. I'd be like a little animal hiding under a tree, I thought, waiting for better, warmer, less insidious times . . .

When I stepped inside, the impression of burrowing continued, with wood and stone everywhere, furniture that seemed to emerge from the walls or rise from the floor, like the whole place had grown organically. In a corner, near the window, was a black Steinway piano. Imagine having enough money to buy a Steinway for your holiday home, I thought. Behind the piano, on grey granite shelves, was a vintage record player with a huge collection of vinyl.

'Fancy, eh? Mr Briers must be a music fan,' the man

said in his sing-song accent. 'And look at that,' he added, opening his arms towards the incredible view, as if he'd made it himself.

He'd gone to a lot of trouble, it seemed to me, to come from another island on a day of choppy seas, and I was grateful. Now he launched himself into the list of things I needed to know: the fuse box and the hot water, the refuse collection and how I should never, ever go swimming in the waters behind the house, because the currents of the Corrywreckan, the ocean whirlpool, were strong and I would be drowned in minutes. Oh, and stay away from the cliffs, they might crumble and take you with them.

Well, thank you. Two nice ways to get killed five minutes from my house. Handy.

I struggled to concentrate on practical instructions; the place was even more spectacular in real life than in the photographs I'd seen, if that was possible, perfectly fused with its surroundings and yet breathtakingly modern. The grass and heather growing on the hill continued onto the cottage's roof, and the floor-to-ceiling windows made the outside and the inside seem seamless. You could stand in the living room and feel like you were on the beach. And tonight, as the afternoon bled into evening, sand, water and sky seemed to be a blur of white and blue and grey, like a Turner painting. *Island on the Edge of Everything*, it could have been called.

Mia would have taken some amazing photographs

here. She would have stood on those rocks to capture more of the sea, and knelt in the sand to look for little details; she would have stood sentry to watch the sky changing, to grab the perfect light . . .

I swallowed. The perpetual lump in my throat still there, always there.

'There's a travelling library, it comes once a month,' the estate agent was saying. 'It's really just a van, but it buys in quite a lot. My wife is one of the organisers.'

'Sounds great,' I managed to say, but I could barely concentrate, my mind was so scattered, so overwhelmed by the *newness* of it all. After two hours on the ferry, with every mile taking me away from the world I knew, I'd landed on Planet Seal. It could have been Mars, given how different it was from everything I was familiar with. I'd always lived among shopping centres and offices and cinemas and busy streets – places that knew no rest, no silence. I'd grown up escaping to places in my imagination, and Seal seemed to have emerged from one of my dreams, a place that was like a miniature Middle Earth.

Seal was *empty*. Empty of almost everything but what was supposed to be there in the first place: nature. When I'd set foot on the pier, carrying all I had on my back, and as I drove north in the car Greg had lent me – a jeep he'd decided he could go without for a while, as you do when you have more money than ways to spend it – I felt that stirring again, a sense of life calling, calling. Everything I was, all that I could think and feel and suffer and need and even love, seemed insignificant in the face of this raw, naked beauty. Ocean and land, the unstoppable movement of tectonic plates and masses of water so big my mind could not conceive; ancient volcanoes and a time when man didn't matter – this was what I saw when I set foot on Seal. I was nothing in the face of nature, and at this point I liked being nothing. It sat well with me if, ultimately, I did not matter, if in the grand scheme of things I did not exist.

'Well, I'm all done. Best of luck on the island.'

I nodded at the man's words and pushed my glasses up my nose with an unsteady smile. I was not concerned with luck. What I needed was *survival*, and that was hard enough. Keep breathing from morning to night and then from night to morning. It was as far as I could go, for now.

The estate agent was lingering. I could feel his eyes on me.

'Thanks,' I said, trying to hurry him. I needed to be alone.

'Have a great holiday,' he replied, and I had the feeling he'd been about to say something else. Something along the lines of *Why are you here? What's your story?* But maybe it was just my imagination.

'Thank you.'

The car lights broke the gathering darkness, and at last he disappeared. I was alone. Alone in the building, as opposed to sharing the space, the air, with another few hundred people, our thoughts and guilt and claustrophobia gathering against the ceiling like cobwebs, like storm clouds.

Nobody but me, the sea and the sky, and a place to walk around, free, my own terrain.

I had an endless shower – a bathroom of cream marble and polished copper – and then stood in the open-plan living room, barefoot on the wooden floor, looking out of the French doors and the full-length windows on either side of them. Only glass and a small stretch of sand separated me from the Atlantic, now grey and raging under a steely sky, the northern night falling faster than I was used to.

I was alone with the ebb, flow, ebb, flow.

Walking into the sea would be an easy solution, of course, but I didn't deserve relief from my endless guilt. I was alive, Mia wasn't. And I would live every moment, every day, every year, knowing that it was my fault.

Every minute I would have to remember it was *all my fault.*

Slowly I opened the French doors and stepped out onto the cold, wet sand. A wind wilder than I'd ever felt before encompassed me and raised goose bumps on my bare arms. It was whipping the sea up into angry foaming waves. I closed my eyes for a moment, to take in the salty scent, the rhythmic noise of the waves eternally hitting the shore. My skin and my hair moistened up, covered by a million tiny particles of salt water. As I raised my chin to the sky, for the first time in months I felt . . . not peace – that would be too much – but a moment where the burden I carried melted into my surroundings, and with it my mind, my soul seemed to fly away on the wind. Blissfully, my own turmoil fused with that of the sea, and they cancelled each other out. I knew a moment of serenity, just a moment, but for now, it was enough.

It didn't last long, soon destroyed by the flicker of a memory – the way my wife had stood on a beach of long ago, a beach so different from this windswept one. The beach I remembered was golden and crowded and sun-drenched, Mia's skin was honeyed. She was wearing a red summer dress, shielding her eyes, messy hair bleached by the sun, her feet sinking in the sand . . .

I opened my eyes quickly, trying to wipe away the painful vision with my hand, and soon my eyes stung with salt. It was then, with tears blurring my vision – maybe just because of the salty wind, maybe not – that I saw the creature. It moved like a piece of the night, black against the grey. All my muscles tensed, as the most primal part of me screamed *predator* – an ancient instinct of fight or flight took hold of me, and adrenaline coursed through my veins. I peered into the lilac light, already too dim to see clearly. The thing was prowling around on strong, fluid limbs. I swallowed.

A *wolf*? On these islands?

Of course not. I was just tired and confused and

everything was new. It came closer, closer, and I could feel my heart beating in my ears . . .

Out of the mist, a dog appeared, a black dog, soft paws silent on the sandy dunes. In fact, a small dog and not much of a threat. I smiled to myself. What a fool. But I was silent, still, just in case. Even small dogs have sharp teeth.

The dog stopped and sat. It looked at me.

We looked at each other.

Are you lost? it seemed to be saying, though it would have made more sense for me to ask that. Which one of us was lost? Both? Or maybe just me.

I decided the best option was to ignore it, so I walked on a little, looking around me in the dim light. On my left was the blurred outline of another cottage, dark and still, and on my right a little cove, a tiny beach with rocks on each side and dunes at its back, like a nest made of sand and seaweed. To my wonder, I saw small, round heads in the shallow water. Seals. And then I realised that some were resting on the rocks that crowned the cove, dark grey, speckled skin fusing with the stone and becoming near invisible. I walked on slowly, carefully, as not to frighten them, but they didn't seem bothered.

Suddenly the sound of barking came from behind me, and the seals disappeared into the waves.

'You scared the seals,' I said to the dog. It was meant as a reproach, but she looked quite proud of herself and wagged her tail, a bushy, feathery thing. She – yes, it was definitely a she – was trying to appease me. 'Go. Go!' I took a step towards her, hoping she would make herself scarce, but again she sat and looked at me, eyes like the seals', soft ears folded on themselves. I walked away, but she followed me on padded paws, panting softly. I opened the French doors and closed them behind me at once, without letting her in. As I made my way upstairs, I caught a glimpse of her nose against the glass. I ignored her black silhouette and pretended she wasn't there. 'Go home,' I said under my breath.

I went into the bedroom, where a bed too big for one man alone and too luxurious for anyone awaited me. As I looked up, I saw a skylight in the ceiling, just over the bed, through which I could see the sky, now black and glittering with silver. A sickle moon hung just to the right, peeping over and saying: *Hello, Matthew, now haven't we made a mess of things?*

I lay on the bed, fully dressed, and sank into it, the silky sheets soft under my skin. It was perfect, comfortable, soothing. Yet the four walls seemed to close on me once again. This sleeping thing wasn't working out.

I needed to go back outside, to where the sea broke against the rocks, violently enough to exorcise me, annihilate me. I grabbed my sleeping bag, stuck the torch I'd brought with me in my pocket and left the cocoon of the bedroom. Part of me wasn't thinking at all, part of me simply felt a hunger, a longing I hadn't known in a long time – except when I hungered for Mia. I *needed* the ocean.

The dog was still in front of the doors, and I nearly swiped her nose with the glass as I opened them up to the beach and the wind.

'Still here?' Black eyes gazed at me. 'Fine. I give up,' I said as I walked on, my torch illuminating my path, and she followed me calmly into the darkness, as if it were a given that she should come with me. We were a strange little party, she and I – a lost dog and a city boy – as we strode towards the cove over the uneven ground: sand and rocks and slippery seaweed to watch out for.

I sat with my back against the rocks, hugged my knees and covered myself with the sleeping bag as I stared out at the sea, the black sky with mother-of-pearl where the moon shone behind the clouds, the shells in the sand, the barnacles on the rocks and the tiny life in the rock pools.

The dog yelped, and I directed the beam of light towards her in a kind of canine *Blair Witch Project*. 'Hey, you okay?' I said and reached across to stroke her head. My heart tightened as I saw her ducking, fearful, as if I was going to strike her. The reflex could only mean one thing: she'd been hit before. Too horrible to even imagine. 'I didn't mean to scare you, dog. I'm sorry . . .'

She looked a lot smaller than when I'd first noticed her, when darkness and the alien nature of the place had made me mistake her for a wolf or some other scary beast. She'd curled up beside me, even after she'd thought I was going to hit her. Her trust melted me. I hadn't the heart to turn her away again, all alone as she was – or maybe it was me who didn't want to be alone. I decided I liked having that little body close to mine, head to tail in a circle. I switched the torch off and snuggled down in my sleeping bag. Slowly, hardly noticing I was doing it, I laid a hand on her warm fur, and with that comforting touch from another living being, the sound of the sea and the dog's soft snoring carried me into sleep.

I woke up suddenly, near-complete darkness around me. The dog was tense beside me, a rumbling sound coming from her throat. I sat very still. A warm gust of wind blew into my face – where could a warm wind be coming from? I fumbled for the torch but couldn't find it. The dog quietened, and silence filled the cove, apart from the song of the sea: ebb, flow, ebb, flow . . .

And then I heard it.

Something, someone was breathing, and it was coming from behind me. I wasn't alone. I felt the hair on the back of my neck rise, and jumped to my feet faster than I'd ever thought I could. The breathing continued – how could I hear it over the sound of the waves, the sound of the wind? It had to be very close . . . maybe now, any second, I would feel a warmth on my cheek. I regretted having thought of *The Blair Witch Project* earlier on. The dog began growling again.

Good. Whatever was out there, I needed to let it know that I wasn't completely alone.

At last my hand closed around the torch, together with a handful of sand, and a ray of light illuminated the darkness. I began moving the beam around, the strange warm wind still blowing on me, trying to find the source of the breathing. What I saw on the rocks made me suck my breath in. The pod of seals I'd seen before was back, but not just them – many, many more. If I weren't so scared, I'd have laughed at the idea of a seal rave. At least two dozen pairs of sweet black eyes were raised to me as I pointed the torch at them, and then moved it at once so I didn't startle them. And then finally I found what I was looking for.

It took a little time for my mind to process what my eyes were seeing. It was the silhouette of a young woman sitting on a rock facing away from me, her contours blurring, long hair flowing behind her. I gasped, and my heart stopped for a second, for an eternity. I knew who that was, and I was terrified of her, but at the same time desperate for her to stay.

Mia had come back. Of course she had. There was a thread tying us to each other, I had always known that. Not even death could cut it, and something had proven that to me already – something I could tell nobody about. My life was made up of *before* and *after.* Before the accident, things had made sense, reality had a place and imagination another – I trusted my mind and my senses. But after . . . after, things weren't so clear-cut. I wasn't sure what to believe, I wasn't really sure my mind was still completely sound. Because when I was in the hospital, just after the accident, a ghost had come to me; and once that thin veil between my senses and reality had been ripped, anything was possible.

I awoke calling Mia's name. Or I thought I was, because I couldn't hear anything, as if I were underwater. All I could see was a white ceiling, and tubes coming out of me, and a woman's face, a woman with cool, soft hands that she laid on my forehead and wrapped around my own hand. She wore blue and she smelled of something pungent, chemical.

Mia? Mia? Mia? A soundless invocation, gentle hands on my chest, pressing me down, trying to calm me. Sounds returned to me, a frantic beeping, my own helpless yelps, and then a disembodied male voice. 'There, there. Calm down. Calm down, now.'

Of course. I was in hospital. The accident.

The accident.

Mia, Mia, Mia, I wanted to shout, but I realised that all the sounds coming out of my mouth were muffled. There was something on my face, and I tried to pull it off, but the nurse put it back in place. What about my wife? Where was my wife?

I am here.

Mia. Mia, my wife, at last, leaning over me. Seeing her was such a relief, I could have cried, and I did, silent tears streaming down my face, under the oxygen mask. Her face was framed by flowing blond hair – oh, she looked the way she did when we were married, pink-lipped smile, tender eyes, the promise of happy years to come . . . Why was she in a wedding dress? The simple white silk one she'd worn when we got married. Why did she look like the Mia of ten years ago? How much I loved her . . .

Mia leaned closer. I tried to smile, although it hurt. Tears of relief kept falling down my cheeks. *You're okay, you're fine*: words of love and relief rushed in, half thought, half said aloud, and I struggled to set myself free from the strange restraints on my body, the tubes, the weight of the nurse's hands on my chest. I would just get up, lean on my wife a little until my head stopped swimming, and go home at last. I would put my key in the door and we would step in quietly, the familiar scent of our house welcoming us . . .

Why? Her voice was calm and sweet. *Why?*

My eyes fixed on hers, and for a moment I didn't understand what she was saying. She came so close to me that her nose touched mine.

I'm gone. You lost me . . . She spaced the words, to make them sink in.

'What? What are you talking about? You're here, you're right here . . .'

'Shh, shh. We'll give you something so you can rest, okay?' The nurse's voice came from somewhere, and her hands disappeared from my chest.

'Mia?' I blinked. My face was now drenched with tears and burning as the salty water inflamed the cuts in my skin. That was my wife. My wife. The woman I loved and treasured. She was there, she was there, leaning over me; she wasn't dead, so why was she telling me those things?

Goodbye, Matthew.

'I don't understand. Mia . . .'

'There you go.' The disembodied voice spoke again, and suddenly the nurse's hand was holding something silvery and shiny and sharp, something meant for me.

Do you not remember? Mia said, and all of a sudden her silky white dress was red and torn, and her face was discoloured on one side, a purple bruise on her temple that seemed to get darker as I looked at it. I gasped, and for a moment there was no breath in me. This is when I die, I thought, as my lungs spasmed, rigid and empty. *Somebody look after my wife! Somebody see to her, please, she's bleeding!* I shouted in my mind, but no sound, no air, no breathing came out of me. Mia spoke again.

Matthew. The text that came when we were on the motorway, remember? You said just a second, it could be work, and it was done. I was gone.

A ragged breath filled my lungs with air and pain, and the silvery shiny object sank into my arm.

I love you, Mia said, and her voice was coming from afar. Slowly her bloody face faded, until darkness swallowed her and me.

*

Was she really back? Had she followed me to Seal to take up our thread, hanging lost and lonely from my hands? Had she returned to carry me away with her? *Please do, please take me with you, wherever you are . . .*

After that visit in the hospital, she'd never come back. That was because, of course, it had all been a hallucination born of trauma and medication.

Or had it?

Maybe Mia's soul had followed her camera and the lost pieces of our life, turned into pixels and captured in digital memory. Maybe that was what she was here for, to get the camera back from me. My knees gave way and my throat was dry as I opened my mouth to call her name.

I shook in terror, alone in the dark. It was all too much. I couldn't take it any more. The black sky weighed on my shoulders and I just wanted to kneel and cry all the tears I hadn't cried in prison, surrounded as I was by fellow inmates and guards. I found words I'd never thought I would say – I'd never been much of a believer – and closed my eyes in a silent prayer. *Please, God, please. Relieve me of this guilt. Please take this guilt away from me, because I can't live any more.*

I could feel her close to me, looking for me. Any moment now she would take my hand and lead me away, any moment now I would feel her cold, cold touch. Terror and yearning mixed in my heart, while the wind carried my prayers away.

When I opened my eyes, the rock was bare; the

figure was gone. It was as if she'd never been there. I was left shaking, still full of the words I'd sent up to the sky in a desperate plea. Alone once again, I dragged myself towards the house on unsteady legs, away from the darkness. The dog slipped inside after me, and I let her.

I took another glug of the whisky I'd bought at the airport, sitting cross-legged on the floor. I'd quickly put together a peat fire, and it burned slowly, steadily in the darkest hours of the night.

'Molly,' I said to the dog. She wagged her tail frantically. 'Molly?' Molly was my pet as I was growing up, a beautiful golden Labrador who lived to the ripe old age of eighteen. The two dogs looked nothing alike, but the name stirred sweet memories. 'Yes? Do you feel like a Molly?' I said, and slowly, cautiously, so as not to scare her, I extended a hand towards her. This time she didn't duck – she closed her eyes in happiness as I stroked her little black muzzle.

Later, I let her come upstairs with me and jump on my wide, empty bed. She fell asleep quickly, while I lay awake, watching the sky lighten through the skylight above our heads.

Mia, was it you?

Was it you?

4

Rose

My quest continues along the line of a story, following a red thread that appears and disappears and gets tangled up and fades under the weight of amnesia. I'm unravelling this thread slowly, as best I can . . . so let's start from the beginning.

I was the princess of a little kingdom until the day of my seventh birthday, when I pricked my finger on the spinning wheel. My kingdom was a white house in a village called Glen Avich, and the three of us – Mum, Dad and me, were its rulers. In my child's life, we were north, south, east and west, we were day and night, we were the seasons and a whole solar system all in ourselves. Our home and our family were everything to me. I wanted for nothing, in body and heart and soul.

Yes, I was the princess of a little kingdom, and I thought nothing would ever change.

But one day, after a rainy, wet walk home from ballet class, my hair still a bit damp and my wellies left one on top of the other on the kitchen doorstep, my parents sat me down. They told me that there was a boy, a little older than me, and that his mum and dad couldn't look after him, so another mum and dad had taken him in, but now *they* couldn't look after him any more either. I sat there gawping – what was this thing of not being able to look after your child and passing him on, like shoes you'd outgrown? That could never happen in my world. Mum – brown-rimmed glasses, sweet-smelling hair, her at-home cardigan – opened her mouth to speak, but I couldn't stay silent any longer. 'He can come here! We'll look after him!'

Mum and Dad looked at each other with a smile. I hadn't disappointed them.

'That's what we were hoping you would say, darling. Yes, he's coming to live with us, and we can't let him down, because he's been let down too many times before.'

'We won't,' I promised. 'What's his name?'

'Jacob. Jacob Blake. But he'll be Jacob McCrimmon when he comes to us.'

After that day, Jacob Blake came into my dreams, appeared in my drawings, was the main topic of the news I wrote every day for my teacher. He became a myth, like another of those stories from my mum's book. A hero who'd gone through so many battles and obstacles to get to us. My parents had a framed picture of him – they allowed me to keep it on my bedside table, the light of my magic lantern dancing on it. At night, I looked at the picture and into his dark eyes. I was too young then to find words that could describe his face, but now I think the word would be *alone*.

It was a long wait. Every day when I came home from school, I asked, *Is Jacob here yet?* I was desperate for him to be there for my birthday, to have him meet my friends and show him off. To me, he would be like another present – a lifelike doll, a little boy with a bow around his waist. But day after day, I was disappointed. By the time my birthday came around – the fifteenth of February – I'd lost hope. I was already dressed up in a pink tulle skirt and little ballet slippers that sparkled when I moved my feet. I was beside myself with excitement. But just before the doorbell started ringing, when all the yummy food was on the table, and the games ready to be played, and ribbons tied to the banister and at the sides of the fireplace, Dad got home – and with him was Jacob. We barely had time to look at each other – him dressed in dark blue, me pink and sparkly like a fairy – before my friends began to arrive. He ran upstairs and sat there looking at us from the top step.

My life had just been turned upside down, and yet I was unconcerned. The sweet, sweet days when my family sorted everything for me, worried in my stead, allowed me to live the happiest, most peaceful life a child could have, are all gone now. But then, everything spoke of happiness. My little friends in their tutus – I'd asked for a ballet party – the presents my grandparents had sent from England and that I would finally be allowed to open, the cakes and sweets on the table; and joy of all joys, *my brother.* The dark-eyed little boy who sat with his face in between the banisters, his body rigid, my mum standing at the bottom of the stairs as a kind of link between him and the people downstairs.

Looking back, it was strange that the arrival of my new brother coincided with my birthday party, a moment when all the attention was on me and not him. Or maybe it wasn't so strange that he should arrive when the star of the show was me: for my parents, the world seemed to revolve around me, and Jacob was a gift in human form, the sibling I'd always wanted but that my mum, who'd already struggled to conceive me, couldn't give me.

Maybe it was then, as I laughed and twirled among my friends while he watched from the top of the stairs, that he started to see his life as a kind of extension of mine.

If I was the princess in this fairy tale, what role did Jacob play?

The prince, the kind gamekeeper?

Or the hunter?

The wolf?

As soon as I had a moment in the whirlwind of excitement, I went up the stairs to him. I held his hand and led him to where my friends were playing musical statues. I loaded a plate for him at the buffet, and he carried it around for a while, then left it somewhere without touching the food. I can't remember exactly what I told him – I gave him words of welcome and comfort the way I knew them, the way they were given to me: are you hungry, are you thirsty, early to bed for you tonight after all this excitement. But I remember exactly what happened next: he took my hand, towering over me from the height of his ten years, and said: *Thank you.*

Just that.

Even as a child, innocent and unaware as I was, I knew it was an important moment. He followed me around, game after game, incongruous among all these six- and seven-year-old girls. Then the time came for the piñata. My friends all had a shot, and finally it was my go. The piñata broke open under my blow, and I was delighted. Except I was still holding the bat when everyone else was on the floor grabbing for sweets. I eyed a rainbow-coloured lollipop and made a dash for it, but my ballet classmate Julie got to it first. I was so disappointed; as the birthday girl, surely I should get the best of everything? My upset was clear as I stood in front of Julie, who clutched the lollipop with a defiant expression on her face. She had, after all, won it fair and square.

We played some more, and my mum brought in the cake. It was perfect – pink and yellow, with yellow flowers – and I forgot all about the rainbow lollipop.

But Jacob was waiting, and when he found the right moment, he took Julie aside and whispered something in her ear. To this day, I don't know what it was, but Julie's eyes grew bigger, and her trembling hands came up to offer the lollipop to me.

That night, when everyone was gone, we were sent to bed. It was early, but we were both tired, especially Jacob, whose eyes were swollen and red like when you haven't slept for ages; the kind of eyes you'd see on a grown-up, not a child. It was no wonder he hadn't slept. He was starting all over again with a new family. With his *true* family.

I lay in my bed, but the excitement of the day – Jacob's arrival as well as the party – had been such that I couldn't fall asleep. My limbs just needed to move, but I knew that if I started wandering around, my parents would reproach me. I tiptoed to the loo, and that was when I heard them talking in their room.

'. . . every night, yes. He sits downstairs, on the floor, under the kitchen table. Anywhere but his bed.' It was Mum.

'Poor wee soul,' Dad replied. 'I haven't heard anything, but I'll go and check. If he's there, I'll get him back to bed.'

'They said he'll just get up again and again.'

'At least I can try.'

'Fine, do it your way,' my mum said. The harshness in her voice surprised me. I didn't know then that that was the first little crack opening between them, the crack that Jacob's arrival had created in our family.

I heard my dad getting up and going downstairs, and then more whispers. I dived back into my room and lay there pretending to sleep. After a while, I heard him leave Jacob in his own room and go back to bed.

I got up again and walked softly to the bedroom at the end of the corridor on the left, the one my parents had made up in blues and greens to welcome the boy of the family. I peeked in, but the bed was empty. And then I saw him, Jacob, sitting cross-legged on the floor, his back hunched and his eyes drooping as he tried with all his might to stay awake. I said nothing, but slipped into his empty bed. Sleep was about to overcome me when I saw him take the blanket from the foot of the bed, cover himself with it and lie down on the floor. A deep, deep sigh came out of him. I felt his body relax, and we breathed in unison in the darkness.

5

Matthew

I sat in front of my coffee, silent, in a low-ceilinged pub imaginatively called the Seal Inn. Soft fiddle music came from somewhere near, but I wasn't sure where. I'd driven down from the cottage in the insomniac haze I'd grown accustomed to, hoping for a chance of a job. After the incident on the beach, the invisible person breathing beside me, I was too terrified to sleep. I'd lain rigid on the bed, the light on, a hand on Molly's warm back, only passing out for what felt like a heartbeat before I saw dawn breaking through the skylight.

I'd opened my eyes ready to see the crusty ceiling of my prison cell pressing down on me, trying to summon the willpower to swing my legs down the ladder of the bunk bed and start another day in confinement. Instead, I became aware of the brightening sky over my head, and the sound of the sea, and the scent of polished wood that covered floor and walls. And freedom. I woke up knowing that I would no longer be surrounded by noise and chaos and the uncomfortable closeness of other tormented human beings, but by sand and heather and grass, alone, swept by a cold, purifying wind.

Life is unpredictable.

Only yesterday, everything was different. And now here I was, sitting with a coffee in some kind of tavern from a hobbit film, rubbing my eyes under my glasses. The plan: to go to shops and pubs and community centres and accept the first job I was offered. I didn't care what it entailed; I couldn't be a social worker any more, so it didn't matter what I ended up doing.

I was born to help people. I took every lost cause under my wing, spent my breaks with whoever needed someone to talk to, listened to my mother's friends' woes, volunteered in the old folk's home. And I was good at it, apparently. I made a difference, I knew I did. With those boys and girls at the shelter, I felt I was truly doing what I was meant to do. I wanted to make things better for them. You know that saying: leave the world a better place than you found it? It's a cliché, but yes, that was what I wanted.

'If there's a bird with a broken wing anywhere, Matthew will take it on himself to heal it,' my father always said, half proud, half worried for the boy I was, the boy who felt too keenly for comfort.

I looked down at my hands gripping the mug. The ghost of the man I was gave way again to the memory of handcuffs and a grey sweatshirt, days and nights in a place where you were better off dead than alive.

Every blow I received from another inmate, I welcomed. Every kind word, I resented. I was to be punished. I was to be destroyed, I *wanted* to be destroyed. I kept Mia's picture under my pillow and made myself look at it every morning, every night, and every time it was the stab in the heart that I deserved, the reminder of my guilt, guilt, guilt. That picture – the debris of a life that was, and then wasn't any more, just like that, in the space of a few moments. In my second year in prison, someone stole the photo. I never found it again, and all I was left with was the memory of her face in my mind, in my heart, ingrained in every cell in my body.

'Hello.' A tall black-haired man approached me. He had a tea towel on his shoulder and a stack of dirty plates in his hand. 'You're the guy who bought Molleson Cottage, aren't you?' His accent was soft and pleasant, like all the islanders. They took English and turned it into something else, something sing-songy, musical.

'Not really. A friend is letting me stay there. I'm Matthew. Matthew Shearer.'

'Cool. Sorren.' He offered his hand and I shook it. 'Nice to meet you. So, how do you like it here?'

'Well, it's . . .' Black sky, black sea, silence, the sound of breathing in my ear, sweat drenching me and a suspended moment in time . . . *It's bloody freaky, that's what it is.* 'It's beautiful. I'm going to stay for a while. I'm looking for a job, actually.'

'Oh. There aren't many jobs going around here.

I suppose your best bet is a fisherman needing an extra pair of hands, if you need something quickly . . .'

'Sorry to butt in, but Fergus was just here,' the girl serving behind the counter called over. 'Hi, I'm Katie.'

'Hi.'

A shy smile, a blond bob hiding reddening cheeks. I pushed my glasses up on my nose. 'So, yes, Fergus is the guy who owns the distillery up in the north of the island . . . He's hiring.'

'I'll believe it when I see it. He's interviewed people before. Nobody was quite right for him. He has trouble with his legs,' Sorren explained to me. 'Him and these other . . . what is it, five, six guys do everything there, and all the traditional way, no technology for them. It's a selling point, I suppose, artisan whisky, nothing to do with the big corporations we have now.' He grimaced.

'That's right. But yeah, he asked me to spread the word,' Katie said. 'He's your neighbour, so to speak. He lives about three miles from you, to the west.'

'Thank you . . . I'll look for him.' I got up, wallet in hand.

'That's on the house.' Sorren put his hands up. 'Take it as a welcome to Seal. And be quick with Fergus. Jobs are scarce here, and the local lads will be all over this chance. It's a good opportunity.'

I nodded. In prison I'd lost the ability or the willingness to do small talk or be effusive, but I was grateful.

For a moment, Sorren's eyes met mine. I looked away at once. It was like he *knew*.

Nonsense, of course. He couldn't know anything about me, unless he read the English local papers. I suppose any man who came alone to an island in the Outer Hebrides, staying in a million-pound cottage but looking like he'd slept on a bench for years, had a story behind him. This was the kind of place that attracted people who wanted to leave something behind. 'Thanks,' I repeated. I couldn't force a smile, so I looked down, flustered over nothing.

I heard the door behind me opening, and Sorren glanced past my shoulder. I turned around and saw a squat man with a beer belly, wearing a police uniform. He was a green shade of pale, and looked very much like he could do with a steadying drink.

'Oh, Mike. You okay? You look like you've seen a ghost!' Sorren said.

'I did. A few of them. I was up at St Fintan's. They had a blackout last night. We all did apparently, but it was at three in the morning so nobody noticed. But they would notice, up at the clinic. It was bad. You know, all those machines they have that keep people alive.'

'Surely they have a generator?'

'Oh aye, they do. That failed too. The power came back after three minutes, but it was long enough. A few patients were in a pretty bad way.'

'But why did they call you? Surely they needed an electrician, not the police?'

'Because they have no idea how it happened.'

'A power cut? We have them every time there's a storm.'

'And when there isn't one,' Katie quipped.

'But the generator failed for no apparent reason, and they check it every single day. Something isn't right. Anyway. Hello . . .' The policeman had noticed me.

'Matthew,' I said. I pondered for a moment the fact that an active investigation was being discussed in a pub by the man leading it. I wasn't exactly an expert on police procedure, apart from liaising with police at the shelter occasionally, but I was pretty sure this was not the done thing. Perhaps in a place that was home to little more than three hundred people, things were different.

'Sergeant Casey. Mike,' he said, and offered me a cold hand. The guy was really shaken.

'He's staying at Molleson Cottage.' Sorren ducked his head towards me.

'Oh, the millionaire. I'm impressed,' Mike teased me, but without malice.

'No, just the millionaire's guest. Well, I'm off. I'll see you around. Thanks again. For the coffee . . . and the tip about the job.'

'Sure.'

'Oh, by the way. There's this stray dog up near my house. I kind of took her in. She doesn't have a collar or anything . . . Small, black. In case someone has lost her?'

'I'll ask around, but nobody has reported losing a pet. Sometimes people come here on holiday and leave their dogs behind. I've seen it happen.'

'That's heartless,' Sorren said. I thought of Molly left all alone on a beach, having to fend for herself, and a hand squeezed my heart.

'If nobody comes forward, I'll look after her,' I said.

'Good stuff. See you soon,' Sorren said, and Katie waved from behind the counter, her cheeks still burning up. I'd never met a shy bartender before.

I made my way towards the door and stopped for a moment to let two old ladies step in. The conversation behind me continued while I was on the threshold, with Sorren asking, 'Are you sure you're okay?'

'I'm fine, I'm fine,' Mike replied. 'Just, I had to go to the silent building. All those beds with people asleep in them. Not a sound. It's like some horror film. And some so young . . .'

The silent building? Like a horror film?

I stepped out. I didn't want to hear any more.

I had no idea where the distillery was, but it was nearly impossible to get lost in the northern part of the island, where there was practically nothing but green, brown and purple fields, sand dunes and sheep. I found it easily. It was a slightly larger than usual whitewashed cottage with a couple of stone outbuildings and a beautiful gold and blue sign over the door. A strong smell filled the air – half sugary, half burnt: the scent of whisky-making. I made my way towards the only door I could see, the omnipresent wind blowing on me, my feet making a crackling sound on the gravel. I regretted not having shaved. It would be hard to give an air of respectability with an unkempt beard and a three-year gap in my employment history.

But hey, what did I have to lose?

'Hello?' I called, peeking through the open door.

'Yes, come in. You here for a tour of the distillery?' A huge man who could have come straight out of *Vikings* stood leaning on a desk. I needn't have worried about my beard; he sported a blond one, streaked with grey. He also had the brightest blue eyes I'd ever seen, laughter lines all around them, and the weathered face of someone who was often outdoors.

'Not really. Sorren . . . you know, Sorren down at the pub, he said you were looking for someone to give you a hand.'

'Oh, yes, yes. Well, that's not entirely accurate. I'm just having a spot of bother with my legs, and there's only the six of us here. I mean, I don't really need anyone, to be entirely honest, I can manage myself, it's just . . . Anyway, who would you be? I've never seen you around.'

'That's because I only arrived yesterday.' Or was it the day before? Time blurred. 'Matthew Shearer.

I live in Molleson Cottage, next door to you.' It seemed as good a business card as any.

'You bought Molleson Cottage and you want to come here to lift barley sacks and clean casks?'

'Just staying there, I don't own it. Long story. And yes, I need a job.'

'Right. Well, you look strong enough. Maybe I should see your CV or something. What did you do before? Where were you?'

'I was in England . . . Bennington, about an hour from London. I was a social worker. I worked with young people with addictions. In my . . . previous life.' I was beginning to babble.

'Right.'

'I'm just out of prison,' I said, and I realised I was trembling, my whole body shaking with nerves, like a frightened animal. I'd been to prison. For manslaughter. This was me. This was my life now.

'Right,' Fergus said. There was no difference between the two *right*s. I had to hand it to the guy. He hadn't even flinched.

'I suppose I'll go, then,' I said.

'Where?'

I shrugged. 'To look for something else.'

'Why? Do you not want this job?'

'Are you offering it to me?'

'On probation. For a week. Then, if you're successful, we'll discuss pay and conditions. Oh, sorry . . . I didn't mean probation in that way . . .'

'No offence taken.'

'Good. So. What do you say?'

'Well . . . thank you. Okay. Agreed.' A wave of gratitude filled me, and I looked down, unable to meet Fergus's eye and reveal how I felt.

'Great. I'll show you around the place, then.'

'Fergus . . .' I had to ask. 'Sorren said the local lads would be all over this job. You don't know me at all. You asked me two questions. And one of them wasn't "Do you know anything about whisky?" Because I *don't* know anything about whisky, except that I like it. I don't exactly come with the greatest references. So . . . why?'

'Because I know a man who needs a break when I see one,' he said simply.

Night, indoors. The world faded to black. A find in Greg's record collection: Debussy. I'd been to Roan again, to buy provisions and peat and coffee, and dog food too. Molly had seemed keen to jump into the car and come with me, but I didn't have a leash and I didn't want to leave her in the car while I ran errands, so I left her outside the cottage. I had a feeling she would wait for me.

I found a bowl in a shop that seemed to sell everything, and a pile blanket, grey with pawprints all over, that I could use to make her a sort of nest she could sleep in. I supposed it wasn't particularly sensible to buy stuff for a dog that might be claimed back by her owners at any moment. But she'd seemed so lost on that beach, in the black night – I wanted to give her a proper place, even if it might be temporary. After all, my own place on Seal was temporary too, and I didn't have the heart or mind to make long-term decisions. I might as well make us both comfortable.

Sure enough, when I got back from Roan and opened the car door, there she was, sitting there calmly with a look that said: *I knew you'd come back.* She had a way of moving silently, almost invisibly, that was very un-dog-like.

'Hey, Molly. I come bearing gifts,' I said aloud. She followed me into the house like she was now a fully fledged lodger. 'Here. This is yours.' I filled the bowl with dog food, then put a small dish of water next to it. I sat and watched her eat and drink greedily – the poor thing must have been starving, and it had taken me so long to see to her needs. The self-centredness of pain, I suppose.

When she had finished eating – she looked slightly drunk with pleasure and relief – we sat on the floor in front of the fire, with Molly snubbing her new blanket to lie against my legs instead.

Little clouds of notes rose from the vinyl and soared up to the ceiling, like whisky fumes. In between notes, the ever-present sound of the sea. There were three miles of darkness between me and the nearest human being, and infinite distance – space, time, life, death – between me and the people I loved.

Without warning Molly, one second earlier a perfect furry circle, turned into a canine question mark – ears up, tail poised, rigid and ready. And then she began to bark and bark, her little body tense with the effort. Her bark wasn't just aggressive – it was frightened.

And suddenly, so was I. *Three miles of darkness between me and the nearest human being . . .*

I switched the music off and laid my hand on Molly's head. She yelped a little, then sat and stared at the French doors, darkness pressing on the glass as if it were trying to come in.

I heard it again.

The breathing.

Let me in, let me in.

I stood frozen, Molly's little body trembling beside me, soft yelps coming from her. Any moment now. Any moment now I would see the dark shape that had come to torment me, the woman who'd come looking for me. What was this, some kind of Edgar Allan Poe style retribution, where I would have to hear and see terrible things for the rest of my life?

Mia, my Mia.

Please go away.

Please come to me, never leave again.

Take me with you, don't let us spend another moment apart . . .

'Mia . . .' My lips formed her name, a whisper in the

golden light of the room as I took a step towards the blackness. I laid my hands on the glass and slowly pressed my face against it to try and see what was outside.

A white face appeared right in front of me, emerging from the darkness like an apparition, and I jumped backwards, a moan escaping me. The thumping of my heart, Molly barking, terror and longing mixed in my mind – for a moment I thought I'd gone crazy. I had to open the door and let Mia in. I had to let her in and be with her, accept her retribution. Maybe her forgiveness.

The white oval of her face, surrounded by black, criss-crossed with black snakes. A small hand rising to rest on the glass, slender white fingers . . .

It wasn't Mia.

Oh God, it wasn't Mia.

Abandonment and despair and relief filled me, and I could have cried. And then I saw that the woman's breath was condensing against the glass in a circle that became bigger and then smaller again as she breathed in and out, in and out. There were no snakes on her face; just her hair, wet against her skin, and she wore a frightened expression. No, it wasn't a ghost – it was a young woman, soaked through, standing outside my door.

'Shh, Molly, it's okay,' I said to the dog, and stroked her fur, my eyes never leaving the young woman's face. Molly was quiet now, except for a low, near-inaudible growl, but her body was still rigid. I put my hand on the handle – unlocked, by the way; maybe that should change – and opened the door. If she was an axe murderer – well, I'd brought it on myself; but she took a step back, looking at me with eyes like saucers, like she was the scared one and not me. I uttered the first words that came into my mind. Stupid ones, I know, but I challenge anyone to do better, given the circumstances. 'Are you all right?'

She shook her head and half closed her eyes against the light. She swayed a little, like the light bothered her, or she wasn't very sure on her feet.

'Don't worry. I'm not going to hurt you. Really I'm not.'

Molly had stopped growling, but I could feel her alertness.

'You shouldn't be out at . . .' I looked at my watch, 'three in the morning. You're all wet. You'll catch your death . . .' The young woman startled, and I regretted my choice of words. Maybe she'd had some terrible experience and needed help. I had to do something.

'You'll catch a cold,' I corrected myself. 'Have you been swimming? Come inside . . . we'll call Dr Chatto.' I'd seen her name on a laminated card in the kitchen, with the rest of the essential Seal names and numbers. The young woman shook her head violently. 'No? Okay. Okay, no. No doctors. We won't call anyone. Just . . . put this on,' I said and slipped my hoodie off.

I handed it to her and she shrugged it on, hiding her narrow white shoulders. 'Are you with someone? A friend, a boyfriend? Can I call someone for you?'

She shook her head again. Was she mute? Traumatised?

'Please tell me how I can help you.' I stepped closer, slowly, carefully – and that was when I noticed that there was seaweed in her hair and around her fingers.

Had she come out of the sea?

'Look. You're soaking. Let me at least help you get dry.'

Still she said nothing. Then she looked down at her hands like she couldn't believe what she was seeing.

Maybe I was dreaming. I'd finally fallen into a deep sleep and was upstairs in bed, and this young woman had come out from some recess of my brain. I offered her my hand. 'Look. I promise you I'm not a psycho or anything. Come in, let me close the door. We'll get you dry and changed and we'll take it from there.'

The night wind made her hair and dress flow to the side of her, brushing against my extended fingers. I didn't think she'd agree, and already my mind was rushing ahead to a scenario where I would phone Sergeant Casey to come and help. But to my surprise, the young woman took a step towards me, bringing a gust of wind with her, and took my hand.

As she stepped across the threshold, the air in the house seemed to twirl and move and rearrange itself around her. She stood there in silence, and then she threw herself into my arms as if she trusted me completely, and I held her with all the care I could muster, like you would hold a little bird. There was a strange pause in the world around us – the wind that had blown through the door suddenly still before starting up again, cold and salty. I held the young woman close, an unstoppable instinct to make contact with another human being. There was a strange scent to her – a sweet one, but also, underneath, one I couldn't quite identify. One that didn't awake good memories; a chemical smell.

She trembled in my arms, alone, adrift. And then I realised that this was the first time I'd had my arms around someone since it happened.

'Mia,' she whispered then, and I had to hold on to her for a moment, or I would have fallen.

'What did you say?'

The young woman looked at me with enormous eyes and said nothing.

I took her by the shoulders and had to restrain myself, because I wanted to shake her. 'Please. Did you say Mia? Did you? What did you say? Who are you?' She was still looking at me, mute, dripping water on the floor. '*Did you say Mia?*'

'I don't know!'

I composed myself. 'I'm sorry. So sorry.' I'd misheard. I was confused, and exhausted with insomnia, not to mention the fright I'd got when she appeared.

Of course she hadn't said my wife's name, I'd imagined it. She looked so frightened, and I felt terrible about having taken her by the shoulders. 'Come, you need a warm shower and dry clothes. Don't be afraid. I'm sorry.'

She followed me to the bathroom upstairs, and I focused on helping her, ignoring the strangeness of the whole situation. I showed her how to work the shower, then left quickly and laid out some clothes on the bed. I went back downstairs and revived the fire – I hadn't managed to work out how to run the central heating yet; I'd zoned out when the agent had explained it.

The young woman emerged clean and considerably reassured, swamped in a T-shirt and tracksuit bottoms. They were so big for her that it looked like there was more fabric than person, but at least she was warm. Her long hair was still soaking; I didn't own a hairdryer, so I led her to the fire and indicated the armchair, but she sat cross-legged on the floor. I wrapped a blanket around her shoulders and made her a cup of tea. I suspected she needed something stronger, but she seemed in such a daze as it was, I didn't want to risk giving her alcohol. I sat beside her on the floor, nursing a dram from a bottle Fergus had given me; she didn't move, nor did she seem alarmed at my presence. She seemed to have relaxed, to be quite at ease, even if everything was surreal.

'So. Can you tell me your name?' I asked. I'd decided she wasn't much younger than me, probably in her early twenties. With a deep sigh, she nestled against me and leaned her head on my shoulder. I froze. This was completely bizarre. Why was she behaving like this?

A sea of contrasting feelings swept through me. It had been so long since I'd been close to another human being, but this strange, nameless young woman with eyes the colour of spring leaves was lost – someone, somewhere must be looking for her. I had to call the police or the doctor, whether she liked it or not. She needed help, and apart from staving off pneumonia for her, there was nothing else I could do on my own.

'Do you not remember your name?' I tried again, feeling the weight of her head on my shoulder, not really expecting an answer. She'd been silent since the beginning. But this time she spoke, and I jumped out of my skin.

'You are . . . Matthew?' Her voice sounded hoarse, as if she hadn't used it for a while.

'Yes. How do you know?' It must have been the Seal grapevine, clearly. The English guy staying at Molleson Cottage, Matthew something.

'Oh, this is good,' she said in reply, extending her hands to the fire. Her lips curled up in a smile. She didn't seem so helpless any more now, but quite . . . composed. Poised. 'I hadn't felt . . . anything . . . in a long time.' She spoke in a matter-of-fact way, as if she were making small talk and the situation was perfectly normal.

'Well, good. Okay. So . . . you're sure you don't remember your name?'

She frowned and thought hard for a moment. 'Sorry. Nothing,' she said, like it didn't matter that much.

My eyes went from her long dark hair to her slight figure, and the way she hugged her knees like a girl from a Japanese manga, small and stylised and almost like a drawing in human form. She looked a lot like someone I used to know.

'Mia, these are . . . beautiful.' I stood in front of a wall full of eerie, dreamy black-and-white pictures, unframed, arranged in a deliberate chaos – overlapping, with little gaps filled with sketches and notes and quotes from poems. A young woman, slight and almost blurred, standing on a beach in various poses. And then, towards the end of the composition, standing further and further into the sea, almost sailing away.

The young woman was Selena, a Spanish student and favourite model of Mia's. I'd seen her pictured perching on a branch high up in a tree, hanging upside down from a circus-style trapeze, dancing among bluebells in a mossy wood, sitting in an empty room against a white wall, her smile lighting up the frame. But I'd never seen her in such a dark setting, on a post-apocalyptic beach surrounded by driftwood and dark rocks.

'Thank you.'

'They're very . . . dark.'

'Yeah. I don't know, they just came out that way.

You were in Manchester on that course, remember, and I was in Devon with Selena, and, well it seemed I hadn't seen you in ages . . .' she said slowly, and shrugged like what she was saying was by the by. She looked down, and away. I was dismayed for a moment to see her so despondent, so unlike herself, but I planted a kiss on her cheek and she smiled, and I thought it would all sort itself out. Yes, she'd been low for a while, distant – but she would be okay. She was overworked, that was all, and . . . well, we'd been trying for a while to extend our family, to no avail.

A woman approached her then and she stepped away from me – I looked for her eyes, but she didn't glance back. I turned to the lonely, forlorn photographs – and it hit me: they just weren't Mia at all. All this grey, the black, and Selena slowly sinking into the dark sea.

I felt uneasy again, more so than ever before.

That night we lay on the same pillow, silence outside and inside the house. She was close to me, but she felt far away – I can't explain why. It's something you pick up when you've lived with somebody for a long time and known them even longer: the shades and slivers of words unsaid, the imperceptible gestures that hold no meaning for anyone but the two of you.

'Mia, listen. Is there something bothering you?'

'No, why? What makes you say that?' Her breath was warm on my neck. She smelled of shampoo and of that honey cream she put on her hands at night.

'Those photographs. I don't know. It just wasn't you . . .

the whole set-up. So . . .' I struggled to find the word, 'forlorn.'

'It was just supposed to be arty, you know, art gallery vibe,' she laughed. She was lying. Mia always laid her soul bare in her photographs; she didn't doctor them to fit in one environment or another. She was truthful.

'Mia, is it . . . the baby not coming?'

'No, no. I have faith, you know, that it will happen.'

'Then what is it?'

'Okay. Okay.' She took a breath, and I held mine. 'While you were in Manchester, I had a dream . . . I phoned Selena and we went to Devon for two days, as you know. I kind of photographed the dream.'

'More of a nightmare.' I tried to laugh, but I was anxious.

'Yes. A nightmare.' The tone of her voice chilled me. I was silent, waiting. My arms tightened around her just a little, to keep her safe. 'It was so real, Matthew. So real.'

'Oh darling, whatever it was, it really was just a dream.'

'I was dead. I was looking from . . . from above. There was a young woman there, standing in water. And I could feel that, you know, I could feel that it was all finished, all gone, and you were cut off from me forever. Everything was dark . . . only this young woman . . . she almost shone like a little moon. She wasn't dead, and she wasn't alive. I can't explain . . .'

'It sounds scary,' I said, stroking her hair. And not like Mia at all.

'It was awful . . . and beautiful at the same time.'

'Hey, hey. I was in Manchester like . . . six weeks ago. It can't possibly still upset you this way.'

But it did, I could feel it. She said nothing; just nestled up against my chest. She laid her arm across me, and finally I felt her close, not just in body but in heart.

'Well, it was just a dream. A silly dream,' I said resolutely, to draw a line under it, to put an end to her fear. I didn't want her to be afraid. I never wanted her to be afraid.

There was a pause. A whisper in the dark. 'Matthew.'

I kissed her hair in reply. 'I'm here.'

'Do you believe in premonitions?'

A cold hand clasped at my heart. 'Nah. Sleep now.'

'Okay.'

Her breathing grew heavier and deeper, but I lay awake long into the night.

'Selena,' I said quietly.

'Is that my name?' After the shower, and with warmer clothes on, the young woman seemed to have changed – she was almost cheerful, almost evening-with-a-friend kind of cheerful, as if we should take a pizza from the freezer, download a film and get settled for the night. It was surreal, and such a contrast with the memories that had flooded me, of Mia's last exhibition. I could see those photographs like it was yesterday – a small, slim young woman on a deserted beach, deeper and deeper in the water . . .

'I don't know your name. But you remind me of this woman I used to know, this Spanish girl . . . Selena.'

'Okay,' she said easily.

The whole thing was so bizarre, I had to pinch myself, something I thought people only did in novels. It was painful, and left a purple mark darkening slowly under my eyes.

The girl protested, 'What did you do that for! That must have hurt!'

'Just making sure I'm awake.'

'You're weird.'

'Oh, *I*'m weird? Okay. Now, you're going to get that hair dry and then I'll take you back to wherever you're staying.'

She looked at me, and I realised that her eyes were more aquamarine than spring leaves. 'I'd rather not,' she said quite calmly, but with a vague disquiet in her voice.

'I don't think you have a choice. Come on, all this makes no sense.' I shrugged and opened my arms to encompass the cottage, the dark night beyond the glass. 'Apart from anything else, someone will be looking for you; you don't want to make them worry, do you?'

'I think everyone is pretty much resigned.'

'To what? That you've run away? Look, you can't

even remember your name; you need help . . . You can't stay here with me.'

'Don't make me leave,' she said in a low voice.

A pause. 'Is someone hurting you? Are you scared of someone?'

She frowned. 'Please stop talking about this.' And then, in a sudden change of mood, 'Oh my God, I'm hungry! I'm starving! Do you have anything to eat?' She got up, crossed the room on silent bare feet and opened the fridge.

'Selena . . . I mean, whatever your name is. I'll be in trouble if I don't call someone.'

'Selena, Selena, Selena . . . I like it. Call me that.' She shrugged. 'It's like being a whole new person. Your cupboards are almost empty? Lots of tins of dog food, though.' She laughed.

'I haven't really bought much yet. I just arrived . . . Look, this is not a social occasion!'

'No need to get intense. I'm just hungry,' she said, as if I were being unreasonable.

'I have beans . . . milk . . . and some kind of cakes, I think. It's—'

'Oh, there they are!' She'd found the packet of French fancies I'd bought earlier. 'Now we're talking. Sorry, it's just that I haven't eaten for ages . . . Oh, music!' she said, walking towards the piano. 'Even better than food!' she added through a mouthful of cake, and laughed. Her cheeks were a little redder now, like she was gaining life and energy. She caressed the piano with her small hand. 'How did I miss it? And all these records . . .'

'Can you play?'

'I . . .' She stopped, lips slightly open, thinking hard. 'I'm not sure. But I know I love music. Will you put something on for me?' She settled herself on the floor beside the piano, taking another bite of cake.

'Well . . . okay.' I shrugged. Good God. This woman was like a tsunami. She'd gone from white and silent to a one-person party. She seemed to have forgotten that I was a complete stranger. I resumed playing the Debussy, and she closed her eyes in delight. The food, the music . . . she was devouring both, it seemed.

I realised I hadn't heard Molly for a while, and looked around for her. She was sitting bolt upright in a corner of the room, perfectly quiet. Yes, she really was unnerved.

When the young woman had finished the cakes, she licked her fingers with pure pleasure and then went to sit at the kitchen island, her legs dangling from the stool. She looked enthralled by the music, and relaxed after the sweet meal. I wanted to press her further – she could not stay here and she could not go back into the night. We needed to come to some understanding. I was about to speak when she opened her eyes again.

'I'll remember,' she whispered. 'I'm sure.'

'Remember . . . who you are?'

'And what I'm here for.'

'What are you talking about?'

'I told you, I can't remember! But I will. In the meantime, can I stay here?'

'No, you can't, sorry,' I said with all the patience I could muster. Suddenly I felt like I'd reverted to my old job, when I needed to repeat the same things a million times, with endless calm, endless understanding, until they sank in. But I wasn't that person any more. And the whole situation was too crazy anyway.

'Why not?' she asked, once again as if I was being completely unreasonable.

A pause, a sigh, then I ran my hands through my hair. 'Selena, we are not having this argument. In fact . . . God, we don't even know each other! I don't know your real name, and neither do you.'

'I told you, I *will* remember!'

'You're crazy . . . Wait a minute. I don't think you're even real. I made you up. Yes, I'm seeing things . . .'

'Okay, so *you* see things and I'm the crazy one?'

'I'm calling for help.'

'If I don't exist, what do I need help for?'

'Enough, this conversation makes no sense. I'm calling someone . . .'

She looked down, suddenly serious. 'Please don't.'

'Sorry. I have to. I don't want to upset you, believe me, but . . .'

I fished the laminated sheet out of the kitchen drawer, found Sergeant Casey's mobile number and looked around for the cordless phone. There was no signal on this side of the island, so I could only use the landline, but the phone wasn't on its hub. I ran upstairs, followed by Molly, so close to me she nearly bumped her nose against my calves. The young woman clearly unnerved her. I turned around one last time to check that our visitor was all right. I felt terrible when I saw her looking down at the floor in distress. But it was the right thing to do, I knew it.

I grabbed the handset from the bedside table and dialled quickly. A couple of rings, and to my huge relief, Mike replied.

'Hello? Yes, sorry to bother you at this time of night. My name is Matthew Shearer, we met today . . . Yes, the guy from Molleson Cottage. Listen, I know it sounds strange, and I know it's the small hours of the morning, but I kind of . . . found a young woman on the beach. Well, at my door . . . Yes, a woman, twenty or so. She can't remember her name, she was alone and soaking wet – maybe she'd been swimming . . . Yes, I know, it's crazy, and the waves *are* huge tonight . . . She's physically okay, just confused. I gave her some clothes to change into . . . I don't know if she's a tourist, I just arrived two days ago! . . . No, she just can't remember . . . Okay. Yes, here, at the cottage. See you in ten. Bye.'

At that moment, just as I put the phone down, I felt a gust of cold air coming up the stairs – a bad sign, I thought. And I was right. I rushed back down feeling vaguely guilty, as if I'd given her away, as if I'd betrayed her – but I knew I'd had no choice. The fire was glowing softly, but the room was freezing. The French door was open, letting salty air in and slowly rendering the room colder and colder. No sign of Selena at the kitchen island, beside the piano, in front of the fire. She was gone – all that was left of her were a few crumbs from the cake she'd devoured, and some strands of seaweed. There was a blue bundle on the sofa – my clothes. She must have changed very quickly and put on the dress she'd arrived in.

I felt goose bumps just thinking of going from the heated house to the freezing Hebridean night in a cotton dress. I ran to the door and looked into the thick darkness; trying to find her would be a hopeless task. I stood and waited, Molly beside me, for Sergeant Casey to arrive.

6

Grace

The first thing I did when I opened my eyes was to look at my bedside table. The silky blue amulet was still sitting where I'd left it the night before. Being an inanimate object, it didn't go walkabout, of course.

Did it?

'Good. You've stopped wandering all over the place,' I said aloud. At the sound of my voice, Hyde slunk in, tiny purple-brown flowers woven into his fur. He'd been wandering too.

I crawled out of bed – I'd been so tired since the *omamori* incident, as if a burden had been taken off my shoulders somehow and I could finally relax, let go. Maybe it was because finally I'd put into words my deepest wish and my greatest desire.

I opened the curtains as I always did, to look at the sky. And that was when all tiredness left me. I stifled a gasp – a column of black smoke was spiralling out of Fergus's cottage. I was fuelled with pure adrenaline as I ran downstairs and out onto the beach, my bare feet sinking in the cold, wet sand. As I ran, I realised the foolishness of my decision: I should have called the fire service first. So much for clear thinking. What I'd been through the night before must have muddled my brain, but I'd been worried for Fergus as it was, with him disappearing from my radar, not calling, not showing up at rehearsals . . .

When I finally got to his cottage, my heart drumming and my lungs full of freezing air, there was a young girl standing in front of the door. She wore a long black jumper and looked pretty much terrified.

'Are you okay?' I panted. 'Did you call 999? Is Fergus inside?'

The girl turned around, and I saw that her height had deceived me – she was just a child, with slanted blue eyes and short black hair with a blue streak through her fringe. She shrugged, clearly to convince me that she was unconcerned, but she was shaking a little. 'I'm fine. No need for firemen. There's a hole in the ceiling, though.' Fergus owned one of the few thatched cottages left on the island, left to him by his grandparents.

'Is there anyone inside?' I repeated.

'Just my jewellery. The stuff I was making, I mean. Melted.'

What? 'Where's Fergus?'

'What are you, the police?'

'I'm a doctor. Is Fergus inside?'

'No, I told you, there's nobody inside!'

'Have you called the fire brigade?'

'Are you deaf? I just told you. No need. I put the fire out myself.'

I wasn't very reassured. 'Are you sure it's out?'

'Look, I can tell the difference between fire and non-fire! There's absolutely *no fire* in Fergus's cottage.' She stressed his name in a strange way. 'Apart from the hole and my silver paste being unusable now, everything is *fine*. Stop stressing.' The girl had just started a blaze and still thought she had the right to be cheeky.

'Okay. That's good. Good.' I put a hand on my chest and panted again.

'Do you need a doctor?' the girl said, a smirk on her lips.

I ignored her quip. 'What on earth were you doing to set the cottage on fire?'

'I was melting silver paste. The blowtorch slipped from my hand,' she said, matter-of-factly.

'You were using a blowtorch?'

'It was a small one. I may look young, but I'm actually fourteen! In some countries I could be married with babies.'

'And that's *not* a good thing. Anyway, you could have been badly hurt.'

She shrugged again. 'But I wasn't. It all turned out okay.'

'Apart from a hole in the ceiling.'

'Fergus can afford to get it repaired.'

I looked at her. Who was this child, making jewellery in Fergus's cottage?

'You're wondering who I am,' she said nervously, and looked down. This moment of shyness was strange compared to the defiance she'd shown just a minute before. She hugged herself in the cold breeze and kind of . . . wiggled. It gave me the feeling that she was trying to escape from her own skin. I allowed myself a smile, now that the tension had subsided a little.

'I am, actually.'

'Everyone who sees me wonders that. Yesterday I was at the shop, and a couple of grannies even asked, "Who are your people?" ' She attempted a smile. She really was shaken, I could see it now. 'I wanted to turn around and tell them I don't have any *people*. You don't get many strangers on the island, do you?'

'Not at this time of year.'

'Well. I'm Fergus's daughter. Susie.'

My mouth fell open at the revelation. Fergus had a daughter? And he'd never told me?

The first time I met Fergus, he was kneeling outside my back door. As you do.

I had just arrived on the ferry, all my belongings plus my brother in tow. I stepped into my garden having no idea he was there, tripped over him and fell face first into a bed of purple heather – thankfully, because back then the garden was still mainly paved, so I could easily have landed on stone and been my own first patient on the island.

'I'm so sorry! I'm so very sorry! Are you okay?'

'I think so. My nose is intact, if not my dignity,' I said, taking his hand and getting to my feet. My first day on Seal was starting with a bit of slapstick – great. I found myself face to face with a tall, fair man with the most startling blue eyes I'd ever seen. He looked Scandinavian, and I stared at him for a moment, taken by his strong features, by those eyes. 'You're in my garden. Should I be alarmed?'

He laughed. 'Don't be alarmed, no. My name is Fergus McLean, I own the distillery up there. I haven't had neighbours since I came back to the island. I was so excited, I decided to organise a surprise for you . . . but you arrived early.'

'Well, nice to meet you, Fergus. Just curious; your surprise was to come and kneel in front of my door? Were you planning to jump up and shout *Surprise*?' I laughed.

'Not exactly. I thought you'd like a bit of colour, and . . . well, this place has been abandoned for so long . . .'

He gestured towards the ground – and there it was, a little rose bush. Exquisite lush white roses with a light pink heart, tucked in against the wall on one side and the hedge on the other, so they'd be protected from the harsh sea wind. I was touched. It was the best welcome I could have asked for, and yet this stranger had no idea how much I loved gardens, and the plans I had for my own.

'They're gorgeous. You've been so kind,' I said. 'Really.' I felt my cheeks flushing like they always did when I was very happy, very sad or very embarrassed – a side effect of my fair Scottish complexion.

I remember that for a moment, just for a moment, the look in his eyes changed from friendly to somehow enraptured, but it only lasted an instant. That night he invited me to the pub with a group of friends, and I was officially introduced to Seal society, not in the doctor's guise but as myself. After that, Fergus and I were there for each other. Always.

Susie grimaced. She was in pain, physical pain.

'Are you sure you're okay?'

'I . . .' All the time we were talking, she had kept her arms folded. Now she moved her left arm slightly, and I caught a glimpse of something bright red.

'Your hand! You're burnt. Please let me have a look . . .'

'I'm fine.'

'No you're not. Burns can become infected very easily, not to mention the pain. You need seeing to. Come, I'll drive you down—'

Right at that moment, Fergus appeared from nowhere, his limp more pronounced than ever. I'd been so lost in the drama, I hadn't noticed the sound of his car coming from the distillery.

'What did you do?' he said quietly. Quiet, for Fergus, didn't mean calm. I noticed he'd asked Susie what she'd done before asking how she was.

Susie shrugged, a mixture of defiance and vulnerability. 'It was an accident.'

'Fergus, everything is okay, there's just a little hole in the roof. Susie is fine, but she hurt her hand. I need to take her down to the surgery . . .'

'A hole in the roof?'

I was beginning to lose my temper, and that doesn't happen easily. 'Yes, but *your daughter* is hurt, she burnt her hand.'

'A hole in the roof?' he repeated, looking at the girl. Who was this man? I didn't recognise him. I didn't recognise my kind, soft-hearted friend. His eyes were so cold, his deep voice had a steel to it I'd never heard before.

'I'm sorry . . .'

'Of course. Of course you'd come and destroy my house.'

I was shocked. His eyes, the same blue as Susie's, were icy. It was taking a while to sink in. Fergus McLean had a daughter, and in the ten years I'd been here, she'd never come to the island. And he'd never mentioned her.

'Fergus. You'll get your roof repaired. But now your daughter needs to come with me.'

Susie had tears in her eyes, and I didn't know if it was from her burnt hand or from her dad being so unconcerned with her. I'd noticed, when she was speaking to me, that she'd never called him Dad, but always by his first name. Now I understood why she'd stressed his name. 'I'm fine . . .' she said again.

'You're coming with me. Now,' I said, and my doctor's voice didn't give her the choice, even if I was still wearing my lilac Tatty Teddy pyjamas.

Fergus signalled for us to follow him and drove us to the surgery in stony silence. 'Do you want to stop at your house and get dressed?' he said coldly.

'No. I want to disinfect your daughter's burn.'

'Fine.' In the back, Susie was silent.

'Thank you,' she said to me when we were out of the car and walking up the slight incline to the surgery. She sounded a lot meeker now. It was probably the pain. 'By the way, are you sure you're okay to go in like that?' She gestured at my state of undress.

'Ach, yes. Nobody will be at the surgery at this time anyway.' My mind went to the nurses at St Fintan's waiting for me to sign off some prescriptions, like every Friday – I would apologise profusely as soon as I made it there.

I opened the door and stepped inside without even wondering why it was unlocked.

Into a waiting room full of people.

Of course. It was the last Friday of the month, when Sharon opened her room at eight o'clock to measure blood pressure, weigh babies and offer a sympathetic ear to any concerns people might have.

'Good morning,' I said with all the dignity I could muster, a hand going to my hair, which I tried, without success, to pat down before starting my walk of shame. Ten steps, ten miles long.

'Good morning, Doctor.'

'Morning.'

'Mummy, why is she in her jammies?'

'Shh! The doctor's very busy and she didn't have time to get dressed! And we don't *point*!'

I had opened my mouth to try and answer when I was interrupted. 'Running a bit late?' a woman by the name of Christine McMillan said haughtily, several generations of Calvinist disapproval weighing down her words. I bristled, but support came from the last place I would have thought.

'She saved me from a *fire*, if you want to know!' Susie snapped.

I had to smile. Mrs McMillan looked like someone had slapped her.

As we disappeared into my room, her whisper followed us: 'Who's that girl? Who are her people?'

7

Matthew

'I know what happened,' Mike said, digging into a pub lunch of steak pie and chips.

I took a gulp of my coffee. It was my third cup; after Mike had left, as bewildered as I was, I hadn't slept at all, and my first morning of work at the distillery had left me shattered. I was in pretty good shape because I'd always played sports and coached the kids at the shelter in football as part of their activities. In prison, I'd gone to the gym every day to try and burn off some of the inner turmoil. But the work at the distillery had been something else. Now I was on my lunch break and feeling muscles I hadn't even known I possessed throb and burn.

'You do? You know the girl? You'd heard something?'

'No. But I know what happened.'

'What?'

'Last night you had one too many!' Mike laughed, his belly bouncing up and down. 'A girl rising from the sea, coming to your place . . . it's a whisky dream, obviously.'

I rubbed my forehead. For a moment, I'd hoped he had an answer. Instead, he was just making a stupid joke.

'She had a shower at my place, Mike. She wore my clothes. How realistic can a dream be?'

'Mmm.' He sank his fork into a cluster of chips. He looked like someone who should have retired a long time ago, with his portly figure and shiny bald head, but I supposed he knew the island and all the residents like the back of his hand, and that counted for something. 'I drove around, you know, after I left yours. She couldn't have gone far. But I saw nobody.'

'You could have easily missed her in the dark . . . Mike, I can assure you. There was a girl at my door in the middle of the night. She was real. And I think I saw her the night I arrived too, except that time I thought she was a ghost because she was kind of . . . floating . . .' Oh God. I shouldn't have said that. Mike dived on my choice of words.

'Right. A ghost. That makes sense.' He wiped his mouth with a napkin and took a sip of his Coke. 'Look, we don't really know each other, and I assure you I take this kind of thing seriously, but if you start talking about ghosts . . .' He laughed and shrugged. What *kind of thing*? I couldn't help thinking. Mysterious girls appearing at people's houses?

'I can assure you she was real. She was wet through, and . . . and . . . she had seaweed in her hair. She wore a summer dress, in October. She seemed confused. She didn't speak, she said nothing. She came in and had a shower . . .' A wink from Mike. I was incensed. I was pretty sure that taking advantage of a vulnerable person was a crime, but Mike seemed to think it was a joke. I wasn't sure I liked the guy. 'There was none of *that*! She was going to catch pneumonia out there in the middle of the night. I didn't lure her to my place, Sergeant Casey . . .'

He put his hands up. 'I know, I know, sorry, I didn't mean anything by it. On the other hand, you're a young man. If you take a girl home, I don't see the problem.'

'Not a girl in that state! I told you, she couldn't remember her own name!' I took a breath, trying to calm myself down. 'She came to my cottage, had a shower, changed into warm clothes, and while I was calling you, she disappeared. Just like that.'

'Right. Look. I'm sorry, I didn't mean to be flippant about this, only it all sounds a bit strange, you will agree with that?' he said, now serious. I nodded, a storm cloud over my head. 'I asked John to drive around a bit this morning. That's my junior officer. He didn't see anyone. She must have been a tourist; maybe she'd had an argument with her boyfriend and had gone out just like she was . . . Maybe she'd smoked something, or taken something she wasn't supposed to take, and there you go.'

'Well, if it was a matter of drugs . . . what if she's passed out somewhere? What if she needs a doctor?'

'Matthew. It's not like I'm not giving this any

importance. It's that I can't chase this girl down. Nobody was reported missing. She's not a criminal. I'll have another drive around this afternoon, okay? But people are coming over from the mainland to look at the electrics at St Fintan's, and I have to be there. We're talking cutting a generator off in a place where people depend on breathing machines. That's what's important now.'

'Okay,' I muttered. *I'm pretty sure the girl said my wife's name. Please help me find her. I need to know more.* But of course, I couldn't say that. I stayed quiet.

Mike chomped on the last few chips. 'You should ask Grace. Dr Chatto. She lives near you; maybe she saw the girl too.'

I sat back and nodded slowly. 'Thanks. I don't know, there was something about her . . . I can't explain.' No, I really, really couldn't. 'She was kind of . . . off key. Uncanny.'

'Did you say she was wet through?'

'Soaking. She had seaweed in her hair and even between her fingers. Who goes into the sea in October? And with the way the sea was last night?'

'The answer to your question is *nobody*. Nobody goes swimming in the Atlantic in October, at three in the morning. Unless . . .' He opened his hands.

'Unless?'

'Unless she's a selkie,' Mike said. And this time, he didn't laugh.

*

I drove back to the distillery, looking forward to the afternoon of work despite being sore all over. Maybe, if I worked hard, the physical exhaustion would buy me a couple of hours' sleep. Today I needed it even more, to take my mind off the mysterious girl; to stop my gaze from wandering onto the beach, looking for her small figure silhouetted against the sky . . .

What I needed was a few hours' sweating to calm my anxiety. I was lucky that vat cleaning was on the cards that day, and I gave it all the energy I had. At Seal Distillery everything was done by hand – I imagined that would be impossible in the big distilleries. But Fergus preferred quality to quantity, he'd told me, and he would keep going like this as long as he could.

This afternoon he seemed distracted. He hovered around me for a little while, checking things that didn't need checking – I didn't know anything about whisky-making, but I'd been given simple tasks, and his main man, Jim, was supervising me carefully. He was in the middle of going over something with me – unnecessarily – when his pocket buzzed and he disappeared, phone to his ear.

'I've been looking for you for a week. You can't just leave her here . . . Lin? Lin, I'm losing you, I can't hear you . . .' I didn't catch any more as he ran towards the office, the only place in this Celtic Bermuda Triangle where phones worked properly. He returned shaking his head and growling, his chin to his chest and his eyes down, 'Trouble with my otter.'

I couldn't have heard him right. Were there otters around here? Troublesome ones? 'I beg your pardon?' I said.

'I said, trouble with my daughter.'

'Oh. I'm sorry . . .'

'Mmm.'

And then a thought crossed my mind. Could it be Selena was his daughter? He was probably in his fifties, so he was old enough to have a daughter in her twenties. 'I don't suppose she was on the beach last night, was she? Around three in the morning?'

'On the beach?' He looked alarmed. And no wonder.

'About twenty or so, long dark hair, green eyes . . .' I continued. Fergus gave a little exhale, and his features relaxed.

'No. Susie is fourteen, and she has short hair and blue eyes, so it couldn't have been her.' He rubbed his forehead. He was very troubled, I could see it. I considered asking him more, to see if maybe he needed a sympathetic ear, but his closed expression told me it was better not to.

'Okay,' I said simply. 'And thanks again for . . . for this.'

'Well, you're not afraid of hard work, I can see that.'

'Look, I'm sorry for your trouble. If there's anything . . .' I began, but his mind was elsewhere, and with a wave and a 'See you tomorrow!' I left. I had one more person to speak to – my neighbour, Dr Grace Chatto.

Twilight had swallowed the sky and the air itself seemed to have turned lilac. I stopped at the house to get Molly – I'd left her snoozing in front of the fire – and walked down the dunes to the beach, towards Dr Chatto's cottage. I could have gone through the small, soft moor at the back of our homes, but I preferred to walk along the seashore. I still marvelled at every step at being out of prison; how four concrete walls crammed with bodies had given way to this endless horizon, to the silvery wind laden with salt and moisture, coming pure and clean from the ocean.

The lights were on in the doctor's home, a whitewashed cottage with a blue door, surrounded by ashes and elms to protect it from the salty wind. I rang the bell and a voice called from somewhere: 'I'm in the back! Come on through!'

I walked along the side of the house and found Dr Chatto kneeling on the ground, tending to sturdy-looking bushes growing out of the Hebridean soil. In the evening light she looked like a young woman, slight and small among her plants; but as I came closer, I saw that her blond hair was streaked with silver and there were lines around her lively blue eyes.

She turned around and got up nimbly when she saw me, rubbing soil off her hands. 'You're Matthew,' she stated. Of course she'd know. It seemed to me that news travelled fast on Seal.

'That's me, yes. Otherwise known as the guy at Molleson Cottage.'

'I'm Grace. And oh, who is this?' Molly was wagging her tail with such conviction that her whole body rippled.

'I found her on the beach yesterday, no collar, no chip. She seems to have adopted me. I've called her Molly.'

'Oh. I haven't heard of anyone losing a dog . . . Maybe some tourists left her. It happens sometimes. It shouldn't, but it does, more shame on them . . .'

'Mike said the same. I'm asking around in case someone claims her.'

'But you hope not, do you?' She smiled.

'Well, I've kind of got used to her.'

'She's lovely. You're lovely, aren't you?' Molly closed her eyes in bliss as Grace stroked her under her ears. 'Come inside, come near the fire, it's freezing out here. I was about to go in myself. Cup of tea? I've made bread, it's still warm . . . It's actually a miracle; I never usually have time. I'm glad you found me home; I've been out on some visits . . .' She was talking to me as if she'd known me forever. 'And I see you're a man.'

I had to laugh. 'I am, yes.'

She joined in the laughter. 'Sorry, I mean, we're doing this Christmas show, just singing a few songs, and we need male voices . . . so many sopranos, we sound like we're on helium.'

'Oh, I can't sing.'

'That would be an improvement on us, then. Apart from Rosalind – have you ever heard Rosalind sing?' I shook my head. 'She's amazing. The rest of us aren't exactly angels. We do our best, and it's going well, actually. We've been asked to tour.'

'That's great.'

'Oh yes. Eilean Community Centre, you know, the next island. It's Carnegie Hall next, for sure!' Her eyes lit up with laughter. In the light of the fire, with her long hair in a side braid, her bright, warm eyes, she seemed to me the embodiment of serenity. 'So, no hope of recruiting you?'

'Sorry, no.'

'Well, just get ready for more of these propositions. There's only a few of us on Seal, and we have the Sea Rescue, the community garden, not to mention the bingo nights . . .'

'Oh God . . .'

'I know!' She laughed again. 'Some initiatives are more fun than others. But you'll be asked to everything . . .'

We were interrupted by the high-pitched sound of a terrified cat. A little blur of black and white crossed the room, followed by a frantic Molly.

'Molly! Come here!' I called, and got up to run after her.

'It's okay, Hyde is fast. She won't catch him. I have a neurotic cat, you see, he sees danger everywhere,' Grace said calmly, spreading jam on buttered bread.

'To be fair, a dog did just enter his house,' I said, sitting back and biting into the delicious bread.

'True, but he tends to overreact. I slip chamomile tea in his bowl sometimes. Maybe whisky would work better. Oh, this is nice,' she said, sitting back in her chair. 'I have a bit of time before Mrs Young calls me to go and see her husband, who will have terrible stomach pains in about . . . an hour, I'd say. Like every Friday night.'

'Does he time the pains? Are they a weekly event?'

'To cut a long story short, Mrs Young does the groceries on a Friday, because that's when her weeklies come out. She always brings home a Victoria sponge. Mr Young can't resist Victoria sponge, but he's a coeliac, which means he shouldn't eat cake . . . and every Friday, like clockwork, he's unwell, and I've got to go and check him out.'

'You're very patient. I would tell him off.'

'But I do! They call me, I give them both a row, they pay lip service, and the following Friday it's the same thing again.'

'I could never have been a doctor.'

'It does require an insane amount of patience. What do you do?' She tilted her head gracefully. 'I mean, what did you do before coming here?'

'I . . .' There was something about this woman that

made me want to open up, to unburden myself. But I couldn't bring myself to talk about my past life. About all that had happened to me. 'I was a social worker. I helped kids with addictions.'

'You need a lot of patience to do that too.' She smiled, and waited. She was used to being a confidante, I could see that – both for work and as natural inclination.

But no, I would not speak, not tonight. I looked down and changed the subject. 'You know, I came here to introduce myself, of course, but also . . . well, something strange happened to me. Maybe you can help.'

'Of course, anything.'

'The night I arrived . . . I saw a young woman. On the beach.'

Grace raised her eyebrows. 'What were you doing on the beach in the middle of the night?'

Good question. 'Well . . .' *I couldn't find peace. I can never find peace.* I stumbled, not knowing what to say.

'Sorry, I didn't mean to sound inquisitive. It's just that it's October, and the beach is freezing. Going for a walk at night is not exactly good for you.'

'I wasn't walking.'

'Oh.'

'I was kind of trying to sleep there.'

'You *were*?'

'I have trouble sleeping, and . . .'

'You'll end up in my surgery. With pneumonia.'

'I'm twenty-five and very healthy.' I shrugged. *I don't care what happens to me* was what I actually meant.

'Well, you won't be healthy for long if you sleep on the beach in October. Anyway. You met a girl there? Oh. Could it be . . .'

'Fergus's daughter? No, it wasn't her.'

Grace's eyes widened. 'You know about Susie? You've been here a week and you know something I had no idea about?'

I laughed. 'Three days, actually. And I've already acquired a dog and a job. Not bad, huh? No, Fergus didn't confide in me or anything. I'm working up at the distillery and he was talking on the phone about his daughter, so that's how I know . . . No, this girl I saw was in her twenties, long hair, white dress.'

'Okay, so it can't be Susie. I'm relieved.'

'No, Susie is fourteen, isn't she?' Grace nodded. 'This woman came to my door, she was confused and cold . . . She had a shower at my place and I gave her clothes and a cup of tea. I was calling Mike when she . . . she disappeared. Just like that. The thing is . . . I don't think she was well. I mean, she wasn't in her right mind.' I neglected to say that she had nestled into me as if she'd been looking for me for a long time, and that I thought she'd mentioned my dead wife's name.

Which I knew said more about my state of mind than the girl's.

'That's concerning. If she wasn't well . . . Do you think she might have had too much to drink?'

'She didn't seem drunk. More . . . spaced. She couldn't even tell me her name.'

'Drugs?'

I shrugged. 'Maybe. I have no idea, to be honest.'

'And you tried to call Mike?'

'Yes. I wanted to call you, but she seemed petrified at the idea of a doctor. I waited for the right time and slipped upstairs to make the call, but when I came back, she was gone. I shouldn't have left her alone. I'm worried. Though she did devour a whole box of French fancies, so she couldn't have been ill or anything like that. Anyway, I'm freaked out.'

'I can imagine. You see, this island . . . well, it's a bit magical. Weird things tend to happen here. I sometimes wonder, is it because of Catriona and her lot?' I raised my eyebrows. She smiled. 'You don't know Catriona, of course. Let's just say she . . . Oh, never mind. You'll find it out by yourself, living here. What I meant to say is that what happened to you is pretty strange, even for these parts.'

'Strange is one way of putting it. You don't think it could have been an island girl?'

'Well, I do know a few girls in their twenties, with long hair, on the island. But I doubt any of them would do this, and if they did, I would probably know . . . So no, I don't think she's local. A tourist probably. Not many of them around now, after the October week holiday, but a few people still come . . .'

There was a pause.

'I spoke to Sergeant Casey this morning,' I said in a low voice. 'He had another explanation. You know, the girl was soaking, she had seaweed in her hair . . .'

'Oh, of course,' Grace said, perfectly serious. 'You saw a selkie.'

8

Grace

I dug my hands into the earth, preparing a little home for my tomato plant, sheltered from the sharp, salty sea wind by a glass greenhouse. I was in the community garden, for self-therapy, really. Gardening gave me a sense of perpetual optimism that everything would work out in the end. That life was, with all its obstacles and grief and challenges, a beautiful thing. That no matter how dry or barren or saturated the soil was, sooner or a later a little green shoot would come, and it would be just right for that kind of soil, equipped to survive and keep going . . .

But as much as digging in the soil relaxed me, I was still worried. I didn't want to admit how much I'd come to rely on Fergus through the years, but I was missing him so much. It was nearly a month of silence now, not to mention his weird behaviour with his daughter.

Oh yes, that. He had a daughter.

'Hey.' A small voice interrupted my thoughts. I turned around to see Susie of all people, wearing the short tartan skirt, white shirt and blue blazer of Eilean High School.

'Hello. How's your hand? Sharon said you'd been to get your bandage changed, like I said. Good girl.' I blinked. I didn't want her to notice my confusion. As if she could have read on my face that I was thinking about her father.

'Hand's fine.' She shrugged. I'd come to the conclusion that shrugging was her favourite way of communicating, just like nodding was her dad's.

'So you go to school on Eilean now?' Seal was too small to have a high school, so kids from the island went to school in the bigger community across the water.

'What do you think this is?' She opened her arms to show off her uniform.

Okay. My fuse was about to blow. Nobody could speak to me like that, let alone a child, Fergus's daughter or not. I cleaned my hands on my apron and prepared myself to give her a dressing-down.

But when I looked into her face, something stopped me from getting properly angry with her. This girl had seen me from the street, she'd come into the community garden just to speak to me – and now she was giving me abuse. Talk about mixed messages.

She needed someone to talk to; that was my immediate diagnosis.

'It's great that you're living here now. There aren't many young people on the island. It's always good when someone new moves here,' I said truthfully, though all the while I was asking myself, *Where is this girl's mum? Why has she never been here before? Why is a mild-mannered man like Fergus being so harsh with her?*

And why did he never tell me about her?

'Not so good for me,' Susie said.

Oh.

'Look.' I glanced at my watch. 'I have a bit of time before I need to go see someone down at St Fintan's. Feel like a hot chocolate?' She shrugged again. 'You'll hurt your shoulders if you keep doing that,' I teased her.

'Pardon?' she said. My sarcasm had fallen flat, clearly.

'Nothing. Ever been to the Design Gallery?'

'Is it where the young islanders go?' Her tone was light, but for some reason she seemed worried.

'No. Not particularly.'

'Okay then. Let's go.'

I stole a glance at her as we walked, trying to see the resemblance to her dad – she was as dark as Fergus was fair, as small as he was tall and broad, but they had the same blue eyes, and similar expressions: gentle, somehow shy. Even with her cocky behaviour, Susie couldn't hide her nature, not from me anyway.

The fashion for the girls on the island at the moment was to wear their hair long, often in a bun on top of their heads. I saw them around, young and easily beautiful, walking arm in arm in their school uniforms, school bags and musical instruments or sports equipment across their backs. Susie looked different, even wearing the same uniform. Her hair was short, and the blue streak added originality, like a rogue note in a music score. And she lacked a certain confidence – while those other girls looked like they *belonged*, Susie didn't, although she pretended she owned the world. There was something strangely innocent about her, like a daisy in a field of roses.

'I thought you were a meddler,' she said suddenly. 'When you came to our house.'

I'll rephrase that. She was like a cactus in a sea of roses.

'Because I ran over when I thought your dad's cottage was on fire?' I said curtly.

'My *dad*? Oh yes. My dad's cottage.' I was puzzled. It was like she wasn't used to hearing that word.

We sat in the light, airy conservatory of the Design Gallery, sinking in the brightly coloured sofas. Abby, the owner, came to us armed with notebook and pen. She was Rosalind's older sister and had a lovely voice too, but the coffee shop was her passion. She'd worked so hard for it to become more than a tourist spot; it was also a gallery and a space for events for us islanders.

'Hi, Grace. What can I get you?'

'Hello, Abby. Hot chocolate then?' I asked Susie.

'And cake? Thanks. That cheesecake on the counter there . . .'

I smiled at Abby. 'Same for me, thanks.'

'No problem. By the way, I love your bracelet.' Abby gestured to Susie's wrist with her pen. Only then did I notice the silver band, to which was secured a tiny shell enveloped in a silver casing. It was simple and beautiful. Susie blushed so hard that even the tip of her nose turned pink. 'Thanks. I made it.'

'You made it?' Abby and I said at the same time.

Susie nodded. 'That's how I set Fergus's place on fire, remember? Melting silver paste,' she said nonchalantly.

Abby brought a hand to her throat. 'Oh my God. Sounds like a dangerous hobby!'

'Only if you have hay for a roof,' Susie pointed out.

'It's not really hay . . .' I said. 'But that's beside the point, I suppose. Abby is right, it is lovely. You're so young, making such beautiful things already . . . I'm really impressed.'

The pleasure on Susie's face as I paid her the compliment was touching.

'I'll make something for you guys,' she said shrugging her shoulders again, as if we were making a fuss over nothing, but I could see how pleased she was.

'Back in a sec,' Abby said, and disappeared to get our order.

'So, Susie. Did you come looking for me in the garden?'

'No, of course not. I was just passing by, I saw you and . . . Well . . . okay. Lorna told me you were there.'

'Well, I want you to know I'm glad you came to see

me.' More blushing and her trademark shrug. I was used to people confiding in me; it happened a lot. And not just because I was a doctor. To be honest, I didn't know why I attracted people's confidences; it was just the way things were. It wasn't like I had words of wisdom for them, some kind of guru-like knowledge – I simply listened, and that, for people in a world where we talk a lot but don't listen much, was enough. 'So, do you like it here, on the island?'

'Well, I was shipped here by my mum because she got married, I hadn't seen Fergus in seven years and . . . yeah, that's my answer.' She was playing with the little shell at her wrist.

'You hadn't seen him since you were seven? And you came to live with him?'

'I had no choice. But he hates me.'

'Oh sweetheart. He doesn't hate you,' I said, but the memory of the iciness in his eyes was vivid in my mind. Mind you, she had just burnt a hole in his roof.

'How do you know?'

'No father hates his daughter,' I replied.

'He does. I don't know why.' She shrugged.

Abby returned with the hot chocolate and cake, a triumph of calories that the doctor in me regarded suspiciously and the woman couldn't wait to attack. Susie dug in with enthusiasm. I watched her for a moment – when she ate, she was like a ravenous little girl just in from the play park. She was at that age where she could be a young woman one moment, a child the next.

I wanted to ask more about Fergus, see if there was a way I could help unravel their situation, but I didn't have the heart to keep talking about sad things. 'You know, Susie, it just came to me. There's a craft fair in Oban next weekend. I went last year and there were quite a few jewellery stands. Would you like to go?'

'Oh, that would be good . . . but how? I can't go on my own, and . . .'

'I would go with you, of course. What do you say?'

'Seriously?'

'Yes, of course.'

'You'd take me to Oban?'

'Yes, why not?'

'It's two hours to go, two hours back. Are you sure?'

'I'm in if you are,' I said, her enthusiasm touching my heart.

At that moment, two girls wearing the Eilean High School uniform came in. I recognised them, of course; they'd been my patients since they were toddlers. The one walking in the front, strong-featured and with a mass of dark blond hair, was Karen McNeil; the other was her sister Mary, a pale, washed-out girl. She was part of our choir, where she sang with a weak, thin voice. When I looked back at Susie, I realised she'd seen them too. She froze for a moment, then grabbed her jacket and bag, mumbled a quick thank you and was gone. Just like that, I was left contemplating the debris of our afternoon snack, unfinished cake and lonely hot chocolate.

I looked at Karen, and she held my gaze with a smile that was a bit too sure for a young girl.

Is that where the young islanders go? Susie had asked. And she'd been relieved when I'd said no. Something was up, and I'd bet it had something to do with Karen McNeil.

I drove home from Roan in the dark and windy night after a visit to a patient. The lights were on in Fergus's cottage. I thought of Susie there alone, and my heart went out to her. There was something about her that tugged at my emotions; maybe because I'd moved about so much as a child, and was always the new girl. Still, I had a loving family, I had my brothers. Susie was there all on her own, or maybe with Treasa, Fergus's housekeeper, who helped him with housework a couple of times a week and left him a meal for his dinner – like me, Fergus was never home. In the most northern part of the island, there were only three cottages; we might have been only twenty minutes away from other houses, and the Seal Distillery was only five minutes from Fergus's cottage, but it was still a lonely place for a wee girl.

Without thinking, instead of turning right towards my cottage, I turned left. I wanted to speak to Fergus.

I was sure that he'd still be working – he always worked late. And in fact, I could see in the distance that the lights were on in his office, yellow against the pitch black. As I stepped out of the car, the sweet, malty scent that was everywhere around the distillery enveloped me. I looked up; the moon and stars were veiled by a translucent blanket of clouds. In the background, as always, was the sound of the sea. After ten years, sometimes I could still be blown away by the beauty of this place, its strange mixture of drama and comfort: on one side of me warm, welcoming lit windows; on the other, the wild, raw noise of Corrywreckan.

I knocked at the bright blue door, not knowing what I was going to say. *You didn't tell me you had a daughter* sounded like I was entitled, and I wasn't, not after I'd turned him down when he'd wanted to evolve our friendship into something else, something deeper.

I remember well when things began to change between us.

I'd noticed that he had begun to limp, to struggle with walking and standing. I was concerned, and mentioned to him that he needed to go and get checked out. I told him I would go with him to the mainland and be with him throughout, but he always put me off. In the meantime, I could see the exhaustion and pain on his face, and I was out of my mind with worry. At a loss, I went to his cousin, Hamish McLean, who set my mind at rest, relatively speaking. He told me that Fergus suffered from a chronic malformation of his knees, which would cause him pain and trouble for the rest of his life, but was not in itself dangerous. I was relieved . . . but why had he not told me? Why had he let me worry so much and plead with him to get checked out?

'I didn't want you to know,' he said, looking down. We were in my living room, Hyde – who adored him – on his knees. My cat would not let anyone else stroke him.

'But why? Why would you be . . . ashamed of something like this? It makes no sense.'

'I'm a cripple. At least some of the time.'

'One, don't use that word, it's horrible. Two, stop the self-pity, it won't get you anywhere! What's happening to you? Is it the pain, is it getting to you? You know I can help . . .'

'It's not the pain.'

'Then what is it?'

'Would you want to be with a crip— I mean, a disabled man? Would you?' I stared at him. 'Would you want to be with me, Grace?'

'Do you mean, in general?' I said in a small voice, feeling like an idiot.

'Well, would you want to be with a disabled man in general, and with me in particular?'

'What are you saying?'

'Grace, you're a grown woman, what do you think I'm saying?'

I shook my head and looked down. I had to bite my lip, because suddenly I was terrified, so terrified I was trembling.

In my fifteen years of solitude I had had a few proposals of this kind, and I always dealt with them coolly.

There had been none of this drama. Certainly no crying, like I was about to do now.

'Grace . . . I didn't mean to upset you . . .'

'I'm sorry, Fergus. Please believe me, it has nothing to do with your legs. You should have told me, because it would have made no difference.'

'I don't stand a chance, then?'

'I'm sorry. It's not you . . .'

'It's not you, it's me?' He smiled sadly.

'It's not like that.'

'Why are you crying? It should be me crying,' he said softly. 'Please, Grace . . .'

'It's because I hate to hurt you.'

'I'm a grown-up too, I'll be fine.'

'And because I don't want to lose you,' I admitted. He walked towards me, leaning on his cane, and held me to him.

'You won't. Hey, you won't. You're going to have to put up with my terrible temper and my limp and my boring conversations for another while yet.'

'Good. That's good.' I sniffed.

'You know what else is good?' he said.

'What?'

He lifted his cane, wooden, with an alabaster handle. 'I get to look like a Victorian gentleman.' I laughed between my tears, and breathed in his malty, smoky scent.

But things were never the same again. And here I was now, once again needing to speak to him.

'Fergus?' I called. After a moment he came to the door, looking tired, shadows under his eyes. 'Oh, Grace. Come in.'

There were moments when his face looked worn, moulded by pain and disappointment – those times he seemed older than he really was. This was one of those moments. Though I didn't know much about Fergus's life, I'd always guessed that it had not been easy, but he never really opened up with me, and this wall between us had been one of the reasons why I'd refused to open my heart in return.

'Thanks . . .' I was hesitant. Contrasting emotions fought inside me. I was worried for him, and saddened by the secret he'd kept.

He was embarrassed too, I could feel it.

'Whisky?'

'Yes, why not. I'll have a wee dram.' He poured me one, but none for himself, and then sat heavily on the armchair beside the fire. He was pale. I wanted to ask him if he was in pain, but I knew he didn't like discussing the problems with his legs. He was being looked after at St Fintan's; that way we kept personal and professional separate.

'By the way, I'm sorry about you having to run to my house in your pyjamas. I can't believe what happened, to be honest.'

'Well, what matters is that nobody got hurt. Except your roof, but that's repairable.'

'Yes.'

'So, you have a daughter.'

'I do, yes.'

Silence.

'And I never told you. I know.'

'It was your prerogative, Fergus. Though I don't really understand why. I knew you had an ex-wife, with whom you lived in London. Why the secrecy?'

'It's a long story.' His handsome face took on a golden glow from the light of the fire, his hands, big and shapely, resting on his knees. I couldn't help feeling a wave of warmth towards him. So many Sundays spent hiking, before his illness reared its ugly head; so many dinners at mine, and long chats in front of the fire, and walks on the beach . . . How could I not have realised that he harboured feelings for me? And yet I hadn't. And when he told me, I retreated.

Maybe that was why he was withdrawing now. But why, two years later? No. It had to be related to Susie's sudden appearance.

'Okay, well. You can tell me when and if you're ready. In the meantime, as she's here . . .'

'She is, yes.' That coldness again. That harshness I'd never seen before.

'Well, I was just wondering if I could have a word about her.'

His face seemed to close up, as if he was shutting me out once again. He stood up laboriously and poured himself a dram too. Maybe it was the pain. It seemed to have grown worse. I'd seen more than once the effects that chronic pain had on someone's personality; maybe that was why he'd changed so much, in such a short period of time.

'My daughter? What is there to say about her?'

'Well . . . she seems to be having trouble adapting, and—'

'She's only just arrived, Grace, what do you expect?'

'Well, okay, but she needs some support, Fergus. It's a huge change, from London to here. I don't think she's having a good time in school, and also . . . some of the things she told me are quite worrying, really. About your relationship . . .'

'Look. I know you're a doctor and everything, but I don't see how . . .' He hesitated.

'How this is any of my business?'

'I wasn't going to put it like that. I know you mean well.'

'Look, forget what I said about you two. Susie just moved here. I suspect she's unhappy, she's having teething problems, you know; it's a bit of a unique place to get used to, Seal. I think she needs a hand.'

'So you took it upon yourself to give her one?' Fergus looked me straight in the eye. Since this whole Susie thing began, it had been like seeing another Fergus, an angry, almost heartless one.

'She came looking for me today, at the community garden. I took her for a hot chocolate. She needed someone to talk to. And you know what? Girls from her school came in and she practically ran away.'

Fergus shrugged and made a show of looking through stacks of invoices. 'Teenagers.'

'Fergus! She told me her mum is not interested in her, that you—'

'She's right. Lin is not interested.'

Lin. Yes, that was his ex-wife's name. He'd mentioned her sometimes, but had never really gone into details. All I knew was that she'd been the one who'd left him and wanted a divorce, and that the whole thing had left him cut to the quick.

'It might just be Susie's perception. I can't believe that a mother . . .' My words trailed away. After all these years as a doctor, I knew enough about people to realise Fergus could be right. Being a biological mother didn't necessarily mean you loved your children. But I had to give this unknown woman the benefit of the doubt; it would be unfair not to.

'Look, Grace. We've been friends for a long time. I always . . .' He looked away. I was alarmed. What was he trying to say? 'I mean, you've always helped a lot with my . . .' He patted his legs. I had the feeling he'd been about to say something else and changed his mind at the last minute. 'I owe you a lot.'

'You don't owe me anything. You've done so much for me too, more than you can imagine.' I looked down, and he waved my words away.

'But now . . . I just can't accept your help. Things are too complicated.'

'Fergus, how old are you?'

'I just turned fifty.'

'Me too. You and I together make a century. Susie is *fourteen.* Fourteen years old. She's come from a city of eight million people to an island where she has to take a bloody *ferry* to go to school. She's away from her mother. She barely knows you, for reasons that are private to you – fine, I won't talk about that. What I'm trying to say is that I'm not offering my help to you, Fergus, but to *her.*'

He was silent for a moment. The table lamp cast a yellow moon on his desk, while the window was a square of darkness. I could feel time trickling away, the ebbing and flowing of the sea as a slow hourglass to measure it. Silence was a wall between us. Again.

I was ready to take my leave when he spoke.

'Ever heard of the Sary's Castle Saga?'

'Sary's Castle? The films? Of course. I haven't seen one, but they're everywhere.'

'My ex-wife plays the main character.'

'Seriously? She's . . .'

'Lin Kruja? Yes, that's her. Her stage name, anyway.'

'That's amazing.'

'Amazing? For Lin, maybe. For me, not so much. When she was a struggling actress, she stayed with me. When her career took off, she left me. Susie was seven. Lin needed me while she was auditioning and earning nothing, but when she began earning millions . . .' His face was tight, bitter, like I'd never seen it before. 'Then I was disposable. And you know what? I didn't want her money. None of it. What I wanted was to be with my daughter.'

'I'm sorry . . .' I said. He did care for Susie then. So why, now that he had her close, was he so cold? It was best not to ask direct questions; he might clam up again. 'And all this happened in London?'

Fergus nodded again. 'Lin didn't want to be here, which was fair enough; this place is not for everyone, and it certainly makes no sense for an actress to live so far away from everything. London was better for her career, so we settled there. I leased the distillery and moved. I was smitten.' He shook his head, a bitter smile on his lips. 'You know what I mean, Grace? She was my world.'

'Yes. Yes, I know what you mean.' I really did. For a moment, my thoughts went back to *him*. My first and only love, the loss that had made me swear I would never marry. Not that I held him responsible for my lack of a family; the choices I made after he left me were mine and mine alone. But it was losing him that made my heart shut down and never dare to love again. I still lived with the consequences now – like when Fergus had tried to turn our friendship into something more. Not many people knew about it, and it wasn't something I would share with Fergus, not now. Not ever, probably, as things stood.

'When she left me, I sold everything I had and

moved back here. She . . . she accused me of . . . terrible things. Things that weren't true.'

I was shocked to see the pain in his eyes. What had she accused him of? And what about Susie? He and his wife broke up, Susie stayed with Lin, and he'd never seen his daughter again until now, when he seemed to resent her so. I wanted to ask more, but I was afraid of having gone too far already.

'And you want to know the irony?' The final word was imbued with so much bitterness, it made me shudder.

'What's the irony?'

'That my wife took Susie away from me, and then, when she had no use for her any more, she sent her back. When we have nothing to say to each other, my daughter and I; when everything is . . . broken.'

It took me a moment to process those heavy, intense words, and I had to fight the impulse to step over and hold him, to give him some comfort. And then a thought occurred to me – if Susie was neglected by her mother, why had she never come to see her dad before? And why did he seem to be so angry with her, so much so that he seemed to be neglecting her too?

'I'm sure it can't be so bad . . .' I began, but at once I realised how shallow, how meaningless my words sounded in the face of his misery.

He turned to face me and opened his hands. 'Why do you think she's here? It's not that I *wanted* her.'

I felt my eyes widen as my body absorbed the shock of those words. For a moment, even the sea seemed to quieten.

'Fergus. She's your daughter.'

'Lin brought her up. And now she says she's done enough. She's getting married again, and this guy really doesn't want Susie around. Apparently Susie has been *obnoxious* with him, Lin's word. So she sent her here. Just like that. From London to Seal . . . I said I didn't want her, I don't even know her, for heaven's sake! I said, send her to boarding school, and Lin was okay with that, but Susie said no. She was sent to boarding school briefly before and hated it. She promised that she would be no trouble, that I wouldn't know she was there . . . And now here she is. Turning my life upside down.'

Yes. Here she was. Left to her own devices, on an island where everyone knew each other and had deep bonds of blood and friendship. And her own father didn't want her. I thought of all the love I had when I was growing up, of my mum and my brothers helping me negotiate every step, of my dad being there after long hours at work, and how different Susie's life was. I had to speak out.

'You know what, Fergus? We've been friends for a long time. I know you'll forgive me if I tell you that you really are acting spitefully. Whatever your wife has done—'

'My *wife*?' He shook his head. 'Grace. You know

nothing. Nothing. And now, please, if there's nothing else I can do for you, I really have to get on.'

I would have found it rude being shown the door this way, except Fergus looked like the embodiment of sadness. But he was the adult, and Susie, for all her posing, was still just a child.

'Fine. Take care, Fergus,' I said. 'But I'll never, ever understand why you don't treasure your daughter. A life is long spent on your own. I should know.'

'You didn't have to be alone,' he said without looking at me.

I found no words to reply to that.

He cut a lonely figure as I closed the door – a stooped man, older than his years, silhouetted against the table lamp. I couldn't see his expression in the dark, but his hand went up to his face . . .

My inner turmoil made me take the long way home along the shore. I drove in darkness, and the fury of the waves echoed my own.

I stepped inside and switched the lights on, Hyde darting past me to go on his hunting expedition.

What I'd just said to Fergus could be applied to me. Maybe I should have given those words of advice to myself.

When Jonathan left me, when he walked away from our home, from our life, he broke my heart. But after a little while, hope came back to me, in a form I was not expecting.

I'd put it down to stress, my period not coming – I would never have thought of another reason somehow. Me, with my degree in medicine, denied the tenderness of my breasts, the tiredness, the strange taste in my mouth when I awoke. Until I couldn't deny any more. The test didn't tell me anything I didn't already know.

There was panic, and a strange sense of joy; and the strongest wave of love I'd ever known. Yes, I was alone, but I would have this baby and raise him or her myself. I would wrap my own family around me, my parents and my brothers, and this baby would be ours, it would be a Chatto. I looked down at my tummy, my hands resting on it. *Welcome, welcome, baby. Baby without a father.*

But it wasn't to be. Where there should have been a heartbeat, there was none – and I cried all my tears on a hospital bed, holding my mother's hand. I had lost my love; now I was losing my baby. It was all finished.

But I was young, and strong, and life took over once again. I was all broken, but I had to go on. And so I did. I found serenity, acceptance, but not love. I never married, I never had children. My parents and my brothers hinted, cajoled, coaxed, argued; but all I wanted in life was to work, and serve, and be useful. I would not give my heart again, only for it to be broken into a million pieces.

One day I woke up and I was forty. Funny, isn't it? Twenty years had come and gone while I worked as hard as I could. I'd seen my brothers getting married and my beloved nephews being born and growing into wonderful young men. I'd seen my parents passing away as peacefully as they'd lived. I'd seen Edinburgh change around me until I couldn't recognise it any more. It wasn't the city that had changed, of course, it was me. I came to the island for a new life, but the mistake I'd made would always follow me: not to trust again.

I'd turned my back on love and motherhood, and now it was too late, and I was alone.

A life is long, spent on your own.

As I got ready for bed, I sat and held the *omamori* in my hands for a long time.

Make a wish.

9

Rose

It's so much hard work, remembering. Sometimes I feel like my head is floating into space, empty of all feelings and all memories. It's a relief to be so far away – not to be. Maybe I could let go, stop this strange existence, sever all ties with my body and just go . . . but something always brings me back. A voice, a touch, a bout of pain pulls me from the grey and forces me back into existence.

And I have something to do, something important to say.

If only I could remember . . .

I piece my life back together slowly, in stops and starts, some bits as vivid as photographs in my mind, some so vague and foggy that they leave me wondering if I'm dreaming, and none of this ever happened at all.

Back in my memory comes the day when I realised everything was changing. I was nine, skinny, with hair that went down to my waist, so that I could put it up nicely when I danced. Granny was over to look after me. My parents wouldn't leave me with Jacob for some reason – they didn't realise that I would never be so safe as I was with him. In fact, they'd gone to speak to his teachers. He was doing well in school, but he kept getting into fights. This time, someone had been badly hurt. I wasn't supposed to know, but I did. Mum and Dad were fighting often too, and the bone of contention was always Jacob. They thought I was in my room, oblivious to everything, but I could hear them hurling insults at each other. Somehow they believed I was unaware of what was happening to our family. That I was too young to realise that we were falling apart.

I was kneeling on the dark red carpet, holding my hands up, parallel with each other, so my gran could wind her wool around them, but when I heard my parents coming, I jumped up.

'Rose!' The wool fell noiselessly, all tangled up.

'Sorry, Granny.' I was nervous, and even more when I saw their dark faces as they came in. Jacob being in trouble was so much worse than being in trouble myself. He couldn't help himself. That was what they didn't seem to understand, that *he couldn't help himself.*

'Where is he?' Dad thundered.

'Gone out with his friends,' Granny said. Even she, usually so sweet with everyone, was perennially angry with my brother.

'He'd better come home soon.' Dad's voice was dangerously quiet.

I shuddered. Jacob had really done it this time. Mum made her way upstairs slowly, step after step, like she had no strength left. I could nearly see the weight on her shoulders; I watched her face become more and more lined as the weeks went by. Dad followed her, and of course it happened again. The fighting. We could hear them shouting, Granny and I.

Granny stood behind me and put an arm around my waist, cuddling me. 'I'm so sorry, sweetheart. They shouldn't be doing this with you in the house. I don't know what's happening to them.'

I freed myself and went to gather the wool abandoned on the carpet, trying to regain some composure. I was about to cry.

'No, I take it back,' Granny said. 'I *do* know what's happening. It's that devil. That *devil.* Since the day he came into this family . . .' Her voice was growing shrill. I couldn't stand it.

'Shut up!'

Granny was speechless, and two pink spots appeared on her cheeks. I'd never spoken to her like that. Or to anyone, for that matter. But I wasn't finished. 'Shut up, shut up, shut up! Leave him alone!'

'He's making you like him!' She sounded incredulous, dismayed.

'He had a terrible time before he came to us. They used to beat him up. That's why he's always angry! And now he's just upset because Mum and Dad are fighting all the time and he's scared because he hates fighting.'

'We're fighting all the time *because* of him, Rose.'

Mum stood at the top of the stairs. 'Your father just will not listen . . .'

'Because we can't do *that*, Ann! We can't!' Dad appeared behind her.

Oh God. A chill went down my spine.

Do what? What was it that they couldn't do?

'We felt sorry for him. We thought those families were monsters. Now I understand . . .' Mum was crying. Again.

It couldn't be.

'Ann. I won't send my son away.'

They wanted to send Jacob away? They couldn't! They couldn't! If they did that, he'd be alone again. *I* would be alone. No, it couldn't be. They couldn't be so cruel. I was filled with panic, and with it came a cold, seething fury.

'Easy for you! It's not like we ever see you! You're always out!' Mum shrieked at Dad. Was that the loving, sweet mother I'd known as a little girl? I didn't recognise this woman. I just didn't know her any more.

'I wonder why I'm always out! You do nothing but shout at me . . .'

'It's him. He did this. We were so close before. All the times we've had to go and apologise on his behalf . . . Always being on edge . . . not knowing if he's going to hurt Rose . . .'

'He would never hurt Rose,' Dad said. And he was right.

'How do you know? I wonder what Niall's mum

would say about this, huh? Niall ended up in a cast for two months when *your* son was finished with him. And you say he wouldn't hurt Rose?'

'Enough. I'm out of here.' Dad stormed down the stairs and outside, banging the door. Granny covered her face with her hands and Mum disappeared upstairs. From the window, I could see our neighbour's face peeking from her lacy curtains. The world was spinning around me. All I could think about was what my mum was planning to do. She wanted to send my brother away.

Everything was falling, falling. I ignored Granny's tears and her calls; I turned around and ran, because there was only one person I wanted to be with.

'Jacob!'

Darkness was falling, and I was too young to be out at night. I was scared, but I had to speak to him. I found him where I'd thought he would be, sitting on the stone wall behind the graveyard, playing video games. He did that constantly. I thought it was an escape from reality for him.

'Sissy. What are you doing here? Come,' Jacob said, taking me gently by the arm and leading me away from his group of friends. I loved it when he called me Sissy. So different from the *Rose* my parents shouted out, when they called me at all.

'I came looking for you.'

'You've been crying . . . I can see it on your face.'

He dried my wet cheeks with the back of his hand. 'Please don't. It's me who's in trouble, not you.'

'I don't want you to be in trouble.'

'I don't want it either.' He looked down. 'I don't know why it always ends up like this.'

'Mum said . . .' A fresh bout of tears. I couldn't take it.

'Hey . . . hey, Sissy . . .'

'She said that we should send you away!'

Jacob paled, and I immediately regretted what I'd said. I was looking for reassurance, but I saw he couldn't give me any, that he was as scared as me.

He recovered himself. 'Look, whatever happens, we'll always be tied to each other, you and me. Always.'

'I want you to promise,' I said. 'Please promise.' These days I felt the ground slipping from under me. I needed something, someone to hold on to. My perfect family had turned into a place of shouting and cursing, and nobody seemed to understand one another. Nobody except Jacob and me.

'I promise, Sissy. I'll always look after you. Always.'

His arms were soft and strong and comfortable, and as he stroked my hair, I relaxed. He was my brother. There could be no sending him away, no matter what my mum said or did.

Devil, Granny had called him.

She didn't know him.

Nobody knew him but me.

10

Matthew

A few days had passed since Selena's strange appearance, and life seemed to have gone on to autopilot. One night I found myself drinking at the Seal Inn with a small crowd of people – not a situation I'd predicted I'd find myself in.

'So, you're off tonight?' I asked Sorren.

'I've been thrown out of my own restaurant.'

'My boyfriend is giving him a well-deserved break. Have you met Fraser yet?' It was Catriona, one of the island schoolteachers, who'd have been more suited to a magazine cover than a classroom. Her blond hair caught the light every time she moved, and her eyes were a bright blue I'd never seen before. No wonder Tom from the distillery turned scarlet every time she spoke to him. I suppose Fraser was a lucky guy – not that her beauty did anything for me, except evoking a vague sense of longing for happier times.

Sorren shook his head. 'I'm *scared*.'

'Why scared? What's wrong with this Fraser guy?' I asked.

'He has . . . ideas on how to run a restaurant. And since he's become my business partner, these ideas have kind of . . . seeped through. Like seaweed soups and pick-your-own-seafood and eating from hand-carved wooden bowls . . .'

'Sounds great to me,' I said.

'You'll have to meet him then. We need to get together,' Sorren said.

'Sure, why not.' I'd been on Seal for a heartbeat only, and people were already opening their arms to me. It was strange and sweet to be sitting here in the warm, fiddle music in the background, drinking whisky made by the people I worked with. I had a sense of . . . respite. From the constant pain, the constant guilt.

A moment to just be.

'Have you done one of his courses, Sorren?' Tom asked.

'Unwillingly, yes,' Sorren laughed. 'Fraser does these survival things . . . living like in the Neolithic or something. People even come from America to attend them,' he explained to me.

'Survival sounds good,' I said. A blue beacon shone on me – Catriona's eyes. She tilted her head; a moment, a question unasked. But someone else filled in.

'What brought you here anyway?' Tom asked. 'I couldn't believe that Fergus took someone on. Working with us, I mean.'

'Well, his legs . . .' I said quickly, randomly, knowing well I wasn't answering his question.

'Mmm, yeah, but . . .' Sorren swallowed a sip of his dark beer. 'Quite a few people went to have a chat with him before he decided to hire someone.'

'Maybe it was just the right time,' I said.

Catriona smiled, a warm, almost maternal smile – although she was a young woman, not much older than me, for a moment she seemed ageless. The face of kindness. 'Maybe it was just the right person,' she said, and I had no answer.

I drove home in the wee small hours and fell asleep with the sound of the fiddles still in my ears.

When I woke, my first confused thought was to wonder what the hard black thing against my cheek was. Of course, Mia's camera. I'd taken it to bed with me and held onto it through the night. Reality fell on me like a landslide, and my limbs were heavy as I went downstairs. Molly followed me cheerfully, in her innocence and simple joy. I stood and watched the rosy tint of the sky over the ocean, Mia's camera around my neck.

The wind on my face was wonderful as I opened the glass doors and listened to the ebb and flow, ebb and flow of the ocean, purple and grey, still asleep, perfectly peaceful. A ripple, a smooth black head appearing and disappearing in the distance. Two birds, three birds pecking the sand – black and white, long, thin beaks, a type I'd never seen. A million little particles of moisture in the air, a million little particles of life.

My fingers clasped around the camera. It was time.

She was there, she was inside there. I had to see the photographs she'd taken, the daily life she'd documented – her life when I was away at work, all the informal shots she took for fun. Maybe somebody else had taken them and she was actually in the picture . . . maybe I would see her face.

I pressed the button. The red light flashed, and I stepped out onto the sand, barefoot.

Mia, Mia. I stood in the wind, between the cottage and the ocean, between my past and the future.

I looked down in the preview square – nothing.

Black. Black. Black.

One after the other, empty photographs-not-photographs. The things that could have been and never happened, maybe.

That was it.

There was nothing there, nothing.

I sat down and cried in the light of dawn, cradling the camera like it was her head lying on my lap in perfect trust.

After a while – I don't know how long – I dried my tears and got up, shaky, emptied of everything. Slowly, step after step on the freezing wet sand, I reached the line where the sea met the land; I looked down one last time, preparing myself for the throw.

'Matthew!'

A voice in the distance interrupted me, and when

I looked over to see Grace Chatto walking towards me, the camera was still in my hands.

Grace

I always woke up at dawn, just to fit in everything I needed to do. I liked to smell the day outside, look around and see what was happening in my world. No smoke coming from Fergus's cottage, which was a good sign. But . . . Molleson Cottage, over there. A figure . . . Matthew. Pacing up and down, walking to the sea, walking back . . .

I had guessed right when he'd come to me. He was a young, handsome man, strong and with kindness in his brown eyes, I could see it. But somehow he was not himself. Like he'd lost a piece of his soul somewhere along the way. Like he was grieving. I didn't know his story, but I could recognise pain when I saw it.

And every empty hand deserved another hand to hold it.

'Hey! Come on, get inside. Bacon, eggs, home-made bread and a side of fried tomato for your five a day. Doctor's orders!' I lifted my covered plate to show him the goodies I'd brought.

Matthew looked at me and blinked. There were deep blue shadows under his eyes; he was barefoot, wearing only jeans and a white T-shirt, and he held something black and boxy in his hands. A camera.

'Grace?'

'Come on, into the warm. I'll put the kettle on.'

He did as he was told, without protesting. I busied myself in the kitchen to make us breakfast – fancy kitchen, all oak and granite – and tried to gauge what was wrong. I didn't like the look of him at all. In fact, I was positively worried.

'Taking pictures of the sunrise?'

'I . . .'

I stopped what I was doing and looked into his eyes.

'Wait here.' I ran upstairs, found his bedroom and lifted a hoodie from a chair. I wrapped it round his shoulders and got to work on the peat in the fireplace. Within ten minutes there was colour back in his cheeks, and he sat with a cup of tea and a plate of bacon and eggs and buttered bread.

'Eat. It'll do you good. Sugared tea for shock, and something to fill your stomach. I promise you, you'll feel better afterwards.'

I laid a hand on his shoulder and stroked his back. He wasn't much older than my elder nephew . . .

'I don't think I can eat.'

'Just the bread, then, okay?' I coaxed him like I would a child. 'Then you can tell me all about it.'

He looked at me, surprised. 'How did you know . . . things weren't right?'

'I didn't really. But then I saw you pacing – I can see

the cottage from my house – and I thought I'd bring you breakfast. I didn't think I would find you so upset. Do you want to tell me about it?'

'You wouldn't believe me.'

'Try me.'

He gulped down the rest of his sugary tea and finished the last of his bread.

'That's my wife's camera. When I came out of prison . . .' I held my breath, 'I took it from our house. I can't remember when . . . I can't remember when I last slept.'

'More tea,' I said, switching the kettle back on.

'Yes, thanks.'

'So . . . your wife's camera.'

'Yes. She's not here . . . She died . . . I . . . We had a car accident. I was driving. So here I am. I thought there would be photographs in there, but there weren't any. Not even one.' He blinked again and looked down. 'She was a photographer, you see. I was hoping . . . to have a bit of her back.'

'There were no pictures in her camera?'

He nodded. 'I thought . . . I thought I would find pieces of her. But there was . . . *nothing*.' He shivered. A proper shiver, deep and violent, that travelled through him and made him pale again.

'No wonder you're upset . . . It must have been a great loss for you.'

He was silent.

'There are so many things I'd like to tell you,' I said.

'And maybe we can talk about your insomnia as well. Why don't you come down to the surgery sometime? We can do this together, okay?' I touched his arm. Even his hoodie was cold.

'It was my fault,' he said calmly. Yes, that was the burden. That was the weight on his shoulders, what made him look haunted. A mistake that had destroyed his life – I'd seen a few of those in my career.

'It was an accident, you said.'

'I was in prison for three years. Now I don't even know if I'm starting again, or ending it.'

Those words chilled me. 'You're starting again, I'm sure.' I got up and handed him the camera. 'You said there were no photos. So go fill it.' He gazed at me for a moment. 'Take this camera . . . What was your wife's name?'

'Mia.'

'Take Mia's camera and fill it. You can show her where you are now.'

Slowly he got up and walked to the French doors. Molly followed him even that short distance – she wouldn't let him out of her sight.

'Grace?'

'Yes?'

'Thank you.'

'Will you do that? Will you use that camera?'

'Yes. Yes, I will.'

'Great. Now go and have a warm shower. I'll heat

up your bacon, and when you come back, I want you to finish it all.'

He rewarded me with a slight smile, the deep warm brown of his eyes lighting up for a moment, and his hair and beard shining copper. He looked very, very young.

We all had to pay for our mistakes, but how many times? And for how long?

As I watched his handsome profile silhouetted against the golden light, a realisation hit me: I didn't doubt he'd told me the truth, but I was sure he hadn't told me everything, just as I was sure that if I probed him, I would get nowhere. For once, I didn't ask any more.

11

Matthew

After Grace had left, I set out to fulfil the promise I'd made to her. I would fill the camera with everything Mia would never see.

And at the same time, I would look for Selena. What did she have to do with it all, this girl who seemed to know my wife's name while she had forgotten everything else, including her own identity? I was worried for Selena. If she hadn't left the island, she had to be somewhere. If she was indoors, in a house or a shop or a restaurant, it would mean she was safe, she was back to her senses and returned to reality. But what if she'd stepped out into the night and fallen, or got lost, or too cold to stay awake – I kept thinking of the clothes I'd given her left there in front of the fire – somewhere so remote that nobody would find her? Yes, there was nothing on the news about a missing girl, but how could we know for sure when we didn't even know where she came from? I would have to scour the land on foot; go into the coves and beaches and onto the moors. And so I began heading westwards, down the coast, followed by loyal Molly, who wouldn't leave my side.

Mia, you could have done something wonderful with this, I thought while framing endless barren, desolate hills covered in brown and purple, just beginning to brighten up in the light of early morning. I shot the mist coming from the sea and settling on the land, so thick that it looked like you were walking on a cloud; eerie, almost other-worldly photographs that were just perfect, even in my unskilful hands. Pewter skies, a corner of pink and orange far away where the sun could get through, a morning of mixed darkness and light, the lovely machair soft and dancing and full of hidden life.

Guide me, Mia. Tell me what you want me to capture . . .

Suddenly there were stones under my feet. I remembered reading in a brochure the estate agent had left that the previous year the sea had taken away a piece of land, and an ancient cottage with it, and someone had died in the storm. The bowels of the ruined cottage were open for me to see. I stepped over them, imagining that here, where the water lapped the land, people had sat and walked around and prepared their food and cleaned their home and talked – and that if you dived and reached the bottom, their things would still be there, covered in seaweed and barnacles and turned into homes for silvery fish. If Mia was here, she could document the smallest details: that white pebble on the grey rock, the tiny salty stream that cut the sand, the stony outline of what used to be the cottage's walls . . .

It was uncanny walking there, as if time had stopped; no, as if time had been jumbled up in an eternal present where the dead and the living mixed. Mist rose from the ground, and it felt like Molly and I were gliding instead of walking. I took a few pictures of her silhouette, blurred against the grey – a little mongrel dog turning into a mythical creature.

After a while of wandering in the fog, I didn't know if it was yesterday, today or tomorrow; I didn't know if those mighty waves had come already or if it was all about to happen and we would be drowned too. I went a bit too close to the water probably – Molly waiting fearfully at a distance – but I needed the perfect shots, and I would take them as near as I needed to go. I came to a ruined church; again I remembered the story: how, at the turn of the century, the waves had come to take away half of the church, and the congregation with it. On that side of the island, the sea had been a bringer of destruction.

Picture after picture, I was showing Mia what was to be my island home. My thoughts kept flowing unchecked as I walked, my feet on sand, on heather, on the hardy grass that grew on the dunes, on the machair, on the barren hills. Molly followed me faithfully.

I felt grateful for all the camping I'd done as a boy, because my sense of direction didn't fail me as we walked south, keeping a wave pattern in our itinerary so we'd cover as much ground as we could. We came to wide white beaches that managed to look inviting and forbidding at the same time, and a gelid wind made my head hurt. From the mist, a brown sandstone building rose, and a sign – St Fintan's Hospital. A faint music was coming from somewhere – strange, music in a hospital. It was some kind of classical piano, slow and sweet, and my mind wandered without being able to stop on anything. I needed something to hold on to – *find Selena* was as good as any buoy to a drowning man. I had a purpose and I had to follow it. But that music, that music was so haunting. I wrestled with myself to get away from the window. The silent building, Sergeant Casey had called it, but it wasn't silent now.

'Come on, Molly,' I called. I needed to hear my own voice over the strains coming out of the sickroom. They were working on me like a mermaid's call, pleading with me to stay. I had to wrench myself away from the hypnotic melody.

The sky was slowly turning from white to grey, and the day was getting darker. I'd walked for hours now. The afternoon shadows had begun to gather when I came in sight of my cottage again, with a camera full of photographs. I had come full circle. But there was still one place left to capture. The wildest place on Seal, the place the estate agent had warned me against.

The wind blew strong and the sound of Corryvreckan was relentless. The rocky cliffs, the breaking waves, the whirlpool turning and turning; it was a wild place, a place that belonged to nature and not to humans. There was a Seal made of whitewashed cottages and the quaint high street with its souvenir shops and multicoloured houses. And then there was another Seal, a rock rising out of a wide ocean, battered by salty wind and besieged by the waves, and up here on the northern side, this wild island was centre stage.

Slowly, carefully, I stepped towards the cliff edge. The grass was brown and damp, slippery underfoot. The wind was so strong that I decided to fall to my knees and crawl. Even so high up – fifty feet at least – I could feel the sea spray against my face, against my hands. The edge was crumbly, rock and grass and sand mixed together, and I held on for dear life. I stuck my head out over the chasm and forced myself to look down. White-topped waves, black rocks, like inky letters on a page. The beach was empty; Selena wasn't there – yes, that had been in the back of my mind. I breathed a sigh of relief as I pressed the button again and again, capturing as many frames as I could with my inexpert hands.

You could have taken some masterpieces here, my Mia . . . If only we could have seen all this together . . .

And now there was the small business of standing up again. My head was spinning from looking down from such a height, and from the wind. But I didn't want to crawl away. I wanted to stand in the elements with my head high. And I did, lifting myself from my hands and knees, my muscles pushing against the wind that wanted to knock me down. I was panting a little, sweating in spite of the cold – the sea looked merciless, Corrywreckan sounded like the gates of the Underworld, and I was elated and afraid at the same time.

I was still breathing hard as I walked back home in the gathering dark. As I came closer and closer to my cottage, Molly began to growl – seals, probably. Darkness had fallen suddenly. The dark on Seal was not like the dark in Bennington; on the island, black was truly black, and if there was no moonlight, you couldn't see an inch in front of you. By memory rather than by sight, I opened the low gate and made my way towards the door. As I reached out for the handle – I didn't need a key; nobody ever locked their doors on Seal, so Fergus had told me – I tripped over something soft. Whatever it was yelped, the high, sweet yelp of a woman's voice, and I landed on her, crushing her slight body, my face in her hair, my hand looking for balance and finding her thigh.

'Selena?'

'Yes. Selena,' she whispered. The croakiness in her voice was now gone completely, and her tone was soft and low. She was smiling.

'Come,' I said, and lifted her up, holding both her hands in mine. I opened the door and switched the light on – long silky hair, aquamarine eyes. She still wore that short white dress. 'I looked for you everywhere. I thought you might be ill or . . .'

As I spoke, she stepped inside the cottage and began exploring. She kept touching things, feeling them with her fingers, her palms. Molly ran in after her, barking. But the dog didn't seem to be looking at Selena – she was barking in her general direction, but jumping about like she wasn't sure where exactly the stranger was.

Selena stopped in front of the record player. 'Music! Can I listen again?'

The warm, soft sounds of Debussy filled the air, and she closed her eyes, swaying gently like a willow. I rested Mia's camera gently, carefully on the kitchen table and watched, drinking in the music.

It was surreal. My legs were agony after having walked for hours; I was weak with lack of food and sleep. Maybe I'm dreaming her, I thought once more. Maybe I'd hallucinated her into being. And yet here she was, smiling, pure. Real. I took her hand and led her to sit down beside me on the plush leather sofa. She followed me, obedient as a child.

'Do you remember now? Why you came here? Do you remember?'

She shook her head. 'I'm sorry.'

'There's something really important I need to ask you. Please listen carefully.' Selena nodded, serious. 'The first time we met, you said Mia. That's my wife's name. She died. Did you know her?'

'I can't remember. But I will. I promise.'

I rubbed my face with my hands, and my glasses fell on the floor.

'There,' she said, handing them back to me. 'Matthew?'

'Yes,' I said wearily.

'I'm hungry.'

I had to laugh. 'Well, I did buy some food. I'm now the proud owner of a few packets of pasta, some jars of pesto and . . . wait . . .' I checked the cupboard, 'blue-berry jam. I thought you might be back, you see . . .'

She smiled. 'Toast and jam! Please. I'll make it.'

A few minutes later, we sat with toast and jam and cups of hot, sugary tea. I'd given her my hoodie, and she clutched her knees to her chest, little white feet sticking out of her dress.

'You . . . disappeared,' I said.

She swallowed a mouthful of her toast. 'You were calling someone.'

'I wanted to help you. I still want to help you. You can't—' I was about to continue, but she interrupted me.

'I don't need help. I'm free now.' She shrugged and swept some crumbs from her lap.

'You're free? What do you mean?' Was someone threatening her? A boyfriend, a husband?

'Yes. Well. I hope so. Maybe just for a while, I don't know.'

'Are you from the island? Are you here on holiday?'

She shook her head and placed a thin white finger on my lips. 'Please. No questions. I can't answer them anyway, I told you, I can't remember.'

'Okay. Okay. But—'

'*I can't remember*,' she repeated, and she seemed so fragile, her skin so pale that for a moment it seemed transparent. What a strange effect of the light, I thought, and blinked until she was solid again.

'Hey, don't worry,' I said. 'It's okay. Look, let's just . . . stay here for a while. In peace.'

'Yes.'

By the time the music ended, when the fire was just embers, she was half asleep and weary. I carried her upstairs, her head against my chest, her arms around my neck, and tucked her into bed, making sure she was warm.

'Get a good night's sleep now. I'm sure tomorrow it'll all be clearer. I'll just be here . . .' I made myself comfortable on the armchair beside the window, Molly at my feet.

'I don't want to fall asleep,' she whispered. Her face was white in the light of the bedside lamp, her eyes circled with blue. In that pose, she looked almost ill, and I was daunted all of a sudden.

'No? Why not?'

'Because I want to be with you. If I fall asleep, I'll be alone again. I've been alone for a long time.'

'My eyes are closing, Selena . . . sorry.'

'Please don't sleep. Please stay with me.'

I was trying, but she had a strange effect on me. Her presence untied all my knots, relaxed my muscles, soothed my mind . . .

'I have to sleep,' I murmured. My last conscious thought was with Mia's camera, sitting downstairs on the kitchen table.

I woke up with Molly's paws on my chest and her wet nose sniffing at my cheek.

I knew Selena would be gone; I was sure, even before opening my eyes. When I finally did, there it was, the space where she had lain, cold and empty but for the questions she'd left behind.

I sat with a cup of strong black coffee and switched Mia's camera on, preparing myself to go through the images in the small preview screen.

The sea, the sky, the moors, the mist, the grey stones of the lost cottage's foundation, the ruined church . . . Wait a moment. There was a shadow in these pictures, a silhouette . . . there was someone in the frame. I zoomed on the image once, twice.

Selena.

I pressed the forward button – she was in the following one too, and then she wasn't, and then she was again . . . She was in almost all the photos, standing on a rock, on a dune, among the heather, hair flowing in one frame, her profile in another, forward, forward, until her face looked straight at me from the screen in what was almost a close-up; as if she'd been standing in front of the camera. She'd been there, she'd been there all along – but I'd never seen her.

12

Rose

Glen Avich, 2009

It was a sweet, golden summer afternoon, and we were playing in our garden. Jacob had made a little house for us out of wooden planks he'd painted white, like a fairy-tale Hansel and Gretel shack. The plan was that we'd retreat there whenever our parents fought. Which was all the time. We'd even carried an old sofa in, a camping stove and a box full of books and comics. He'd slipped some pages from my ballet magazines into poly pockets, so they wouldn't be damaged by damp, and pinned them up on the walls.

'It's perfect!' I clapped my hands in happiness.

At that moment, angry voices rose from the house – a man and a woman. I couldn't decipher their words, but I recognised who was speaking. Niall's parents. Niall was a schoolmate of Jacob – and he was a bully. He'd pushed my brother once too many times, and Jacob had finally lost his rag. Big-time. But I'd thought it was finished now, that it had been resolved between them. Instead it looked like Niall's parents wanted an explanation for their son's broken wrist. But Jacob was sorry; I knew he was, because he'd told me.

I wasn't sorry. I thought Niall deserved it.

Jacob just couldn't keep his promise to control his anger. He tried, but he couldn't. There was always someone making him angry, something landing him in trouble. He never argued about it being his fault, he never complained he was being picked on. But now that I was at school with him, at Innerleithen High School, I could see it. They never left him alone, never gave him a chance. They goaded him like a bull, the dark, surly, silent boy who'd come from nowhere, and would probably go nowhere too.

Mum and Dad didn't listen to me. They didn't believe me when I said that yes, Jacob had his faults, but circumstances had put him in a cage he couldn't get out of; that other people liked to see him roar, helpless, like a lion in a circus. His temper was a river in flow, and soon we'd alienated many people in the village – a terrible thing for my mum, who came from a solid old Glen Avich family and lived for appearances. Adopting Jacob had been part of it; they were the kind of people who did good in the world, who reached out. They were model parents, and elders in church, and Jacob beating up their friends' children didn't quite fit the picture.

Jacob knew how much my parents resented him.

He knew when Mum stuck my Mother's Day card

on the fridge, but not his surprisingly beautiful drawing of her in our garden.

He knew when she whispered with her friends and looked his way, then enjoyed playing the role of the martyr who'd given all of herself and was now offering the other cheek.

He knew when they organised a family holiday and left him with Granny while we flew to sunny Spain.

He was out of his mind with the pain of another rejection, and I tried and tried to make him better. My love for him had not wavered; he was my brother, my big brother, who protected me and looked after me and never, ever raised a hand against me. He was the one who used to tell me bedtime stories when I was wee, who waited for me outside dance school when the nights got dark, who made beans on toast for us when Mum was on shift and Dad was out working in the evening, which happened more and more often.

'I don't want to stay here any more. They hate me,' he said one particularly blue night.

'Please, don't say that,' I begged him. Every time he mentioned leaving us, I went into a panic. The loving, all-knowing, all-powerful parents I'd thought I had – looking at them with the eyes of a child – had turned into bitter, detached creatures who did nothing but quarrel.

And they blamed Jacob for everything; the state of their marriage, their shortcomings, everything that didn't go their way was because of Jacob.

Yet I still loved them.

The voices moved to the front garden, and now I could hear better. My mum sounded drained, and for a moment, I felt sorry for her. 'I'm so sorry. So sorry. Of course we'll deal with it. Yes, I know we've said it before, but . . .' There was silence for a moment. Niall's parents had left. There went another set of friends; not that I cared. Then our parents' voices coming from the kitchen. We could see them through the French doors, my mum running her hands through her hair, my dad lighting a cigarette.

'I can't believe this. He promised!'

'Look. Let's call Jacob and get this over and done with . . .' My dad's calmer voice.

'I don't want to even look at him, Thom!'

I gazed at Jacob. He was stony-faced, looking down, his long eyelashes shadowing his eyes. 'What happened?' I whispered.

He shrugged. 'Nothing you don't know already.'

'I'm going to call the police,' I heard my mum saying, and all the sympathy I'd felt for her dissolved. 'I can't take this any more.'

'Ann, the police for a kids' fight? Come on . . .'

'He torments me,' Jacob said softly. 'Niall.'

'I know,' I whispered. I was barely twelve, but I could read the situation better than my parents did. Jacob had been a silent, sullen, easily angered child who'd turned into a teenager with a chip on his shoulder, full of a rage inside that he just couldn't control.

Some kids found it entertaining; goading him was their pastime. It was worth getting a blow or two to see this quiet, impenetrable boy lose his temper to the extent that he couldn't control himself. He was constantly being set up. And the people who should have stood by him, his adoptive parents, simply joined the chorus of *Jacob is a bad apple.* My mum did so with anger, with scorn; Dad with resignation, like a martyr determined to carry his load.

Jacob was alone.

Or rather, he would have been alone had it not been for me. I was all he had.

I saw things nobody else noticed, I knew things about him nobody else did. I could see his distress, how hard he tried to fit into a normal life after all he'd been through. At the end of a bad day, he still spent the night on his bedroom floor like when he was a child, cross-legged, unable to loosen his muscles, to relax even just enough to lie down.

But he was also full of kindness that, it seemed, only I could see.

He used his paper-round money to go to Swan's, the dance shop in Aberdeen, and buy me the pink cross-over cardigan everyone at class had and I desperately wanted. He kept Granny's peat shed stocked, he went for her groceries, he did all those little jobs my father couldn't do for her because he was always out at work. One day, my mum said how much she'd loved a pergola she'd seen on a travel programme; Jacob made one for her, painted blue, trailing over it the ivy that grew on the trellis. Another time she had a sore back and the chemist had run out of the arnica patches she used; Jacob cycled to Innerleithen to buy them, but they'd run out there too. He cycled all around the local pharmacies and came back three hours later, wet and muddy, with the patches.

All the little things he did for us, and nobody noticed.

Because he carried this persona on his shoulders, the boy who always got into trouble, the boy who couldn't keep his hands to himself, who threw desks in class and punched people in the lunch hall and spent the rest of the time in his room, playing video games.

Devil, my granny had said, years ago.

But he wasn't a devil. He'd been a chronically underweight baby because nobody had bothered to feed him. He'd been beaten as a two-year-old because he couldn't sit still. He'd been a three-year-old who ended up in hospital because his mother had crushed a sleeping pill in his milk. He'd been a four-year-old left to sleep in the garden for nights at a time because he wet the bed. I wasn't supposed to know any of that, but I heard my parents talking when he first arrived, and I knew more than they imagined.

'Hey. We'll sort it,' I said in a low voice. The sun lit his dark hair with orange streaks; his strong frame was folded in on itself as he withdrew, like I'd seen him do so often. All the joy had gone out of that summer day.

But I couldn't have imagined what would happen next, how much our lives would change. How everything was about to break, irreparably so.

I stood as close as I could to my brother as the little house behind us, assembled only that morning with its coloured posters and recycled furniture, turned into a memory of a world just fallen apart. We heard them going upstairs, and then no more sound came from the house. This was even worse than the shouting.

'Jacob. Rose. Come inside, now.' Mum peeked from the back door. She was white-faced, and so were we, I imagined, a cold breeze hitting us while the summer afternoon turned dark in that sudden Scottish way. Mum waited for us, arms crossed. I thought she would be wound up tight, full of resentment, waiting to explode – but she seemed drained. She stepped back inside slowly, stooped, like a woman defeated. My stomach was in a knot. We followed her, and I could feel Jacob's tension; I felt it in my mind, on my skin. My dad stood by the piano, grim-faced, waiting for us. Something was afoot. Something not good.

'Sit down, children,' he said. We obeyed, and I stole a glance at my brother's face. His expression frightened me. When he looked like that, usually it meant he had to go for a run or carry heavy things up and down or just fight with someone to get it all out. And *children*. That was another little sting, for his benefit. He wasn't a child any more, but my mum would not stop calling him that. She felt powerless in all this, and the only way she had to assert herself was to belittle him, to humiliate him.

'We're sorry—' Dad began.

'We have something to tell you,' Mum interrupted him. Her eyes were red-rimmed, her lashes wet – she'd been crying.

'I thought *I* was going to explain, Ann. Can you give this to me at least?' Dad burst in. Of course. It had all turned into point-scoring between them.

'If he goes, I'm going too!' I shouted, unable to stop myself any longer. Everyone looked at me. I was usually a shy, quiet child, and I could see they were shocked.

'Don't be stupid,' my mum snarled.

'Don't call her stupid.' It was Jacob, his voice not much more than a whisper.

My mum turned towards him, and for the first time I saw it in her face – fear. She was afraid of him, I realised.

'It's me going, not you!' she almost shouted.

The room fell quiet as we all absorbed her words. The words I'd never, ever thought I would hear.

She was this family.

She was this house.

She was Mum. She couldn't go.

A plea flew from my lips of its own accord, sounding a bit like the yelp of a puppy. 'Mum . . .'

'I'm sorry, Rose. I can't take any more,' she burst

out, as my heartbeat went *thud, thud, thud* in my child's breast.

'Where are you going?' My voice came out small.

'I'm going to stay with Aunt Cheryl for a while—'

'But we *need* you!' I cried without letting her finish.

There were tears in her eyes. 'Oh darling. Look . . . I'm moving to Aberdeen, not Australia . . . I'll see you all the time . . .'

Dad seemed a lot older all of a sudden. 'Ann, we can still work this out. It doesn't have to be this way . . .'

'Yes, it does. I'm sorry. I'm so sorry. Sometimes . . . one mistake can change everything,' she said, looking at Jacob. So that was pretty clear. He was the mistake they'd made. This child they'd pinned so much hope on had disappointed them, destroyed them ultimately.

But he hadn't. They'd destroyed themselves and they couldn't see it.

I was in floods of tears while my brother just sat, not crying, not speaking, not moving. He was taller than both our parents, big strong hands resting on his knees, his hazelnut eyes looking down. The dark, withdrawn, sweet brother I adored. He might look like a man, but he was still a boy. And this boy who'd got into trouble for fighting so many times was also someone who looked after his younger sister, who dealt with our eternally bickering parents and generally kept it together whenever my mum locked herself in her room to cry in peace and our dad had to go somewhere – somewhere being his work, his mother's house, the pub, wherever he could go to be away from us. Yes, Jacob was the one who kept me from falling apart. Yet they blamed him for everything.

'Well, I think there's nothing more to say,' he said very calmly, and stood up. I was proud of him. My Jacob was different from the one the outside world knew. He wouldn't lose his temper, even when my mum's decision to leave was laid at his door, instead of her taking responsibility for her own choices.

'No, nothing more to say. You finally did it, Jacob,' Mum said.

I trembled with the injustice of it all. 'No, no! Tell them what Niall did to you!'

Jacob shook his head.

Mum found Dad's cigarettes and lit one, filling the air with nauseating smoke. 'What? He looked at you funny?' She was trying to humiliate him again. 'And you thought it was a good idea to beat him black and blue for it?'

'It took them two days to get your name out of him, Jacob. Niall was scared that if he told on you, you'd kill him,' Dad said, his hands shaking as he rubbed his forehead.

Jacob slowly lifted his eyes and gazed at Dad from under his long black eyelashes. For a moment everything I knew seemed to blur, and reality shook and trembled like my father's hands.

Because with that one look, Jacob had told me what

he was capable of. Like he was saying: *Yes, I could do that.*

I swallowed, my mouth and throat dry.

Mum straightened herself, rigid, wide-eyed, as though she herself couldn't believe what she was doing; she held her cigarette in a gesture that seemed final, irrevocable. I panicked. My eyes were full of tears, and all my effort was going into keeping them in. I failed, of course, and ended up sobbing like the little girl that I still was. 'Dad, please, you can't let her go . . .'

'No, of course not,' Jacob said, still sounding very calm. 'All this makes no sense. I'm the problem, I'm the one who should go.' He was reasonable, even, as if we were discussing the options for building a new conservatory, or where to go on holiday. It was surreal and sad to see him negotiating another separation when he'd had so many already, and withdrawing deep into himself where nobody could hurt him. 'I'm calling the social worker. I'll go somewhere.'

'Jacob, please, no . . .' I cried. I was pulled in both directions; I loved them both, my mum and my brother. I was torn. Our eyes met.

'It's okay. In a year I can live by myself.' *Don't worry, I'll come back for you,* his gaze said.

'And do you think that will sort it? I begged your father . . . Thom,' she corrected herself, and Jacob winced. A little reminder that he was not of our blood. 'I begged Thom for years to send you away, I told him that having you here would destroy us. I realised it straight away, when I couldn't even come and get you from school without having someone come to me and say, *Your son hit my son, what are you going to do?* Every. Single. Day. Until people didn't even speak to me any more. But you know what really did it?'

Jacob looked straight at her. The pain in his eyes burnt through me. And it was my parents doing this to him. The three people I loved most in the world were tearing each other apart.

'It was that Thom and Rose cared more for you than for our family.'

'We'd committed ourselves, Ann,' Dad said. 'We would just look like idiots if . . .'

I stared at him, aghast. He returned my look as if to say, *What?* He hadn't even realised what he'd just said.

'That's why you kept me. So you wouldn't look bad.' Jacob's voice was very quiet. 'So you wouldn't look like idiots.'

'Whatever the reason, Thom and my daughter . . . they always sided with you. They made their choice. What do you say, Rose? Me or Jacob? Tell me now.' Mum spoke cruelly, and when I did not reply, she opened her hands as if to say, *I told you*. I just glared at her, wondering which one of us was the child. She shook her head. 'It makes no sense for me to stay.'

Jacob stood slowly and went to the back door. I was torn in two, wanting to run after him, wanting to convince my mum to stay; my heart and soul were ripped apart. And then my mum offered me one last chance.

'You can come with me, Rose. If you can bear to leave *Jacob*.' She said his name like it was a bad word.

'What?' Dad was shocked. Mum ignored him and came to hold both my hands. The sudden show of affection after all that conflict made me burst into tears again.

'You can come with me to Aberdeen and we can start again. No more trouble. No more being scared in our own beds . . .'

What? Had she been scared in her own bed? I was horrified. I'd been scared too, very much; but of their fights, certainly not of Jacob. A wave of rage drowned me, and I was done with this crazy conversation. 'I'm not coming with you. You're abandoning us! Jacob is my brother and you hate him! You're . . .'

And then we heard it, drowning out my voice. The bangs, the crashes, the thuds. Dad and I ran out. Jacob had torn apart the white house he'd built for the two of us. He'd ripped the planks away from their nails and banged them on the ground until they broke. He stood there, panting but composed. Why was he wearing red gloves?

No. Those weren't gloves, they were his hands.

'I haven't hurt anyone else this time,' he said.

I had no idea how to bandage anything, but I tried. Jacob's poor hands were flayed. Dad was in pieces and unable to help, so he'd gone to the pub. Mum had left quickly, a trolley and a suitcase materialising nice and ready out of the wardrobe. She'd been planning this for a while.

'She asked you to go and live with her?' my brother asked in a quiet voice. His tanned skin had faded to white. I was desperate to make him better.

I froze. No point in denying it. 'I said no.'

There was a silence, dripping with dismay. 'Do you think it's my fault that she left? I mean, I know she said it was . . . but what do *you* think?'

'She went away because she wanted to. She just tells herself it was you.' I thought for a moment, trying to choose the right words. 'She doesn't know you. You're her son, but she doesn't know you.'

'I'm not her son.' I froze for a moment. Did that mean he didn't feel like my brother either?

'You know why I was put up for adoption? I mean, after I was taken from my real family. And why all those foster families let me go?' he asked quietly.

I shook my head. I was lying, of course. I knew he would feel so humiliated if he realised I knew about everything he'd been through.

'Good. Because I never want you to know what happened to me. A lot of it I couldn't remember, you know. The social workers said I'd removed those memories. They told me what happened. They told Mum and Dad. Bottom line is, they all left me.' He shrugged, as if it didn't matter.

I held his clumsily bandaged hands gently. I remembered his eyes the night he'd arrived as if it had happened yesterday. They hadn't changed. He still had child's eyes in a young man's body. His hands were shaking, and no wonder – the pain must have been excruciating. Pink streaks were already seeping through the gauze.

'And what about you? Will you leave me?' he asked seriously, so seriously that it felt like both our lives depended on it. Like we were hanging over a chasm and only the other person's grip could save us from falling.

I had no doubts about my answer.

'Never,' I said fiercely. I didn't feel twelve years old; I felt ageless and bent over a heavy burden. My family had been dismembered and it was left to me to comfort Jacob and keep things together.

He stood up, and my face was against his chest. He wrapped his arms around me, and I felt his strength, his resilience. It was then that I let go and cried in his arms, my burden dissolving as everything about him told me: *I will carry this for you.*

My parents had failed me. Jacob never would.

The look he had given my dad when he'd mentioned Niall's fear that Jacob would kill him floated before my eyes, but I pushed it away, and pretended it had never happened.

13

Matthew

'So. How are you liking it here?' Fergus said, lifting a bag of barley with surprising ease. In spite of the ongoing trouble with his legs, his upper body was strong, and he was so tall that he handled the sacks like they were bags of sugar. But I knew by now that he tended to overdo it, and I kept an eye on him. We'd just received a delivery, and there was a lot to do. I'd worked at Seal Distillery for just over a week, and every single bone and muscle in my body knew it. It was the best job I could have found, with the way it pounded my body and rested my mind. If only I could get some sleep . . .

'You mean the island, or the job?'

'Both.'

'Well, I'm enjoying both. Thanks for this. For giving me a chance.'

'You're welcome. Oh . . .' He swayed a little.

'Hey, hey . . .' I took the sack from him.

'Shit.'

'Don't strain yourself.' I could see he felt demeaned

by not being able to do as much as he used to, and I sympathised. It must have been hard.

'Well, you know. This is my place. I built it from nothing. And it's all being taken away from me.' He shook his head. 'Right now, my life is one big almighty mess. Every single bit of it.'

For a moment, I was taken aback. Fergus had seemed to me a reserved man, one who didn't talk much about himself. I scrambled for words of comfort. 'In the work I did before, I didn't need my legs. Just my head. Leave the sacks to me and Jim and the others; you can make the decisions.' I surveyed the low white buildings and the small woods behind them. 'You are the centre of this place, Fergus. Legs or no legs.'

He gave me a long, even look. 'What were you in prison for?' His eyes were very clear, direct. I had to swallow as I formed the answer in my mind. It hurt, it always hurt.

'I was in prison for manslaughter. My wife died, another couple was involved . . . I was driving . . . Manslaughter, yes. I killed them.' Suddenly my head spun, and I didn't know if it was because of what I'd just said, hearing it aloud. Selena's appearance in the photos I'd taken with Mia's camera haunted me. It was like I'd lost my grip on reality, like every time I was alone, a dream world took the place of the real one and left me uncertain of what was real and what was not.

Fergus was silent for a moment. A gust of wind made its way among the trees with a low swooping sound, like a hunting owl. Branches rustled and leaves danced, and I stood with my story, with this burden on my back.

'I'm sorry,' he said, and he held my gaze like he wasn't afraid of my pain, my shame. Most people were. There was nothing left to say. I lifted the sack and we began to walk towards the storehouse. One down, forty-nine to go. Oh well.

'See that?' He pointed to the sky. All I could see was grey clouds gathering over a white sky, hastening eastwards.

I blinked. 'No?'

He laughed. 'Exactly. It's the angels' share. You see, when it's maturing in the casks, a small amount of whisky evaporates and rises into the sky. It's like a little tribute, I always think. We get to keep this gift, but we need to give a little to the angels. You can't see it, but it's there now, going up, you know. And I think, if the angels' share is there but we can't see it, maybe the angels are there too, drinking it, but we can't see them either.'

Is Mia with the angels?

I was silent as I put down the sack of barley. If only it was as easy to lay down the pain, I thought.

It was then that I saw her. Selena. She stood amongst the ash trees, slender and slight like a young tree herself, barefoot, hair blowing in the wind. For the first time I noticed that her white dress had lacy sleeves. I thought I must have fallen asleep on my feet and was dreaming.

I have something to tell you.

'You okay? You don't look good.'

'Yeah. Yeah. Just . . . I didn't get much sleep last night. And . . . any other night really. Fergus, do you mind if . . .' I gestured towards the trees, towards Selena. His eyes followed my hand.

'Sign off early? Ah, sure. It was a long day. For someone who normally only uses his head and not his muscles,' he teased me.

'Thank you.'

Fergus disappeared into his office; I tried to stop myself from running to her, but I couldn't.

For the following five days, she visited me every night. Five days of appearing at the distillery, young willow among the ash trees; five days of sleeping in my bed with me in the armchair, half watching her, half dozing. Five nights of disappearing.

On a cold purple evening, twilight having just dissolved in a triumph of lilacs and pinks, Selena and I sat side by side on the rocks of our little cove. The pod of seals keeping guard on one side, Molly on the other. I just wanted to stay there with her, my arm around her shoulder and her curled up into me, cosy in the zipped-up fleece I'd found for her. I didn't want to talk, to spoil the moment, and I could tell she didn't want to either. Sometimes words were so strident, so unnecessary.

I took her gently by the shoulders, making her face me. I closed my eyes and touched her forehead with mine.

'Selena,' I said simply. 'Don't go.'

She stroked my hair slowly, slowly, until I closed my eyes. It seemed that even the wild Atlantic air was still, silent, while the sea continued its ebb and flow, ebb and flow.

The nights in the hospital, unable to close my eyes . . .

The nights in prison, claustrophobia tormenting me, the heat and noise and constant alarm of so many people around me . . .

Standing on the hard wooden floor of Molleson Cottage, wondering what would become of me, wondering if I would ever take a full breath again . . .

They were all swept away when Selena was around, as my body finally gave in, as my brain stopped screaming and my nerve endings stopped hurting.

'I'll try. I'll try to stay,' she said, as if somehow it wasn't her decision.

I held her tight, drawing her close to me. If I stood guard, she couldn't go. It was as if I kept her tethered – once I wasn't there any more, she disappeared too.

I knew our time of innocence would come to an end. And soon, I suspected. But not now. Not yet. We lived in a suspended bubble with no yesterday and no tomorrow.

'I have a message for you,' she said softly. 'It's from Mia.'

For a moment I could not speak, I could not think, I could not even breathe. And then, a voice calling me.

'Matthew! Hey! Oh, Molly, hello!' I turned around to see Grace waving, her silver hair blowing behind her. Molly was running to her, and I waved back, reluctantly – this wasn't the time . . .

I could feel it, I swear I could. It was like a shift, like everything around me jumped for a moment and then readjusted itself. It was then that I knew she was gone. I was alone on the rock, hanging on to her words like a climber to the rock face.

Don't fall, don't fall.

After a few disjointed words – Grace laying a gentle hand on my cheek: *Are you sure you're okay?* – I found an excuse and went home, feeling her worried gaze on me.

Something had changed inside me – something that had been waiting to change for a long time – and rage came at last. I was furious at everything and everyone, furious at the universe itself. I turned into another person, someone I didn't know. I threw the first thing I saw against the wall, a heavy vase. It shattered with a noise that made Molly cower, but I barely noticed. There were a thousand jagged edges on the floor, against my skin, inside my heart. I bled as I took my shoes off and walked on them barefoot, but I didn't care; there was blood on the white sheets as I destroyed my lonely bed, tearing the linen into pieces, roaring like an animal kept in a cage for too long, too long.

Why did you leave me? I maybe shouted, though I'm

not sure – the words that came out of me were confused, too full of grief to make sense. *Why, why did you leave me? That's never the way things were meant to be . . .*

It was about all that I'd lost and that would never, ever return.

That night, Selena didn't come back. Nor the night after, or the one after that. Exhausted and wakeful, I sat on the rocks with Molly and a bottle of whisky, in almost perfect darkness.

A message from Mia, my Mia.

In my loneliness, my drunken stupor, I thought I saw someone, a near-transparent silhouette, glimmering hesitant, feeble, like she was trying, trying but couldn't make it all the way to me – lands and seas between us, an ocean of existence that kept us apart.

The next day, with a pounding headache and sore bones after a night spent in the almost-December freezing wind, I found myself clutching at straws. Maybe Selena had come back but hadn't found me. She'd always found me before, but maybe . . .

'Fergus?' My boss's office was appealingly warm, with its fire glowing on this grey, icy morning.

'Yes?' He raised his head from his papers. 'What can I do for you?'

I felt like an idiot. No: I felt crazy. Demented. *You haven't seen this girl who comes to me; she says she has a message for me, but she can't remember what* . . . Oh, wait a minute. Actually, he had seen her once, though they didn't speak. The first night she'd come for me at the distillery.

'You haven't seen that girl around?' I said. 'You know, the one who came looking for me a few nights ago . . .'

'A girl came for you?'

'Yeah, do you not remember? I asked you if I could go early . . .'

'I don't recall seeing anyone.'

That was strange. Selena had been standing not far from us, the wind blowing among the trees and in her hair . . . but then what *wasn't* strange in this whole story?

'A young woman, dark hair, white dress,' I continued, feeling more and more absurd. Fergus was shaking his head.

'I never saw her, no. Are you sure she's not a figment of your imagination?'

Good question. Good question indeed.

I shivered, a deep shiver that travelled through my body and made my teeth chatter.

'Someone walked over your grave,' Fergus said.

'I have to go,' I blurted out without giving him time to reply.

Out into the wind, running on gravel and machair and sand to Grace's cottage, too distressed, too addled to even think. My knocking on her door broke the silence, and then I called out over and over again, my own voice startling me. 'Grace! Grace! Are you there? Grace!'

I heard her steps coming towards the door. 'Matt, hi . . .' she began, and then she saw my face. 'What's wrong?'

I was panting, breathless. How could I explain everything that had been happening? How should I word my question when everything sounded crazy? 'Remember three nights ago, I was sitting in the cove . . . that cove over there . . .' I turned towards the beach and the sea, now shrouded in white mist, thickening before my eyes.

'Yes, yes.' She raised a hand patting the air down as if to try and soothe me. 'The cove. Come inside, Matt, come on . . .'

'I can't right now, Grace. Please listen. I was sitting there the other day, remember?'

'Yes. Matthew, you're scaring me.'

'There was a girl sitting with me. That girl I told you about, the one who . . . appeared on the beach, remember?'

'Yes, I remember that too . . .'

'She was there, wasn't she? Sitting beside me in the cove. When you saw me . . . us?'

'Matthew, look, come on in and let's sit down for a moment.'

'Selena. She was there, wasn't she? Beside me?'

'Matthew . . .'

'Please, did you see her?'

She took a breath – I could see the worry on her face, and I knew the answer already. I could almost feel the cold hands of the gathering mist behind me, on my neck, on my hands as she spoke.

'There was no girl. You were alone.'

I'd lost my mind. She really had been a figment of my imagination. But if she was a vision, it was a vision I wanted to have. I put the Debussy on again, calling her, calling her. The floor-to-ceiling windows were black, and if I came close to them all I could see was my reflection. So I opened them, and welcomed the icy air in and around me. For a moment, I imagined the cold, cold sand hardening into crystals and scintillating like a million stars, sunk and crushed onto earth. And then I knew I was not alone, I knew it in my bones, in my nerves, in my muscles, her presence filling me from hair to fingertips.

I have a message . . . from Mia.

Once again I switched the camera on. The invisible girl whom only I could see . . . she was there in almost every frame. She was there.

'Are you real?' The question came out of me like a prayer. 'Am I crazy? What is it that you have to tell me?' My words resounded, low and pleading, in the empty house. They soared up to the sky, mixed with the music, like the angels' share.

14

Grace

Two hours there, two hours back, and if you didn't have sea legs, you would suffer. I thought that Susie would mind – after all, she'd been so negative about everything concerning Seal – but instead, she stood on the deck for a long time, her eyes half closed in the wind, her face barely visible under a Fair Isle hat with a huge pompom on top that made her look even younger. I could see she was thinking hard. She certainly had a lot to process, with all that had been happening to her in the last couple of weeks.

After my fraught conversation with Fergus, I needed a break from him; he needed one from me, for sure, because his silence continued. I texted him to ask if Susie could come to my house after school. Lorna would be there, and it was better than being on her own in Fergus's isolated home, with his cleaning lady only going in a couple of times a week. Lorna wasn't supposed to come to my house every day either; I'd asked her so that Susie could have a warm fire and some company to come home to, and a home-made dinner. I had no intention of interfering in Fergus and Susie's relationship, or in the whole strange business going on with her mum; but she was just a child, really, and very much on her own. If I could help in any way, I would.

My message received a short, simple answer – a *Yes, thank you* that was like the pale ghost of all conversations past, full of confidences and jokes and laughter.

I missed him.

Fergus and his booming laughter, his kindness; the way he always had time for everyone and hardly ever for himself, the way he had so often helped people in need and did so in great secrecy, without ever asking for gratitude or recognition. When my brother had developed an infection nobody could give a name to, and was dangerously ill, it was Fergus I called. He drove me to the ferry, then from Oban to Edinburgh, and didn't leave my side for a moment throughout the ordeal. When finally my brother was declared out of danger, I cried in his arms.

That was Fergus, and in this girl, whatever her story might be, I saw his eyes, light blue and kind, and a generosity of heart and soul that was rare to find.

'Hey, you're staring at me,' Susie laughed.

'Sorry. I love your hat,' I scrambled to answer. I could hardly say *You remind me of your dad, and you know, there could have been something between him and me, but I rejected him, and now . . .*

'Thank you.' She patted it. 'I got it in the Design

Gallery, it's from Shetland. That's my phase two. After making jewellery, I'm learning to knit. Oh, I'm cold. Fancy a hot chocolate?'

'Always.'

We sat on plastic chairs near a window and sipped our hot chocolate from plastic cups. Susie took out her phone and showed me pictures of her jewellery: bracelets, necklaces and brooches made from silver paste, fabric, shells, little beads and even tiny rocks.

'You have a lovely eye, you know? Just like your dad. He designed the logo of his distillery himself, and the labels – the stylised drawing of the sea eagle, and the barley sheaf . . .'

'I didn't know. I don't know much about him.'

'You'll get to know him now that you're here.'

'Mmm. Maybe. He doesn't really speak much to me.'

'It will take a bit of time, I think.'

'Yeah. Oh, look at this one, that's pieces of velvet packed tightly together to make an extra-long necklace . . .'

As she was scrolling, a photo of a boy came up. He was wearing the Eilean uniform and had a shy, surprised smile, like someone who didn't expect to be photographed. I had to suffocate a smile as Susie grew scarlet to the tips of her ears.

'That's Ewen,' she informed me before I could say anything. I wouldn't have asked – too intrusive – but I admit I was dying to know the background story.

'Oh yes, I know him. And his parents.'

'And his grandparents, and his uncles, and his dog, and his neighbours . . .'

I laughed. 'I see you've twigged how it works on the island. True, I know his whole tribe.'

'Yeah.'

'Mmm.' I nodded, still trying not to smile.

'What?' She laughed. 'Ewen is a *friend*. I mean, I've only known him for five minutes, but he has the potential to become one. I think he'd like to be more than that, though. But I've known him for such a short time . . .'

'Well, he's a nice boy. And he's from a nice family.'

'It's not like I have to marry him, Grace!'

'Oh, sorry, sorry, I know. You're just *children*,' I teased her.

'We're not! Oh, stop it.' She laughed again, her cheeks still pink. 'Anyway. There's a problem.'

'What problem?'

'Karen likes him too.'

'Karen . . . Is that Karen McNeil?' I remembered Susie running out of the Design Gallery when Karen and Mary had made their appearance.

She nodded. 'Someone told me she's been after Ewen since they were, like, in nursery. But he likes *me*. So she's turning people against me. They always play this stupid game, Bet You Can't, and try to humiliate me.'

'What's that?'

'It's like some kind of Truth or Dare, except it's always a dare. I bet you can't . . . eat dog food, or touch the janitor's backside, or—'

'What?'

'I know. Like they're five years old. I bet they came up with this game in nursery – they were there all together, you know. I'm the only newcomer.' She rolled her eyes. 'Anyway, Karen hates me now, 'cause everyone took it for granted she and Ewen would get together, and she has lots of friends, she's like the Queen Bee of the Islands, so that made me even more of an outcast than I was before.' She took a big breath.

'That's rotten. I'm sorry. Surely there must be some nice girls that are not under Karen's thumb.'

'Yeah, a couple. I call them the Anti-Karens in my mind. They were happy I arrived, kind of another arrow for their bow. But we're like three against thirty, you know what I mean?'

'Yeah. I had my share of mean girls to contend with in my time.'

'Did you?'

'Oh yes. You see, I changed schools a few times . . . countries too. I was always the newcomer, every two, three years or so.'

'You were? Why?'

'We travelled a lot because of my dad's job. So I know what you're going through.'

'But I bet you never moved to an island in the middle of nowhere . . . like a *castaway*.'

'No. But I did attend schools where everyone except me was from that country. Everyone had black hair and black eyes except me and my brothers, the three blond foreigners who didn't know a word of the local language.'

'Could you not have gone to an international school?'

'My parents didn't want us to. They thought it was better for us to mix with the local children. And mostly they were right. When I was about your age we lived in Tokyo for a while, and I had a best friend, Tetsuko. We were inseparable. She made all the difference for me. She made me feel like I belonged.'

'I'd love a friend like that,' Susie said. She looked out to the grey sea. 'Are you still in contact?'

'Not for a few years now, but I'd love to find her again,' I said. Oban's houses were coming closer and closer; soon it would be time to gather our things and prepare to get off the ferry. Susie was lost in thought.

'I speak to my mum sometimes. On the phone,' she said suddenly, unexpectedly. I held my breath.

'That's good . . .' I ventured.

'I thought sending me away just for a couple of arguments with Cole was overreacting a little,' she said, and her voice trembled. 'I asked her if I could go to Burlingame with her, but she said no.'

'Where's Burlingame?'

'Near San Francisco. Cole is from there. My stepfather, her new husband. You see, when my mum and dad broke up, years ago, she was really busy with her work, shooting all over the place. She asked Dad to have me, but Dad said no, he didn't want me . . .'

'Did your mum tell you this?' I struggled to believe it, I really did. It seemed so unlike Fergus, to reject his little girl. But then he hadn't even mentioned her to me.

She nodded. 'So it was good of her to keep me, I suppose, otherwise it would have been boarding school, and I was only seven. I went for a while, but I hated it, so she took me out. But then she met Cole. I tried to get on with him, but I couldn't. I really couldn't. He's mean. Not just to me, to everyone. You see . . .' She hesitated.

'Hey. You can speak to me, you know? If you need to talk, Susie, I'm always here, and it won't go any further.'

'Thanks. Okay.' She breathed in. 'The thing is, Mum is very rich. Very, very rich. And I think that's why Cole is with her. She's about your age, and he's very young. He wants to be an actor too.'

'Right.' I refrained from passing any judgement; things weren't always what they seemed.

'I don't like him, and when I don't like someone, it shows. I can't keep it in. He wanted me out of the way. I knew that Dad didn't want me all those years ago, so I thought it would be boarding school for me again. I was so surprised when he agreed to have me.' She frowned. 'I miss my mum, though. But I speak to her on the phone,' she repeated. It was like she really wanted me to get this.

'You can tell her all about life here.'

'Yes.' A pause. She looked down as passengers began to walk past us, towards the exit. 'Sometimes she doesn't answer the phone. Well, she hardly ever answers the phone. I don't really call much, there's no point. In fact I've only spoken to her once since I arrived . . . but not to her really, just her secretary. I heard her in the background. She was busy.'

'Susie—' I began, without really knowing what I could say to comfort her.

'We're here,' she interrupted me, and got up as the ferry slowly made its way into Oban harbour.

By the time we were off the ferry, she'd found her smile again. We hurried through the grey streets, under the drizzle; in the air, the scent of sea and frost and winter, and the first tentative Christmas decorations peppered here and there.

The fair was in an art gallery, rented by a craft shop that had just opened – a clean, simple white space where the brightly coloured stands stood out like tropical flowers.

'This is great,' Susie said in a low voice, and I noticed that she'd slightly rolled her *r*, the Scottish way.

'It's probably not what you're used to. I suppose in London these kinds of things are much bigger . . .'

'I don't know, I've never been to a craft fair before,'

Susie said from under her hood. Her fringe, half black and half blue, was plastered to her forehead and she was dripping, but she looked happy. 'Do you often come to this kind of thing?'

'Well, do you want the truth?'

She nodded. When she smiled, her eyes were half-moons, startlingly blue like her father's, in contrast with her raven-black hair. She was a beautiful child and would become a stunning woman. And here she was, smiling at me, growing every day a little, and all away from her mother's eyes. It was a mystery that her parents would allow such a thing to happen. They had something so precious and didn't seem to value it at all.

'The truth is that . . . well, after I saw the lovely bracelet you made, I thought it would be nice to encourage you.'

She stopped. 'You came here . . . for me?'

'Yes, of course.'

'As in, had it not been for me, you wouldn't be here?'

'Well, yes, you certainly widened my horizons.' I smiled.

She looked at me like this amazed her. Then she glanced away, embarrassed by the intensity of the moment. 'Thank you,' she murmured, slipping her hood down, and those words meant so much to me.

We returned to the island after darkness had fallen, bone tired but satisfied, laden with bags of colourful craft materials and treats. I drove Susie back to Fergus's cottage, and on the doorstep, she threw herself into my arms.

'I had so much fun.'

'Me too, sweetheart,' I said. Over her shoulder, I saw Fergus opening the door. She freed herself from my embrace and ran inside, and he looked at me in a way I couldn't decipher. Once upon a time he would have asked me in, and we would have had a long chat and a laugh while sipping a dram, setting the world to rights as we always did.

I missed him, I thought for the second time that day. Would the wall between us ever come down? Would I find a way back to him; would he allow me in?

What was in that look? I wondered as I drove back in the dark. He didn't seem angry. He certainly wasn't indifferent. What was he trying to tell me?

The question followed me to my cottage, was there as I washed and changed, drank my tea and went to bed. And then, as I lay with my eyes closed, Fergus's expression suddenly made sense. I opened my eyes and blinked. The look he'd given me was one of *regret.*

But regret for what? For all that he was missing with his daughter . . .

Or for me?

15

Rose

Glen Avich, 2011

'Will I see you later then?' Julie said, and she tipped her head in that graceful way of hers. There was a hint of sparkle on her eyelids – she'd put make-up on after the ballet class, and I knew why. She was hoping to see David, the boy she had a crush on. Julie and I had been friends since we were in our prams, but she'd outgrown me. Compared to her, I was still a child, although at fifteen years of age she was only a year older than me.

'Sure. Well I hope so,' I said tentatively.

'Promise? Everyone will be there.'

'I'll try.'

'Just try?' She was disappointed.

'Julie . . .'

She rolled her eyes. 'I know, I know. Jacob.'

I shrugged. It was hard for me to understand my family situation, let alone describe it to someone else. Try to explain that Jacob and I were linked by a promise that kept us together, kept us afloat . . . And how even if our little world had begun to feel so tight around me, too tight, I just didn't feel strong enough to fight for more freedom.

Even if I longed for it.

'You shouldn't let your brother tell you what to do. If *my* brother tried it . . .' Julie snorted with laughter. Her family came out of a storybook: housewife mum, engineer dad, two children, a dog, a perfect house and holidays in Spain. She'd seen all the trouble we'd had with Jacob's rage, and she was there when my mum left, yet she still couldn't quite imagine how hard things had been at home. Or how chaotic my life would have been if Jacob hadn't held the threads of our household in his hands. Yes, this boy who was perpetually in trouble for getting into fights, and worse, had taken charge of me when my mum left and my dad was as good as gone. I was only twelve back then; he was fifteen, and we'd made a family. I was responsible for him as much as he was for me. I couldn't just go my own way and leave him behind. I didn't want to, anyway.

I almost always didn't want to.

No, Julie could never understand.

'He doesn't tell me what to do. And I don't do everything he says. It's just that . . . there's only the two of us now. He does the best he can to keep me safe.'

'Safe from us? The wild young people of Glen Avich?' She laughed, but then saw my serious face and asked softly: 'What about your dad?'

'Comes home late, leaves early, goes away for days. We hardly ever see him.' I shrugged. 'He has someone. He's not involving us in that, though. I don't even know her name.' It was painful talking about these things. Admitting that my father had pretty much given up on us, on our family. As for my mum, I saw her once in a while. She would have liked to see me more often, but it seemed such a breach of loyalty to go and visit her without my brother. She had rejected him completely, forcefully even, without a chance of reprieve. She'd never given him a proper chance; she'd never even tried to understand what he was going through. And when things got too much for her, she'd upped and left.

I had been the princess of my little kingdom, as my dad used to say – and now that kingdom was gone.

'I'm sorry, that's rotten,' Julie said.

I shrugged. We stopped at the crossroads where we parted ways, and Julie hugged me. 'You know I'm here if you need to talk, honey.'

'I know.'

'Well, I hope to see you later,' she said with a wave, turning the corner towards her house. I kept going, quickening my pace. In the distance I could see our windows, all lit up, and Jacob's silhouette in the kitchen.

'I'm home!' I called and stepped in.

'Hey.' Jacob appeared in the hallway. He still had his jacket on. 'I'm just in too. Sorry, work ran late. I haven't started cooking yet.'

I smiled. Jacob took his role of looking after me very seriously, including cooking every night for the two of us. I was training hard regularly after school; I'd set my sights on Balletnorth, one of the most prestigious schools in Scotland, and I had to put in the hours. As for Jacob, he'd found a job in a video game development company, surprising everyone. His school career had been fraught to say the least, and nobody expected him to find a well-paid, sought-after job, especially so young.

Nobody but me. I'd always believed in him.

Now his days of getting into fights and drinking in the school toilets, of vandalising our tiny train station with his friends and generally talking with his fists were over. He was still full of rage inside – I could see it in his eyes sometimes – but he'd learnt to control it.

'Chinese?' he said. 'We don't have much in the house . . .'

'Well, I . . .' Maybe now was the moment to tell him about the night they'd organised at Julie's. Maybe he'd be okay with me going. At that moment my phone chimed, and I put my ballet bag on the floor to check it.

'Who's texting you?'

I looked up briefly. His long black eyelashes hid his eyes, and his tone was calm, easy. But I knew he wasn't just making small talk. He *really* wanted to know who was texting me. He always did.

'Julie. There's a thing at her house tonight. Her parents aren't in, she's phoning in pizzas and her brother is getting chips . . .' I wanted to keep my voice as calm as his, but I couldn't help betraying a note of pleading. And I was angry at myself because of it.

Was Julie right? Did Jacob tell me what I could and couldn't do?

'And getting a few cans in?' he said. I could hear it. That hint of ice that told me he didn't like this. I knew I would end up staying home.

'No! I don't think so. I don't know. Anyway, you know I don't drink.'

'Of course, the drinks would be for the boys.'

'Probably.'

'So, a nice gathering with beer and boys.'

I'd fallen into his trap. I kicked myself. 'Jacob, come on, you make it sound like some crazy alcoholic party. It's just the dance girls, Julie's brother and a few guys from the village. That's all. Julie really wants me to go. She kind of really likes this guy David, and . . .'

He took his jacket off and I followed him into the living room. 'Oh. And who do you *kind of* like?'

'Nobody. I'm just going for Julie.'

'She's not worth it. She's not worth your time, she never was.'

'Jacob, she's a friend!' I said to his back as he bent over the fire, getting it going.

'Some friend. She doesn't like me.'

'She might not like you, but she likes me. Anyway, she just thinks you're too protective of me. And sometimes I . . . sometimes I agree.'

He stopped and straightened up. 'Do you?'

'Yes. They get together all the time and I'm here with you.'

'Is that so bad?'

'Of course not. But not all the time. Sometimes I just want to be with my friends. I don't understand what's so wrong with it.'

'You're safest here, you know that.'

I lowered my head. Jacob and the sofa and a DVD and just being home, the two of us, was tempting. But I was fourteen years old. I needed to see people my age, I needed my girlfriends. Why could he not understand that?

'Jacob, you can't always keep me with you! You're my brother, not my jailer!'

A heartbeat, silence, his face white, his eyes full of hurt and, I could see it, fear. Guilt took a bite out of me. I regretted my words.

'I didn't mean that, I'm sorry. It's just that I need friends. That's normal, Jacob, surely you must understand that . . .'

He turned away for a moment, hiding his face, then turned back and offered me a bright smile. His eyes were shining – a bit too much, I thought, and trembled inside. I had crossed him. 'Absolutely. Off you go.'

I looked at the black window. 'Jacob . . .'

'Go on. Get changed and go. I don't want to hear another word about it.'

I looked down at my legs, and realised I was still in my dance gear; I'd just thrown a long hoodie on, and trainers.

'Jacob, don't be like this. Please.'

He shrugged and opened his arms. 'If something happens to you, well, I'm sure your friends over at Julie's can take good care of you.'

I didn't say, *Why do I always need someone to look after me? I'm a teenager, not a toddler!* I didn't say that, because Jacob's words had given me a knot in my stomach. It was so dark outside, and it felt like an unspoken threat was lurking. But here I was safe. And what about Jacob? If I went out, he'd be alone too, after a long day at work. We didn't even know if Dad would come home or sleep out.

'Do you not want to get changed? Here's your coat then,' he said, going to grab it from the hall and handing it to me. 'Come on.' He opened the door and stood in that steady, unyielding way of his. Cold air hit my legs in their white tights.

'Jacob, please. Stop.'

'Stop what? Do you not want to go?' he said in a low voice. With Jacob there was no shouting; he had a horror of it. The quieter he got, the angrier he was.

'No, it's okay. I'm staying,' I said with a smile that stretched my lips a little. 'I'm sorry.'

He closed the door slowly, deliberately, and I was

rewarded with his arms around me, and a kiss on top of my head. He cuddled me for a moment, and I unknotted. How could I ever have thought of leaving him alone? How could I have thought it would be better for me to be at Julie's than with him? He was my family. My protector.

So where had that word come from – *jailer*? And why did my skin feel so tight on me . . . ?

'Chinese, then?' he whispered in my ear.

I laughed between my tears of relief. He wasn't angry any more. He wasn't disappointed in me. But I'd given in once again. This delicate balance between us, I knew it couldn't last. Sooner or later . . .

'Oh, you know how this is going to end! You'll barely eat, and I'll scoff the lot.'

'Well, you need energy, with all that dancing you do.'

'Not *that* much energy!'

'Let me do your hair, then you can get changed and we'll get set up for the night.'

'Okay.' He loved doing that, unpinning the chignon I wore for dancing.

I sat at his feet in the living room, where the fire was now burning sweetly, peacefully. One by one, leisurely, he removed all the pins that kept my bun together, letting my long hair fall to my shoulders, to his knees. I sighed at the blissful feeling of his fingers on my scalp, so tight for hours.

'Your hair is lovely,' he said to me for the umpteenth

time, and the sweetness of his voice made me sit back and close my eyes. As he ran his hands through my hair slowly, slowly, making me feel like I could purr, all fretfulness fell away from me. I'd made the right decision. We were home and we would look after each other. My phone chimed over and over again in my bag, but I ignored it. My last remaining doubt – had I made the decision or had he? – dissolved under his touch.

16

Matthew

I came downstairs expecting rain and grey, but I found a bright morning – dark blue sky over the sea, a soft mist at each side of my view, and pewter clouds in the distance. They'd come from the Atlantic and then blown away, off to the mainland. I blinked in the bright light and made myself my usual extra-strong coffee.

Molly was still subdued. 'I'm sorry I scared you yesterday,' I told her. 'I'm sorry . . . good girl, good girl . . .'

Grace had phoned twice to make sure I was all right, and again in the morning, just as I'd opened my eyes. I'd found reassuring words, I apologised for last night's madness: I'd got confused about things – I didn't specify what things – but everything was okay now. I was about to go back upstairs to get dressed, cup of coffee in hand, when a flash of white on the mat in the hall made me do a double-take. A letter. It was too early for our postman – it must have arrived yesterday and I hadn't seen it.

The envelope had a slight mother-of-pearl shine to it, and it was sealed with the letter H. I recognised it at once.

It was from Hannah, Mia's sister; from my other life.

I was tempted for a moment. I could have slipped the letter in the fire, never to know what my wife's sister had to tell me. What would change, anyway?

Hannah's heart didn't know hatred.

Hannah's forgiveness had been a lot worse.

I held the letter in my hand as though it was burning me, and stood in front of the French doors. I needed the ocean to back me up while I opened the envelope, my hands shaking.

Dear Matthew,

I don't know if this letter will get to you. I haven't heard from you for three years now, though I've tried many times, so we only know that you are alive from Greg. I wonder why you've chosen to go so far away from us, and I don't mean geographically.

I don't even know why I'm writing this letter, as I know there will be no reply. Maybe I just want you to know how much we miss you, all of us, me, Nick, the boys.

You know what helped, Matthew, throughout this terrible thing we've gone through? That you loved my sister so much. I always knew that. When I can't sleep or when I'm sad, I always think how happy you made her. There was never Mia without Matthew. When I came into the world, the two of you were already best friends. I never knew any different.

Matthew, my sister was a part of you, and you were a part of her. You took such good care of her. Of us too. I understand if you don't want to get in touch, though it breaks my heart. You've always been like a brother to me, you know that.

I can't even begin to imagine what you must be going through, with such a burden to bear. Greg did say that maybe it was better for you if I didn't get in touch for a while yet. But I couldn't help it, I really wanted to send you this photograph I found.

What photograph? I looked inside the envelope – there was nothing. I glanced about and saw something sticking out of the letter box. I pulled the rigid brown envelope loose and opened it slowly, carefully. And there it was.

A photograph of Mia; a photograph of us. We weren't much older than children, probably thirteen or fourteen, standing in Mia's garden. She was smiling, I looked awkward and bespectacled, as usual, and at the bottom of the picture there was the top of a small dark head – Hannah's.

Ben and Michael are now almost five; you wouldn't recognise them, they're so big! If only you'd come to Bennington, come and see us . . . I hope one day you'll be able to forgive yourself, like I've forgiven you.

*

My ferry ticket was in one pocket, the photograph in the other as I stood on the shore on the darkest day I'd ever seen on Seal. After a call to Fergus, and leaving Molly in Grace's loving hands, I left the island, not knowing if I'd ever return.

17

Rose

Glen Avich, 2013

I was waiting for Jacob around the corner from my mother's house. She didn't want to see him, so he was picking me up in front of a little row of shops. I was so relieved to be going home. A week with Mum was more than enough. She spent most of the time bad-mouthing Jacob and Dad. She said she'd spoken to Dad, that I was under Jacob's thumb through and through, that I should get away. That he had managed to manipulate me like she'd thought he would – he was 'the prince of manipulation', apparently. She asked me over and over again to come and live with her. I wanted to say, *If you care so much about me, why did you go in the first place?* But I didn't. There were many things I wanted to say but didn't, to many people.

Add the fact that she had found love again with Martin, as she put it in that nauseating way of hers. I didn't even want to acknowledge Martin's existence, though I had to admit he was a decent man, and he was nice to me.

I looked around me impatiently and zipped up my jacket in the chill wind. Behind me, people were going in and out of the Spar, the laundry, the kebab shop with its smell of roasting meat. I wanted out of there, and home.

And not just to see Jacob. There was another reason, but it was a secret . . . I checked my phone in my pocket, and yes, there was a message. I smiled and had begun to reply when finally Jacob's car appeared. My heart soared as his familiar figure stepped out.

'At last. Time to come home,' he said and held me in his arms.

I knew his scent, a mixture of soap and woodsmoke and moss. He swallowed me in his embrace, and I was cherished and secure and protected again. I was still the princess of my kingdom, I thought with satisfaction as I took my place beside him in the car, except now it was smaller. It was a kingdom of two.

'How was it?' he asked as he turned the key in the ignition.

'You know how it was.' I smiled. 'We spoke every day. And you texted me like twenty times a day!' I pretended to mind, but I liked it.

'How is she?' Jacob always asked after Mum. Mum never asked after him. Except to find out if he'd got into some kind of trouble again. The fact that my brother was doing so well, holding down a great job, getting paid more than she or my dad would ever manage, keeping his temper in check and making the village change its mind about him – all this bothered her. She didn't want to know; she wanted to hold on to the idea of him as a troubled little boy, constantly up to no good. Maybe, in a dark corner of her mind, she wondered what would have happened if only she'd stayed around a little while longer; maybe it was occurring to her that I'd been right: Jacob just deserved some time, some stability, and of course, what he'd never had from a mother before – love. Or maybe she was just jealous of how close the two of us were.

'She's good. Apparently Martin adores her. I don't really see the signs of it, but there you go . . .'

'How is Martin with you?' Jacob asked. There was the usual hint of possessiveness in his voice, and it bothered me.

'He's all right. No, really, he's not a bad guy at all, he's nice, actually. It's just that they . . . No, never mind.'

'She keeps asking you to move in with her, is that it?'

'Yes. Both of them do.'

'But you won't.'

'Of course I won't! Never.'

'Rose?'

'Yes?'

'Why do you keep looking at your phone?'

'I'm not.' My stomach churned. I cursed myself. I'd been so careful up till now.

'Are you waiting for a text from Mum?'

'Yes.'

There was a moment of silence. He didn't believe me, I could feel it. And I knew why. I was keeping something from him, and he could always sense when that was the case. There was a moment of silence while we drove, and then my phone chimed. I was holding it loosely in my hand, and before I could do anything, Jacob snatched it.

'Jacob!'

'*I can't wait to see you.* And who would this be?'

'Jacob, you're driving. Give it back!'

I saw his handsome profile change, harden. A glimpse of the old Jacob came back, a creature of compacted, compressed rage.

'Who is this, Rose?'

'A guy. I'm sixteen, Jacob. I don't see the problem. It's not even serious.' I didn't want to see him angry. I didn't want to see him scared, which was what he was when he was angry. But he'd just snatched my phone and read my message. He'd gone too far.

'Who is it?'

'Jacob, please . . .'

'What, I'm not allowed to know who my sister's boyfriend is? And why have you kept this from me, by the way?'

'Because I knew you would react like this,' I said. My voice trembled slightly, and I hated myself for it. I should be strong. I had the right to see whoever I wanted. He had no right to police me. But no mention of rights was going to change the fact that he was shocked, and distressed, and that I'd made him so.

His lips were a thin line, and the moors on both sides of us were suddenly passing by a lot faster.

'Slow down, Jacob.'

'Who is it?'

'It's Gary, okay?'

'Julie's brother.'

'Yes.'

I was nearly relieved. Keeping it a secret from Jacob had been quite a feat. And in a village like Glen Avich, I'd known that sooner or later we'd be found out. That was the only advantage of staying with my mother: that I could speak to Gary whenever I wanted, that he could come and spend time with me. But now Jacob would have to accept it. He was my brother, not my keeper, my warden. And Gary was a good guy, not one of Jacob's former friends, losers who thought getting drunk in the graveyard was the height of self-expression. I was happy. I was working hard at school and training even harder, and everything was good. Maybe Gary wasn't the love of my life, but I was sixteen, it didn't matter.

So why was I keeping him a secret? Why was I so frightened?

And what exactly was I frightened of?

We got home to a silent, dark house. Jacob was quiet, and I was on the verge of tears. I'd waited so long to come home. We were supposed to cook together and watch one of those stupid horror films that should scare you but actually made you laugh, and we would crack the same old jokes about characters going down into dark cellars when a killer was around and never thinking it might be wiser not to.

Instead, though, Jacob was seething. I could feel it. Like the yellow sky before a storm, like the static in a cat's fur – little signs told me that something was coming, that although Jacob was saying nothing, the careful balance I'd built between my home life with my brother and my relationship with Gary had just shattered. If you could even call it a relationship – texts and letters and kisses down at the bridge where we couldn't be seen, that was all. Gary hated that I wanted to keep us under wraps. He kept saying he would come and speak to Jacob and we'd all be friends.

I wasn't so sure.

'Rose?' Jacob peeked into my room as I sat miserably on my bed. For a moment I perked up, thinking he'd come to make peace, but when I saw his expression, my heart sank again.

Strange. My girlfriends had often said that my brother was handsome but scary. He was the resident heart-throb at school, because of his rebel reputation, but any girl who came near didn't last long. I'd always thought all that giggling and those comments on how strong and dark he was were silly, but I could see where they were coming from; I couldn't deny how attractive Jacob was. But as for him being intimidating, no, I didn't really see it.

Until now.

'Yes?'

'I need you to call Gary and arrange to see him.'

'What? Why?'

'So I can go in your place and make things clear to him.'

'Jacob!'

'Rose, you are sixteen. It's my duty to look after you.'

'That's right, I'm sixteen! I can have a boyfriend!' One day in science class, they'd showed us a video of a butterfly trying to free herself from her cocoon to fly away. It was a long and painful process, with the butterfly laboriously squeezing herself out – not the glittery, colourful liberation I'd imagined. At that moment, I felt like that butterfly.

'A boyfriend? Are you crazy?'

I saw red. 'No, you're the crazy one! Mum always said that, and maybe she's right!'

Oh no. I'd said something horrible. Truly, truly horrible. Jacob would never forgive me now.

'Jacob, look—'

'It's okay,' he said calmly. But his jaw was working.

'It was a stupid thing to say . . .'

'It's fine. Honestly. Don't worry.'

I pleaded with him, but he insisted there was nothing wrong, that he knew I hadn't meant it, and he said so all the way downstairs, where he put his jacket back on. I panicked. He was going. He was leaving me, just like Mum and Dad. What had I done? And for who? A guy I wasn't even that into.

'Where are you going?'

'Back to Aberdeen.'

'Aberdeen? Why?' Had he hit me, it wouldn't have hurt more.

'Rose,' he said sweetly, reasonably, and his sweetness killed me. 'Why do you think I stay living in Glen Avich, even though I work in Aberdeen?'

'Your home is here.'

'I commute over an hour and back every day. And you know why?'

I lowered my head. 'For me.'

'Exactly. But now I don't need to, do I? You have Gary looking after you.'

'That makes no sense! Gary is my boyfriend. You are my brother. Jacob, please don't go.'

'I'll see you later, Rose.'

I heard the door closing downstairs – not slammed, but closed calmly, in that controlled way he had when he needed to take a hold of the storm inside him. Then he was gone.

I stayed in my room, without eating, without changing, without answering the phone, which kept chiming, chiming – Gary and my mum calling over and over. The night went by slowly. I looked out of the window and realised I was alone in the world. The ghosts of the family we used to be resounded in my memory – Mum, Dad, and the beloved little girl who used to be me.

You're going to have a brother, Mum was saying.

And then there he was, the dark-eyed boy with terrible memories and the overwhelming desire to belong. And the demons inside that spoiled everything he touched.

But not us, not me and him, as close and complementary as any brother and sister could be. No, it was me who had spoiled that relationship. Because I had reached out, outside our warm, suffocating little world. The world of two that smothered me but that I couldn't live without. The butterfly could not free herself from her cocoon; she needed it too badly.

Finally, at four in the morning, I sent two messages. One for Gary:

It's over, don't look for me again.

And one to Jacob. A message that killed me and healed me at the same time:

He's gone from my life. Please come home.

18

Grace

'So how was it?' I asked, handing Susie a towel. She'd been at a knitting workshop held in Eilean. The heavens had opened while she was there, and her hair was soaking, but she was beaming. I'd collected her from the ferry and taken her to Fergus's house.

Crafts were turning out to be a saving grace for her, giving her confidence and helping her settle; she'd also decided to come to choir with me, and she put her heart and soul into it, carefully pronouncing the Gaelic words with a London accent that made her sound even more adorable.

It had become the norm for me to do these things for Susie – take her places, give her dinner, look over her homework. There was an easy companionship between us, with Susie shifting from cheekiness to vulnerability in a way that never failed to melt me.

'It was so good. So good. Okay, the average age was like seventy-five, but they could knit! I can take their patterns and do really modern stuff with them, you know . . . Wait, I'll show you the stuff I made.' She jumped up to get her bag.

'Dry your hair first, you'll catch cold!' I called after her.

She turned around, laughing. 'Yes, Mum!'

I froze. She realised what she'd said and blushed. Our eyes were locked into each other's and then, embarrassed, we looked away. The warmth in my heart was half sweet, half painful.

'Come on, seriously. Get dry,' I said, to dispel the intensity of the moment.

'Okay,' she said, and she ran upstairs to her room, carrying her bag with her.

I was hanging her soaking jacket on the back of a chair to dry in front of the fire when she appeared downstairs, her hair still wet and an expression on her face that chilled me.

'Grace . . .'

'Susie, what's happened?'

She came into my arms and burst into tears, the deep, heartbreaking sobs of a child. 'They . . . they put a video of me online!'

'A what? Come, come, dry your tears . . .'

'Come and see! It's horrible.' She led me back upstairs and into her room, and we sat on her bed. She grabbed her phone, still sobbing. 'They put a video of me and Ewen on YouTube. We were . . .' she shrugged, 'you know, kissing and stuff. And then . . .'

'Oh Susie, listen, I know it's embarrassing . . . these social media things can be horrible. But tomorrow everyone will have forgotten it, I promise . . .'

I tried to comfort her, but I'd gone cold inside. Was it one of those horrifying situations where they set someone up and secretly recorded them? It couldn't be. Susie wasn't even fifteen. Was I being naïve? What did I know of the connected world of today?

She handed me the phone without saying a word. I was afraid to look, but when I did, relief doesn't begin to describe how I felt. She and Ewen were kissing, a sweet, half-clumsy, half-knowing kiss, recorded from far away.

'Oh darling, yes, it's embarrassing, they shouldn't have done this, but . . .'

She shook her head and pointed to the phone again. The video wasn't finished. Ewen was on camera, and this time he was being recorded from up close. He was rubbing his lips with his hand.

'Oh my God, that was disgusting! Keep her away from me! I'll never do anything like that again. It's the last time I play Bet You Can't with you crazy people.' More rubbing of his lips, laughter off screen – and then the camera turned to show Karen McNeil laughing so hard she had to hold her middle.

I felt sick.

'Susie . . .'

'Don't say anything, Grace.' Susie was grave, sombre. Her little face looked grey. 'Don't say anything.'

'They don't even deserve—'

'I'm leaving.'

A heartbeat.

'What?'

'I'm not going back to that school. Ever.'

Her face was pale and resolute as she began to pack. I pleaded with her, told her we needed to get to the bottom of things, that I would go and speak to Karen's parents, and Ewen's, get her dad to come with me. But she didn't stop packing her things, she didn't say any more.

When she'd finished, she stood at the window, her hands on the sill. She'd been here for such a short time, but I couldn't imagine the island without her.

Had my daughter lived, what would she have looked like?

The thought was a stab in my heart.

'Susie. Where are you going to go? Your mum . . .'

'Boarding school. That was my mum's plan anyway. She didn't want me to come here, she wanted me to go to this place, Bray School for Girls in Chesterfield. We even visited it. I hated it. I wanted to stay with her, I didn't want to go away just because she was marrying that guy . . .' Another bout of tears. My heart broke and I wrapped my arms around her. She really was just a kid, and a lost one.

'But if you hated the place, why go? We can sort this out.'

She freed herself from my embrace and shook her head. 'No. I'm not going back to school. Look at the comments! Everyone under the age of twenty in the Western Islands saw it! Everyone is laughing at me.'

I didn't know what to say. I was livid on her behalf. And scared as well. I didn't want her to go. But I didn't know what to say. She rubbed her face with her hands.

'The thing is . . .' she said in a small voice, 'Karen is a bitch. Okay, that's fine, I'd guessed that. But Ewen . . . I thought he liked me. For real.'

She looked completely desolate. The bag with her knitting work lay abandoned on the floor, like the debris of another, more innocent life. I stood beside her and tucked a strand of wet hair behind her ear.

'I'm so sorry, Susie. But believe me, I'll make sure they don't get away with it.'

I was on the warpath. First, the distillery. I glided over the gravel as fast as I could and made my way into the office. Fergus was at his desk, and as I stormed in, he looked up with a hint of pleasure at seeing me – a split second where our eyes met and we were simply pleased to be together, in the same room at the same time. But reality soon flooded in as I told him everything that had happened; how his daughter was back home in tears because of the cruelty of some of her schoolmates. How betrayed she felt after the boy she'd trusted had turned out to be so . . . vile.

For a moment Fergus looked furious, on the verge of wanting to teach the boy a thing or two – but then his expression changed. He gazed into the fire, and his face was blank. He was indifferent to his daughter's plight.

No. He wasn't indifferent. He was *feigning* indifference, I could feel it. My twenty-five years as a doctor had taught me enough to see beyond a mask.

But why? If he cared, why not show it?

'Fergus, she's very upset. Will you go to her?' I said as calmly as I could.

'She'll be okay.' He rubbed his left leg. He was in pain.

'She needs you!'

'She doesn't. She never did.'

'Fergus, you really are an idiot sometimes, you know.'

There was a moment of silence, where he took my words with his head bent.

'She wants to leave the island,' I said.

His eyes widened imperceptibly. 'It's for the best. She can go home to her mum.'

'She's not going home to her mum, Fergus. You know very well that her mum won't want her back; she's not even answering the phone when Susie calls her!'

'How do you know?'

'Because Susie told me. She confides in me. She doesn't have anyone else to speak to, in case you haven't noticed. But she was putting down roots here. And now she'll probably end up in a boarding school she hates.'

'That's her choice,' he said. He began shuffling some papers on his desk as if they were all-important.

'You can't possibly tell me you're happy about it? What could she have done to you? She's only fourteen.'

He shook his head. 'I'm not happy, no. But I am relieved.'

'What . . . How can you be relieved?'

'Grace, you don't know . . .'

'Fine. Fine. From now on, Fergus McLean, don't ever speak to me again.' I went towards the door, defeated. He had put up a fortress of pretend indifference and half-spoken words, and I couldn't breach it. I didn't know how.

'Given that you're a doctor, you don't listen much, do you?' he said unexpectedly. He got up from his desk with some difficulty and came to stand beside me, leaning on his cane. Even stooping slightly, he was taller than me by a head. A sudden wave of tenderness swept me, for this man whose burden I could feel but couldn't give a name to.

'I would listen if you spoke,' I said in a low voice. He looked away, into the fire, and I took a long, deep breath. 'When I was a wee girl, I collected writing paper. My dad travelled a lot, as you know, and wherever he went he brought me some writing paper back. I remember once he went to Hamburg and came home with the most exquisite writing set, with a pen and stamps . . . I was over the moon. I still have it, actually. He wasn't home much, but when he was, he took me for hot chocolate and asked me how things were; we chatted for *hours*. He did that for each of us, you know, me and my brothers, so we'd all have time alone with him. That's what a dad does. I took Susie for a hot chocolate too – the power of memories, I suppose. I'm not a mother' – the slightest stab of pain in my heart, as always – 'but this much I know.'

'What are you trying to say to me?' Fergus said softly. 'That I'm a bad father? Because you have no idea how much I loved that girl.' He seemed resigned to the way things were, like they would never change. Whatever the situation was, he felt it was forever.

'Loved? And what about now? Because she's not dead, you know, she's very much *alive* and very much *here*. And she's trying. She's trying to reach you!'

Fergus laughed, the kind of laugh that sounded more like a sob.

'What's so funny, Fergus?'

'That of all the people involved in this sorry mess, you're blaming the only innocent one.'

'More innocent than a young girl?'

'Susie is not innocent. If you had any faith in me, you would believe me.'

'And if you had any faith in me, you would explain why you're saying this. You would tell me what's behind this thing you and Susie have got going, this mutual hostility. You would tell me what really happened with Lin . . .'

A pause, in which he was still, rigid, his mouth slightly open, as if he wanted to speak but couldn't.

My heart went out to him, and for a moment I would have loved to go to him, hold him, try and take away whatever was making him suffer so. But his coldness towards Susie stopped me. She was just a child, just a child who needed her parents, and neither of them seemed to be able to set aside their own feelings, whatever they might be, to look after her.

'Right. Okay,' I said, deflated and terribly, terribly sad, turning to go.

'Have you ever been betrayed?' he called to me; and maybe, at that moment, he was about to open up. But I was too angry, too dismayed to listen to any more self-pity.

Oh yes. I've been betrayed.

'Whatever she's done to you, Fergus – or even whatever her mother did to you . . .' He lowered his head. 'Have you ever heard of forgiveness?'

I stepped out of the office into the blustery evening and walked away, my tears blurring the sea and sky into one.

The man had everything, and was throwing it all away. He was turning his back on life, just like I'd done all those years ago; but when I'd made that decision, there had been no other injured parties but me. The child, my child, so wanted, so loved, had gone before she could even draw her first breath. But Susie, Susie was alive, and beautiful and clever and sweet, and she deserved better than what these two selfish parents were offering her.

Yet still, when I made it to my kitchen and stood at the counter, darkness outside my window and inside my heart, I regretted it. I regretted not having held Fergus to me and told him he could lean on me, that he could tell me what was troubling him, that I would help.

And I wished I could have told him how much I'd come to regret the day I'd rejected him and refused his love. How I'd come to realise that when I'd said he was a friend and could never be anything else, I was lying to him and to myself.

19

Rose

Glen Avich, 2015

I kept flexing my toes, my legs, and slowly, slowly bending my torso at the waist, raising my arms and dipping one side, then the other, to make sure my muscles were warm and supple and would not cool down while I waited. We were all doing that, all us girls – and a few boys – auditioning for Balletnorth. And the way we stood in a line along the corridor, warming up, made us look like sea anemones floating languidly in the water.

My heart was beating in double time with fear and excitement. This was my moment. This was the moment when I would prove to myself and everyone else how hard I'd worked, how far I'd come, how I deserved this. How all those extra hours of training I'd put in had been worth it.

Jacob was there, of course. The auditions were closed, so he had to stand in the hall with assorted parents. I hadn't even thought of asking my parents to come.

'God, I hope it's over soon,' the girl beside me said. She was pale and blonde, her hair nearly white, with thin lips and elongated blue eyes. There was the slightest trace of a foreign accent in her voice.

'I know. It's nerve-racking.'

'Where are you from?' she asked.

'Glen Avich. Down the road. You?'

'Kind of Birmingham. My parents are Russian. Roxana, nice to meet you.'

'Nice to meet you. I'm Rose . . .'

'Rose McCrimmon, you're next,' a willowy woman with a clipboard called, stepping out of the audition room. A ripple went down the line of dancers, and I swallowed.

'Good luck,' I heard Roxana whisper, but I couldn't reply.

The floor felt empty and daunting, and the examiners wore no expression. My mouth and throat had dried up, but my body knew what to do. I went into autopilot, and gave it all I had, down to the last drop of energy, of skill, of hope, of ambition that I carried in me.

'How did it go?'

In one fluid movement, like it was the most natural thing in the world, Jacob enfolded me in his arms. I was limp and yet charged, electric all over, still in my simple black leotard and black tights, a black velvet ribbon threaded in my chignon. I didn't know what to tell him. I simply had no idea. I thought I'd seen a hint of appreciation in the examiners' faces, especially the woman with the clipboard, but I might have been wrong.

'Well, we'll see,' I said into his chest, and freed myself from his embrace. 'I'm going to get changed. See you here in five minutes.'

The changing rooms were full of girls as wired as me, and a couple of them seemed to have been crying. I swamped myself in my oversized blue tracksuit and let my hair down my back. Roxana was slipping on her denim skirt just beside me. 'You guys are so cute! How long have you been together?'

'Sorry?'

'Your boyfriend. He's gorgeous, by the way, if you don't mind me saying.'

I laughed. 'He's not my boyfriend. He's my brother.'

'Oh. He's really sweet to you. My brother wouldn't dream of hugging me in public! Can you introduce us?'

I shrugged. 'Sure, another time. Good luck, I hope you get in,' I muttered, and slipped away. I caught a glimpse of her on the way out, getting into the back of a car with a plump, smiling woman in the passenger seat and a blond guy at the wheel. Roxana waved frantically, but my eyes met those of the blond man – clear and elongated like Roxana's. His hair was as golden as Roxana's was pale, and his long fingers held the wheel assuredly. There was something about him that made my gaze linger, and we looked at each other for a little longer than we should have.

'We're all good. Yes. You? Dad? Dad? You're breaking up . . .'

As usual. It was the first time he had called in weeks, and he'd decided to do so from his mobile, on a train. I knew he wasn't going to phone back, not for a few weeks anyway. We'd spoken for about seven minutes; he probably felt it was plenty. Jacob and I were an afterthought now that his partner had given him a new daughter. My half-sister, who replaced me very well, apparently, as my father contacted me less and less.

'Failed call again?' Jacob came in from the night, filling the hall at once with his strong, warm presence. He always came home late, while I only worked a few hours a day, teaching dance in Innerleithen and training the rest of the time. I'd decided to put off university and try to become a professional dancer, but since the audition at Balletnorth, my faith had been wavering.

I knelt in front of the fire and took my frustration out on the peat, piling up the blocks like I wanted to pulverise them. 'Yep.'

'Nothing from Balletnorth?'

'Nothing. Still nothing.' I sighed and rubbed my hands together to clean them. 'How long does it take to send a letter out, honestly!' I grumbled. 'This wait is killing me.'

'I know. Come on, let's go out for a drink and a bag of chips; it will take your mind off things.'

'Mmm. I don't think anything can get my mind off this. And I can't have chips. Ballerinas don't eat chips.'

'Life is not life without chips. Or we can go out for a bag of salad . . .'

'Ha ha. Anyway, dinner's ready, just give me a second to wash my hands.'

'Rose?'

'Yeah?'

'What's this?' I turned around to see that he had a crumpled, muddy letter in his hand. 'It was under the mat. It must have slipped out of the box and—'

'Oh my God!' I ripped the envelope out of his hand. 'Oh my God . . .'

'Is it them?'

'It's them! I don't want to look . . .'

'Hey, hey, it's fine, it's fine. Do you want me to open it?'

'Yes please. And then don't tell me. I mean, tell me, but prepare me first. No, tell me straight away . . . Or maybe it's better if . . . Oh my God, you're opening it . . . wait, I'm not ready . . .'

'You got in.'

'*Wait!* Don't tell me just yet . . . What?'

'You got in.' He was beaming.

'I did?'

'You did!'

I jumped into his arms, laughing and crying at the

same time. I'd made it. *We'd* made it. The dream formed in my room long ago, when I'd danced in front of the mirror in my white leotard, my head barely reaching halfway up the glass, had finally come true. And I couldn't have made it without Jacob. Never.

'Hey. Are you okay?' I'd caught a glimpse of his face as we disentangled ourselves from our embrace, and he seemed troubled.

'Of course. I'm so happy for you.'

'Only . . .'

'Only, stick around,' he said, and shrugged. He wasn't looking at me. At that moment, a shift happened in our world as I perceived it.

I don't need him as much as he needs me.

He doesn't make me stay; I choose to stay.

I tilted my head to one side and gazed at him with infinite tenderness, once again seeing the little child he was when he first arrived. A frightened child. My child, in a way. From my protector to the one I was there to protect.

20

Matthew

I wandered through the streets of Bennington like the stranger I'd become. It was all alien, all kind of offbeat. This place used to be my home. Here I was born and went to school, here I met Mia, here we built our life together.

Here I destroyed it.

Here I spent three years in a box with three other men, looking out at a concrete courtyard framed by barbed wire, a crooked basket hanging on one side, and rusty outdoor gym equipment of which I knew every crack, every dent. And that was when Bennington turned from my home into a foreign land. My time in prison alienated me from this little place on the outskirts of London. I could have been anywhere, in any place where hundreds of men were crowded together and punished for something they'd done.

The life I had before – that life felt like yesterday and like a thousand years ago at the same time. No. It felt like today. It felt like it was here with me now, always. The moments we spent together, the two of us, would always be with me. Matthew and Mia. That was the way it should be. That was the way it should have been forever.

The closer I got to my sister-in-law's house, the more memories came back to torment me. Memories I had locked away carefully, like some unstable material that, if disturbed, would explode in my face. For a moment I thought I would turn away and run, and find shelter on Seal again; never face my demons – just let them devour me inside. But this wasn't just about me. Hannah had reached out to me because, for some reason, she wanted to see me. Maybe for her, seeing me was some kind of closure. I couldn't turn away from her any longer.

I didn't need to ring the bell; Hannah was waiting for me, looking out of the window. How many times I'd walked up this driveway with Mia, how familiar it all was . . . And yet, everything had changed. The man I used to be had died with Mia in that car.

Hannah threw herself into my arms and held me close to her. I knew it wasn't just me she was holding; it was her sister's shadow. Like me going back to the house we used to live in, hoping for a scent, a memory, anything that linked me to what I'd lost. Hannah was clinging to me to catch a memory of her sister, of the love that bound them, of the life they'd had together.

Because my face reminded her of Mia, my voice reminded her of Mia, because I could tell her things about Mia, because I held the key to a part of Mia she didn't know; I had memories of Mia that eluded her.

'Matthew,' she whispered, and the sound of her voice, so similar to her sister's, made me quiver with solace and pain.

'Hannah,' I murmured in her hair, and I clung to her for just the same reasons she was clinging to me.

Tell me about Mia.

Give me back a piece of her.

For a moment, just for a moment, let's pretend, you and me, that she is still here.

We sat at the kitchen table; it was one of those family meetings that was too formal to be held while slouching on sofas. I accepted an offer of coffee, though I knew already I would not be able to swallow.

'We thought it'd be better if we talked first, before you saw the boys,' Nick, my brother-in-law, said.

'Yes. Good idea.'

'So how are you, Matthew? You've lost weight . . . but you look well. I love the beard. Very Gerard Butler.' Hannah smiled, but her eyes were still shiny.

'Yeah.'

'Oh my God, I have so much to ask you.' She ran her hands through her hair. She was dark where Mia had been fair, but their faces were so similar. I had to grip my hands in one another because I couldn't stop the nervous shaking. The yearning threatened to overwhelm me.

'I . . . I'm sorry I didn't get in touch. I was grateful for the things you said when . . . when it happened.'

'There was something I wanted to tell you, Matthew,' Nick said. He took a breath and looked away. 'After it happened, I . . . I started running. A lot. In fact, I ended up running a marathon, you know? I had so much resentment inside, so much bitterness for the unfairness of it all . . . I had to get it out somehow. One day I was running in the park, and I remembered something I'd completely forgotten. I was about three years old. My mum was cooking dinner one night and had just taken a pan of potatoes off the stove. The TV was on, something funny came up and she turned around quickly to see. I was just beside her and she poured boiling water on my head and shoulders. It was so agonising I passed out. They took me to hospital; it was horrible. My mum was cut up, beside herself with guilt.'

'God. That's terrible.'

'But it wasn't her fault. I mean, it was, and yet it wasn't. You did something stupid, and you lost everything. But people do stupid things all the time, and most times nothing happens. And then the day comes when there are consequences . . .'

'I used to read texts in the car,' Hannah said. 'Nothing ever happened to me. To us. I knew it was stupid, but I did it anyway. I got away with it. You didn't. I never did it again.'

'It's still my fault.'

'You made a mistake, you got your retribution a million times over. You paid. You pay every day . . .'

'Yes. I pay every day, every night. Forever, really. I mean, there won't be a day when I'll say okay, I've forgiven myself now.'

'That's why I wrote to you, Matthew. To ask you to stop paying.' Hannah looked down.

'I don't understand.'

'I tried to get in touch with you, because I knew you were coming out of prison. Three years is a long time . . .'

'I deserved it.'

'. . . a long time to be alone and to suffer the way you did. I was desperate to tell you all this, but you wouldn't speak to us. I called a few friends, but nobody knew your whereabouts. Until I got to Greg. He gave me your phone number as well, but, well . . .' she shrugged, 'I preferred to write. I'm so glad you came. What I wanted to say to you is this: my sister may be gone, but you're alive. You have a duty towards her. You have to *live*.'

Time stood still for a moment.

And then started running again.

The journey back to Seal was full of wonders; like I'd never been here before, never seen the vast expanse of the sea, with its secret geometry of waves ebbing and flowing, and the profile of the islands in the distance, their cliffs falling into the ocean, their purple-brown hills rising round and soft, smoothed down by millions of years at the mercy of the elements. Like I'd never seen the seals swimming beside us, and the sky that was blue and grey and black and white all at the same time, opening and closing like an accordion. My hand was in my pocket as I stood on deck, curled around something very precious; but it wasn't time to do what I needed to do, not yet. And then Seal appeared in the distance, small and remote and far from everything but itself.

I drove along dark roads, chasing my own headlights, as shadows thickened and the sky turned inky. Finally, after having travelled from dawn to dusk, I was back in my cove. I couldn't wait to go and get Molly from Grace's house, but first there was something I had to do.

I didn't have a torch with me, so I guessed every step on sand and rock until I got to the water. There I took the picture Hannah had sent me out of my pocket, crouched down on the sand, and slowly, lovingly, gave it to the sea to keep.

21

Rose

Aberdeen/Glen Avich, 2016

I peeked from backstage. The lights, the music resounding from the amplifiers on each side, the red velvet curtains that smelled of dust and excitement, and so, so many people in the audience. Our families and friends, and among them, scouts for the big companies in England and Europe. The end-of-year show was important in many ways. But for me, that night was even more crucial.

I felt my hairband, decorated with tiny purple tissue flowers, slip down on my forehead. 'Oh, no!'

'Come, I'll sort it!' Roxana said, and stabbed another pin or two in my hair to hold it all up.

'Thank you.'

'Oh, sweetheart!' she said, and hugged me tight. In the year we'd spent at Balletnorth we'd become very close. She liked to call me her sister, though I was careful about that term – I didn't want Jacob to be resentful of her like he'd been of my old friend Julie. 'It'll be okay, you'll see,' she said with her hands still on my shoulders.

She wasn't talking about the show, as important as it was.

Afterwards, I was going to tell Jacob that Roxana's brother Peter and I were to move in together. The blond man I'd seen in the car the day of the audition had come to mean everything to me, in a way I'd never thought possible. And tonight, he was in the audience, he and his mother sitting beside Jacob. Jacob had no idea that Peter and I were together. Every time I stayed at Peter's flat, I told him I was at Roxana's. Peter hated having to keep things secret, and so did I, but I had to be careful. Jacob couldn't stop me, not any more. But I was desperate for him to accept Peter, to accept us, for us to be like a family. I didn't want to lose him; I didn't want to hurt him.

'Rose, listen,' Peter had said to me as we sat at his kitchen table, drinking coffee before he went to work and I went to school. I couldn't do it often, staying over at his flat, because Jacob liked to have me home at night. When I did, though, it was bliss. Usually.

But in the last few weeks, Peter had kept pushing me to move in with him. I wanted to, but it was all so complicated. And now, when he spoke, I tensed up. I knew what he was about to say. And I was right.

'This makes no sense. You go up and down from Glen Avich every day, you're exhausted, and we hardly ever see each other . . .'

'I know. It's hard.'

'It's not hard, Rosy. Your brother drives you here

and back when he goes to work, right? It's the way he likes it. It means he can keep an eye on you, spend more time with you. He's a control freak; he wants everything done his way.'

'He had a lot of bad experiences when he was a wee boy . . .'

'Oh here we go again. Rosy, wake up! He's not a wee boy any more. He's a man! He should have a girlfriend of his own.'

'He hasn't found the right person yet.'

'Because he's too busy clinging on to you. Look,' he sighed, 'I don't care if your brother has a girlfriend or lives in eternal chastity; all I know is that you're not a child either. You're nineteen and hiding me like I was a dirty secret.'

'Please don't say that.' I pushed my coffee away from me. I knew he was right, but I wasn't ready to be called out on it.

'Look, I get it, okay? I get that he's traumatised, that your parents aren't exactly mother and father of the year. I get that Jacob is the closest thing to a family you've had for years, and I'm sorry you had it so hard . . . If I could go back and sort it all out for you, I would, believe me. But you're not children any more. It's not the two of you against the world. You're adults, both of you. And he has to accept the fact that he's your brother, not your boyfriend.'

Those words sent a chill down my spine. 'I know.

I know. I'll speak to him. It's just that . . .' I shook my head.

'What?'

'You don't understand.'

'What don't I understand, Rosy?' he said, and he sounded weary all of a sudden.

'That he's been let down many times. That he's my family, my responsibility.'

'He's not your responsibility! He's a man, a grown man!'

'Peter, I can't . . .' But I knew I was repeating the same argument over and over, that there was no winning or losing this conversation, no right or wrong – it was just a matter of choice, and the choice fell on my shoulders; not Peter's, not Jacob's, but mine. 'Peter . . .' I began, but he looked at me in a way that made me fall silent. He didn't want any more words. He wanted me to do something.

'If you don't speak to him, Rose, I will.'

'No. This is down to me.'

'Then do it.'

'Yes,' I said, but I must have looked unnerved, because he tried to reassure me.

'It'll be good for him too, can you not see? He'll get himself a life.'

'He has a life.'

'Not from where I stand. Look. We'll be together. You'll be twenty minutes away from school, how good is that? And a whole hour away from Master and Commander there. I mean, what can he do?'

'Don't speak about him like that. And I'm not afraid for me. I'm afraid for him.'

'Sorry. I'm sorry. I know you care for him – of course you do, he's your brother. We can be friends. I truly hope so.' But his eyes said, *Unlikely*.

I got up to go and get ready. Coffee and buttered toast lay untouched, the wreckage of our fraught conversation. While I was pulling a T-shirt over my bra, Peter took me by the arm and pulled me close to him, as gentle as he always was. 'Rosy?'

'Yes.'

'Do you love me?'

'I do, Peter. I really do. I . . . I've never felt this way before. Before you . . .'

'. . . there was never anyone worth fighting for.' He finished the sentence for me.

'I'll tell him after the show, okay? I can't have any grief until then. I need to concentrate.'

'After the show, then,' he said. He kissed me like I was his very reason for being, and I allowed myself to dream that the two people I loved the most in the world would find a way to live side by side.

Now the night of the show had arrived at last. We stepped on stage to the sound of sweeping chords; we turned and jumped and bent and raised our arms and smiled our ballerina smiles, we told a story with our bodies and made it look like it was no effort at all, while our muscles screamed and trembled with the strain. But it didn't matter. Dancing was all that mattered, showing the world what we could do. With the final bow, we were drowned in clapping and cheering, and I was bursting out of my skin with joy. Backstage, Roxana and I hugged each other, jumping up and down. All around us, giggles, selfies, hairbands coming loose and a small sea of ballerinas swaying, rising, falling. The show had been a success. A year of hard work, so much sacrifice, had all been worth it. And each of us was thinking: have I been noticed? Did someone important see me? Have I been earmarked for a big company? So many variables – not just our talent and skill, but things we couldn't control, like our height and the shape of our legs . . . this part was a genetic lottery.

I too was wondering if someone had noticed me. But for now, I had more pressing thoughts. I'd been thinking for weeks of what to say to Jacob, choosing the words, writing and rewriting the script, trying to find the way that would cause as little fallout as possible.

Our families and friends were waiting for us as we came out. Roxana and I were holding hands, both smiling, both buzzing. She ran into her mother's arms, and I froze.

They were both in front of me, both waiting to hold me.

Peter and Jacob.

It was a split-second decision. My boyfriend, my love, my life as an adult. My brother, my family, my roots as a child.

I ran to Peter, my freedom. He held me to him and kissed me with a touch of possessiveness – I heard his mother making a happy, surprised sound. For a moment, I hid in his arms, and then I knew I had to face what had just happened. I looked up, and there he was, Jacob, standing pale and unsmiling, a bouquet of pink roses in his hands.

'Let's go home, Jacob,' I said, and even in the din of the theatre, my voice felt to me as if it was resounding in an empty space and bouncing off the walls with an echo. After this, things would never be the same again. My mouth was dry; I was tingly with panic. I needed to take matters into my own hands, not Peter's, not Jacob's, not anybody's but mine, for once.

'Are you sure? Because we could all go for a drink. We must celebrate!' Peter's mum exclaimed, and rested a hand on my arm. It was a simple, quiet way to say she was happy about Peter and me, and I was desperate to give her a hug, but my eyes couldn't leave Jacob's. Roxana was smiling and saying nothing. I could see the strain in her expression.

'Another time, Mrs Krol. But thank you,' I said.

Peter and I locked eyes. Peter nodded slightly. He was satisfied, for now; I'd chosen to go to him. But I could see the storm gathering on Jacob's brow.

I hugged Roxana and Mrs Krol quickly and said my goodbyes. 'I'll call you later,' I whispered to Peter.

'I'm not ready to say goodbye,' Jacob said coolly, and my heart stopped. His voice might have been calm, but I knew him well, and I could hear the discordant notes in it. I wished I could have just told him everything in peace, alone; but when I'd been faced by the two of them standing there waiting for me, I'd had to make a choice.

And for once, I hadn't chosen Jacob.

Now I could see him smouldering, and I was desperate to take him away from the theatre. My classmates were there, and my teachers, and the school patrons, all mixing with the crowds. If a fight started now, I would die of humiliation.

'Please, Jacob,' I said simply. 'Don't.'

'Come with me.' He gestured to Peter; Peter didn't need to be told twice. They made their way out under curious gazes, and I could feel my cheeks burning with shame. I followed, while Roxana, to my gratitude, kept her mum inside. Mrs Krol was looking from me to Peter and Jacob on their way out, confused. I felt sorry for her. It wasn't easy being involved with the Jacob and Rose binary stars, revolving around each other and repelling everyone else.

We stepped into a side alley, grey and stony and shining with dampness in the light of the lamp posts. Old posters were peeling off the walls, theatre programmes wet and muddy on the ground. From there, we could hear the excited flurry outside the theatre.

'So. What's going on?' Jacob asked reasonably, like all this was something he had to sort out, that he could somehow unravel and solve it and then everything would go back to the way it was.

'Your sister has a boyfriend.' Peter shrugged. 'Problem?'

'Peter . . .' I tried, but it was too late. There was no hope now of doing things my way; they were locking horns over me, and at that moment I hated them both. Part of me wanted to go to Roxana and simply be a young woman having fun and living life without having to constantly appease someone.

'The problem is, I didn't know. Nobody thought to tell me, eh, Sissy?'

'Sissy? What is she, five years old?' Peter sneered, but Jacob ignored him.

'I was waiting for the right moment.'

'Mmm. So, I assume that when you stayed over in Aberdeen with Roxana, you actually stayed over in Aberdeen with Peter,' he said slowly, like he wanted to get the facts just right. Like I was on trial.

'Yes. She's *nineteen*, in case you haven't noticed. She can stay out if she wants to.' Peter opened his arms. And then, before Jacob could reply: 'Jesus. You look at me like I'm some kind of predator! Me and your sister have been together for over a year now, I've always been good to her, and now that we're going to live together—'

'What?'

'I was supposed to tell him!' I cried out. 'Me, not you! Peter, leave us!'

'I couldn't trust you to do it. You were scared of telling him, that's what it was. You're scared of him.'

'Peter, please, go,' I said in a quieter voice. Two women on the main street had stopped in front of the alleyway and were looking at us, trying to be inconspicuous.

In the muted light, my brother moved his gaze to Peter, slowly, slowly. Sometimes, when he was angry, he had the circumspect moves and mannerisms of an animal waiting to pounce. And now I saw it again, the look of long ago, the one he'd had in his eyes when my father had talked about Niall, the day my mum had left.

'Jacob, I really was going to tell you,' I whispered. 'Please, let's go, and we can talk this out together, you and me.'

But Peter wouldn't let it go. He was smaller and slighter than Jacob, but he didn't care. Maybe because he didn't know what my brother was capable of.

'For God's sake, you're her brother, not her dad! And even if you were her dad, she has the right to do what she likes. She's my girlfriend, Jacob, accept it. Get a girlfriend yourself, get a life. It's not like you'd have trouble in that department; look at you, the girls go crazy when you turn up at the school. All you have to do is let her go and make a life for yourself. Rosy, tell him!'

'Rose. Her name is Rose.'

'What?'

'Rose. Not Rosy.'

Peter blinked. 'You're crazy.'

It had to happen. Looking back, it was just a matter of time. Peter prone on the wet pavement, Jacob punching him hard, with a fury that made it impossible for Peter to defend himself. The screams, the blood, the strangers hauling Jacob off him. Peter would not call the police, but they came anyway. He reassured them it was all sorted, it was a family argument, all over now. I didn't know how he managed to convince them, but he did. And now we were a pale, cold cluster of people by the side of the road. Roxana and Mrs Krol had run out when they heard the commotion, holding Peter and trying to drag him away, me trying to do the same with Jacob.

'Come home with me, Rosy,' Peter called. He had a hand to his nose, blood in his hair. Blood on Jacob's knuckles.

'Let her go, Piotr. They're crazy. Crazy!' his mum shouted, white with fury. Roxana was avoiding my eyes. They were going the same way as Julie; I would lose them.

But Peter, loyal as he was, ignored them. 'Please, Rosy, come with me.'

I wanted to. I really wanted to. But Jacob's face was white. So white, I was scared he would fall. Instead of looking angry, he seemed terrified. I knew he was shocked at what he'd done, shocked at having fallen into it again, the rage, the violence, when it had taken him so long and so much hard work to become a different person. But now both of us could see that he *wasn't* a different person, not really. The boy who hit and broke and smashed was just hiding inside the settled adult, still scared, still lashing out. *Oh Jacob. I'm sorry. Please don't be upset. I won't leave you, I won't leave you.*

'I have to go home, Peter. I'll call you later.'

'Rosy!'

'He has nobody!' I hissed. 'Only me. The three of you go home together. Jacob, come with me.' I spoke to him tenderly but firmly, and once again I thought how stupid, how blind were the people who thought I was in his power, that he was the head of our family of two.

I drove us home. Jacob was limp on the passenger seat, dumb after what he'd allowed himself to do. I was scared for him. He was in a haze, mute and staring, the street lights reflecting on his face, his hands. But as soon as we got home, he seemed to shake himself. He murmured something about going for a shower, and I dragged myself to my room and onto my bed. Only then did I realise how sore my muscles were, not from the dancing, but from tension. I was drained.

I lay on my bed in a foetal position for a bit, watching my phone light up and then darken again. Peter was calling me, but I wasn't ready to talk. I had to speak with Jacob first.

Finally, he knocked at my door. He came in wearing a white T-shirt and sweatpants, his hair wet from the shower. He looked younger than his years, those long eyelashes that everyone noticed damp and low on his tired eyes.

'May I?' He waved towards my bed. I nodded. 'I'm sorry, Sissy. I'm so sorry I hit him. I should have welcomed him, and instead I did a terrible thing.'

I was astonished. I hadn't expected an apology. I allowed my heart to open a little, sat up and crossed my legs.

'Oh Jacob. You think it's either you or him . . . you think if I go and live in Aberdeen I'm going to abandon you, like the other families did . . . like our parents did. But I won't. Never. I'll always be there for you.'

He sat close to me, wrapped his arms around my waist and hid his face in my hair. He was holding me like a delicate thing that could shatter at any moment, but it wasn't me in danger of shattering. 'You don't understand, Rose. It's not about me. It's about you. You can't trust him.'

'Oh Jacob,' I whispered, and once again, as we held each other, I was his protector, not the other way around. I was the one taking care of this traumatised man. 'Who says?'

'Did you trust our parents?'

I nodded, ever so slightly.

'Exactly,' he said. He held me tighter. It was just

a moment, but his fingers dug into my skin, and I trembled.

Everything was under control, I thought as I sat surrounded by boxes. In a week's time I would be in Aberdeen with Peter. Jacob had called him and apologised for losing his temper, and Peter had forgiven him, or so he said, though apparently his mum didn't want anything to do with my brother ever again. I couldn't blame her. Peter's face was still bruised and tender. Roxana had phoned me to say I'd lived with crazy for so long, I couldn't even tell what was normal and what wasn't; to keep my psycho brother away from her and from her family. I mentally added her to the list of friends I'd lost because they were scared or freaked out by my brother.

'You have an insane amount of toiletries,' Jacob commented, still panting from his Sunday run. He'd just come in, wearing his black Nike gear and running shoes. The contrast between my recollections and his cheerful random comment made my head spin.

'I have the bare minimum!' I laughed.

'How many bottles do you need to wash your hair?'

'Four. And a couple of jars as well; you know, treatments.'

'Right. Of course.'

Just a week before, he'd been punching my boyfriend so hard he'd drawn blood, and now we were laughing together. It looked like the only reminder of what had happened was his raw knuckles, and the fact that Roxana had blocked me on WhatsApp.

But it wasn't so. Neither of us had forgotten. And he had stopped sleeping again, sitting on the living room floor, worn out and yet rigid, his eyes open and red-rimmed, waiting for dawn. I was worried, and I felt guilty, because I knew it was me moving out that was doing this to him. Part of me wanted to say: *I won't go, you can sleep, I'll hold your hand like I did when we were wee* . . . but I couldn't. I had to make this move, for myself, for Peter, and for Jacob too.

'Look, I was thinking,' he said, taking a bottle of water from the fridge. 'I need to go down south for a thing. Why don't you come with me?'

'What thing?'

'Need to see the boss down there. It's quite important, you know, a project I've had my eye on for a while. I hope he'll decide to develop it here in Scotland. And that I'll be in charge of it . . .' He took a glug of water.

'That's great, Jacob – well deserved. You work so hard . . . I'm proud of you.'

'Don't congratulate me yet, it's not in the bag.'

'But I'm optimistic. Why not? Did he not call you a prodigy in that email?'

Jacob rolled his eyes. 'He's prone to exaggeration. Do you want to come?'

I opened my mouth to say no, that I would stay in Glen Avich to finish packing.

'It can be our swansong,' he said, shrugging. 'All

these years of living together, and now you're moving out . . . We can have a few days of shopping and eating and a bit of partying. Book somewhere nice. You know.' He smiled bashfully and looked down. 'To be completely honest, it's a big thing and I kind of would like some support. I've been working a long time for this . . .'

'Okay. I'll come.'

'It'll be fun.'

I smiled. A nice hotel, shopping and eating out didn't sound bad at all; but what I really wanted was for it to be just the two of us, away from tensions and arguments and looming changes.

'I'm looking forward to spending time with you, Sissy.'

'Me too. I really am,' I said, and pronouncing those words made me realise how much I'd missed him, how I'd suffered for the distance and silence between us. Yes, it would be good. The two of us, alone.

Like it used to be before Peter came along.

22

Grace

I was back home at last, after a round of home visits that had left me weary. It wasn't like me, being drained so easily. I made myself a cup of tea and sat at the kitchen table. The house felt so empty, so silent. By this time tomorrow, Susie would be gone.

Now more than ever, I felt there was no way back between Fergus and me. I didn't even recognise him any more. It was like my Fergus had been replaced by someone I didn't know, maybe even someone I didn't want to know. And yet I wasn't ready to give up on him. There was a wall between us now, laid down by my rejection of him as a lover, and then by Susie's arrival – I could feel it as if it was real, solid, made of stone.

If only I could turn back time.

I took a sip of tea and looked out into the blackness, dark branches tap-tapping against my kitchen window. I thought of the *omamori* hanging from my ash tree.

Tap-tap. Tap-tap.

It couldn't be. It couldn't be the talisman going walkabout again . . .

The tapping continued, even louder. I got up with some apprehension and slowly walked towards the window, the black silhouette of the trees barely visible against the dark purple sky. Suddenly a white face in a black hood took shape beyond the glass and made me jump, scalding my fingers with hot tea. *Tap-tap*, she knocked with light fingers.

Susie. I breathed a sigh of relief, but my heart was still thumping as I opened the door. 'Sweetheart . . . come in. You almost scared me to death there.'

'Sorry.'

'It's okay. You shouldn't be walking around alone.'

'I'm not completely alone,' Susie said with a weak smile. Behind her I saw two bright emerald eyes shining in the darkness. Hyde. 'He came to get me. Seriously. He came to get me and brought me here.'

I smiled too, though with a heavy heart. 'I wouldn't be surprised. Did you speak to your mum? What did she say about boarding school?'

'Well, I asked her if I could go home, actually.' She lowered her hoodie and took off her jacket, while Hyde darted between her feet and straight to the sofa. 'She said we don't have a home in London any more and that Burlingame is not my home.'

'Right.' A white-hot anger towards that unknown woman burnt inside me once again.

'It's okay, Grace, honestly. I didn't really want to go

back to her anyway. Being here . . . you know, it opened my eyes. To the way she really is.'

'I suppose there's no point in asking you once again if you'll stay?'

She looked at her feet. 'I can't go back to that school. And it's not like there's much choice around here.'

'No. So . . . where will you go?'

'She said okay about boarding school.'

'But you hated that place when you visited it!'

'Yep. Whatever. She doesn't care.'

'But I do. Susie, I'm so sad that you're going. I'll miss you terribly.'

Because you're the closest thing to a daughter I've ever had.

Because it seemed to me that you were a second chance for me. A second chance for me to be a mother.

But this wasn't about me, it was about her, it was about Susie finding her place in the world the way she chose.

'I'm sorry too. Now I'll never get a chance to get to know my dad.'

'To be fair, he's not making it very easy for you.'

'I know. Grace . . . there are things I really don't understand about my dad. He's been saying stuff . . .' She shrugged.

'What stuff?'

'I don't know . . . things about when him and my mum broke up. Like it was my fault that I stayed with Mum instead of going with him. You know, like I had the choice . . .'

'Oh Susie. I think before you go, you really need to have a good long chat with your dad. You two need to sit down and talk it all out. He can't say no.'

At that moment the doorbell rang. It happened often; people on the island just dropped in on each other for a dram and a chat. I was nearly sure it was Lorna, because we often had a blether or watched something together in the evenings, and then joked we were part of a two-person Lonely Hearts Club.

But when I opened the door, breathing in the damp, salty air of the night, there was no sign of Lorna. Instead, a boy stood in front of me, a bike leaning against my garden gate behind him.

It was the boy in the video, Ewen.

Except he didn't look half as cocky. He was sheepish, his head hung low. I bit my lip. It was not my place to take charge and give him the biggest telling-off of his life; I was sure he'd come to see Susie, not me, and she'd handle it. With a bit of help, if she wanted it.

'Susie. I think this is for you.'

'Yes. Sorry. Thank you, Dr Chatto.'

'Who told you I was here?' Susie appeared at my shoulder.

'Your dad. Fergus. Mr McLean. Sorry . . .'

I frowned. I had to remind myself what he'd done, or I would feel sympathy for him. He was scarlet, his hair plastered to his head from cycling in the damp wind.

Susie crossed her arms. 'After more material for your videos?'

Go, Susie, I thought. She was heartbroken, I knew it, but in front of him she was showing all her strength.

'Ewen, come in,' I said. 'I think you're here to explain yourself. I'll go out and leave you to—'

'Please stay, Grace,' Susie said, and all of a sudden she seemed a lot more vulnerable.

Ewen came inside, and we stood in an awkward triangle around the fire.

'They removed the video,' he said.

'I know. Grace made them. She spoke to Karen's parents and they weren't very happy. Anyway, if you've come to apologise, there's no need. I'm over it,' Susie said, and there was a forlorn echo to her voice that broke my heart. She *wasn't* over it.

'I haven't come to apologise. I've done nothing wrong.'

'What?'

'It's true. It was Karen. She did it, all of it!' he burst out.

'A big girl made me do it? What are you, three years old?'

I bit my lip, trying not to smile. What was it they called girls like Susie nowadays? Badass? Oh yes, she was badass.

'Somebody filmed us when we were . . . well, you know . . .' He shot a shy glance at me. 'When I was kissing you. I had no idea . . .'

'Right. Sure.'

'It's true! And the things I said . . . Karen set me up.

Remember that game they're obsessed with, Bet You Can't? I agreed to play, like a dick, really . . . Sorry,' he said, looking at me.

'You're in my house, watch your language,' I snapped.

'Of course, sorry.' I'd lost count of how many times he'd said it since he arrived. 'I mean, like an idiot. My bet was to lick the bin in the playground . . .'

'Lick the bin? Oh Ewen, you *are* an idiot!'

'I know. I know. Anyway, I did it. It was horrible. But hey, everyone laughed, ha ha ha, it was fine, finished, over. And then they told me I was on YouTube. I wasn't bothered, I thought it was just a bit of fun. But then I went to see, and Karen had sort of fused the two videos together . . .' he brought his hands one in front of the other, 'and made it look like I was talking about you, that I was saying you were disgusting, and to keep you away from me . . .'

Susie's eyes widened. 'What?'

I gaped.

'All those things I said, I was talking about Karen making me do that stupid Bet You Can't.'

'I don't know if I can believe you,' Susie said in a low voice.

'You will when you see this.' He took his phone from his back pocket, pressed a few buttons and gave it to Susie. She tapped the screen. I couldn't see the video, but I could hear it. It was Ewen's voice.

'I decided to do this because I want to apologise to

Susie McLean. Susie, I'm so sorry. I had no idea they were making a video, and I had no idea they would cut and edit my words to make it sound like I was talking about you. You're not disgusting, you're the best. I don't want you to stay away from me, I want you to be with me . . .'

I glanced at Ewen. He was even redder now, like a boy-shaped beetroot. Good on you, I thought. This was brave for a fourteen-year-old lad.

'I don't care if people in school laugh hearing this. You coming to Seal is a . . . a really cool thing. I'm happy you're here. Don't let anyone bring you down. You're the best. I said that before. But you are. Well, see you later. Bye.'

By then, I was smiling and trying to hide it. Susie looked very serious, her eyes lowered to the screen. She gave Ewen the phone back solemnly. 'Now I believe you. Thank you.'

Ewen shrugged. 'You're welcome. I mean, it was the least I could do.'

'Next time I see Karen, I'm going to slap her,' Susie said calmly, coolly.

I should have scolded her.

I didn't.

23

Matthew

Being back on Seal was like coming home. Everything seemed brighter, sharper, like reality was clear again and not blurred any more. Fergus, Tom, Sorren, Catriona and especially Grace welcomed me back like they'd missed me, and that was precious to me. I didn't think I could feel happy to be anywhere ever again – but I was happy to be on Seal.

As I got ready to go for dinner at Grace's house, an adoring Molly jumping up at me after our short separation, I reflected on Selena.

What weird tricks the mind could play, especially if it was a muddled mind, full of pain. I'd turned a girl into an apparition, a young woman who was clearly troubled into some kind of message-bearer. I'd even made her say Mia's name.

I was relieved that now I could put Selena back where she belonged – into my imagination. She existed, of course she did – I couldn't have made her up. But she certainly wasn't a supernatural apparition.

She'd escaped Fergus's eyes, and Grace's, but this didn't make her magical and didn't make me crazy.

I took hold of the tin of biscuits shaped like a London bus that I'd bought for Grace, and walked into the purple evening. For once, my step was light, lighter than it had been in years. Molly followed me happily, and a baby moon, sweet and white, was glimmering in the sky. Night was falling, but the light was on in Grace's cottage. Soon I would be chatting, drinking, sitting beside the fire with my friends.

At first it looked like a little mound of clothes, but then I saw the white hand, the strange shine of her dress in the darkness, the way she lay. I ran blindly towards her as the waves threatened to swallow her and take her away to sea. She was curled up, her hands together, her knees to her chest. I knelt beside her – her long hair was wet, but it wasn't water, it was sweat. Her skin was scalding, and there was a sickly flush to her cheeks.

'Selena . . .' I called her name and gathered her to me. I moved her onto the dry sand, away from the greedy waves. Blindly I grabbed the torch I'd dropped and stuck it in my pocket.

'I came for you. You weren't here,' she whispered.

'I know, I'm sorry. But I'm back now. I . . . Selena?' She was trying to open her eyes but wasn't quite making it. I could feel her ebbing away from me. Molly was running circles around us, scared to come closer. She'd always been scared of Selena, I could see it now, but at the same time she wanted to be around her. Selena was to her like one of those strange, high-pitched sounds that terrified dogs and yet enthralled them.

Selena's head kept falling backwards as she lay on my lap. She needed help. I had to get her help. I had to take her to Grace. I picked her up – one arm under her knees, the other around her shoulders, her head tucked into my chest and her hair streaming downwards, limp and wet – and started walking as fast as I could, Molly at my heels.

It was almost dark before I reached Grace's cottage, winter night falling at breakneck speed. The sound of Corrywreckan was as loud as ever, louder, it seemed to me, than the waves on the beach. Selena was burning up, but now she was shivering too. *Hold on, hold on*, I whispered as I walked. *I'm sorry, I'm sorry.*

Not again. Not again. I can't lose you too.

She trembled so violently, almost convulsively, that I stopped and fell to my knees. I laid her on the sand, my arms around her, her eyes closed. And then, the impossible happened.

It was like seeing a wave coming away from the shore, a river changing its course and meandering away from the sea.

Like throwing a stone and seeing it rise up into the sky.

In the feeble light of the torch, half revealing, half hiding, she began to shimmer and blanch – and slowly, slowly dissolve into transparency. I could make out the sand and the little shells and stones through her, and then I could see them outright as she trembled and waned, until she was gone.

I was alone on the beach, folded in two, my hands empty.

It was like she'd never been there, she'd never even existed, and I was left without a rational explanation, without faith in my own sanity, without a compass telling me what was north and what was south. The world of reason had been turned upside down, and this time I knew I wasn't crazy.

24

Rose

LONDON, 2016

'This is gorgeous!' I walked around our hotel suite, opening drawers and looking out of the window and twirling in front of the mirror like an excited child. I was happy, happier than I'd been in a long, long time. I'd carried the secret of Peter and me for so long, dreading the moment I'd tell Jacob, and now it was all out in the open. The worst was over, Jacob had come round, and I was sure we would overcome Roxana and Mrs Krol's animosity.

Yes, we would be a family, like those extended families other people seemed to have, or the ones you saw on TV, with children and aunts and uncles and cousins and in-laws getting together for Christmas and holidays and birthdays. Jacob would be loved and accepted. We would both be. And everything, everything would turn out fine . . .

'It's the best one in town,' Jacob said, stunning with his long eyelashes shadowing his liquid brown eyes, his broad shoulders, the confident way in which he spoke and moved. I thought of what Peter had said to him: to get a girlfriend, get a life. His words had come from a place of anger, but he was right: it was time for Jacob to flourish too. I would never be away from him, never. Yes, things were changing, but we'd be side by side as always.

'We're going to have a great time,' I said.

He looked at me, and I could see his eyes widening. 'Sissy.'

'What?' I laughed.

'I don't know. You looked so happy all of a sudden.'

'That's because I am.'

He smiled back – how his face changed when he smiled, when the frown lines in his forehead finally smoothed. When he didn't look like he was holding on to a buoy with all his might, trying not to drown.

'Yes. We're going to have a great time,' he said. 'I'm off now. Wish me luck.'

'Good luck.' I gave him a peck on the cheek.

'I won't be long, and then we can hit the town and do whatever you want to do.'

I watched from the window as he crossed the road towards the car, and I thought that life couldn't get any better.

We had an enchanted day, and a night of celebrating. The next morning, at our breakfast table, he got the call he'd been waiting for. I abandoned the croissant and grapefruit slices in front of me and stood beside him in the street as he spoke.

His face was dark, and he replied with monosyllables. My heart sank.

'Look, I'm sorry . . .' I began when the call ended.

'I convinced him.'

'What?'

'My boss. I convinced him. They'll do the VR project in Scotland, and I'll lead.'

'Jacob! But you looked . . . lugubrious!'

'Nobody's ever said that to me before, cheeky. Anyway. It's all good. And we still have the whole day ahead of us. Come on, let's finish breakfast and then we'll go treat you before we drive home.'

He was strange. Yes, there was something strange about the whole thing, but I decided to ignore it. When it came to Jacob, I was skilled at ignoring things, at keeping all the good and throwing away the bad, the scary, the painful like it had never happened.

We finished breakfast and went out exploring, the two of us, shopping and chatting and laughing together. At one point he fixed his eyes into mine, he held my hand and softly, so softly, stroked my cheek. We gazed at each other for a moment, and then he looked away.

Another thing that never really happened.

A few hours later, Jacob lay with his head on the steering wheel, still and white. His eyes were open and blinking, but I knew that it didn't matter, that he was dead all the same because of the way his spine sat at a strange angle.

I too was lying forward, on something white and soft. I knew there was something terribly wrong with me, but I was perfectly calm, perfectly peaceful, floating away somewhere no one could reach me and my body didn't hurt. Everything was beginning to blur – maybe I was crying. People were banging on the windows, but they were far, far away.

There was a trickle of blood coming out of Jacob's mouth, and more came out as he whispered his last words to me; words I would carry with me into the deadly sleep that was just beginning: *I love you.*

25

Grace

I enjoyed every moment of our Christmas concert, but I couldn't stop thinking about the turkey I'd left cooking in the oven back home. Once or twice I was in danger of singing *I'm dreaming of a white turkey* and *We wish you a merry turkey.* Christmas had come so quickly – the village seemed to have barely started decorating the freezing streets of Roan when it was already time to gather for Midnight Mass. In Edinburgh, the shops would be overflowing and there would be lights everywhere, but here it was a quieter affair, peaceful, without the frantic busyness of shopping centres. Lit trees peeking from the windows, people coming back from the mainland with gift bags and provisions, the schoolchildren putting on a small show in St Fintan's, chocolate and shortbread tins pouring into the surgery – and before I knew it, it was Christmas morning and time for me to play and sing.

I was going to have a motley crew over for Christmas lunch: Fergus and Susie, Matthew, my receptionist Lorna and local old biddy Mrs Gibson, the last three being alone with no family around. I hoped I hadn't miscalculated cooking times and wouldn't end up going home to a cremated bird.

When the last notes reached the sky, everyone was beaming. The community centre reverberated with applause, and then silence fell again as Rosalind sang a beautiful Gaelic Christmas song, a cappella, giving me goose bumps. I really thought people should come from far and wide to hear her. The room was overflowing with emotion, full of memories and stories in the true language of the island, and for a moment we all felt connected, a small community who'd all been born in this little corner of the world or had chosen to live here. From my place at the piano, my eyes met Fergus's, and for a moment, things between us felt the way they used to be. Two souls who'd met by chance, two souls who understood each other. The moment was soon over, but the sense of togetherness remained after the concert. He took my arm as we walked to the cars, and the warmth I felt inside surprised me.

I left him and Susie at their car, and I drove back with Lorna and Mrs Gibson. I was looking forward to lunch; to our collection of singles and strays, held together by mutual affection. The six of us were a family for one day, a family for Christmas. And I was happy.

Matthew hadn't been at the concert – I'd already gathered that he was the solitary kind, who didn't enjoy taking part in community events, so I wasn't surprised. He was sitting on my doorstep, and when he saw us, he dragged himself up. He looked terrible.

'Matthew? Hey, are you okay?'

'Yes, yes. Just . . . no sleep. The usual.'

'Mmm.' I looked at him through narrowed eyes. I suspected there was something more than insomnia.

Mrs Gibson frowned. 'That's what kept you up last night, eh? Partying?'

'Not exactly, Mrs Gibson,' Matthew said, and I made a mental note to persuade him to come and see me after Christmas. There was something in his expression that I really wasn't happy with.

'You look like you've seen a ghost,' I said.

'Maybe I have. There you go, to keep the party going,' he said, and handed me a bottle of Seal whisky. No point in asking questions now. I would catch him alone later.

'Fergus is bringing a couple of those too,' I said. 'I suppose inviting the owner of a distillery was a good idea, eh, Fergus?' I joked, as he and Susie approached us, having parked the car.

I noticed it immediately, the change of mood. Fergus looked thundery and Susie dismayed. Words must have been exchanged in the car. Not today, I thought, and fixed a determined smile on my face. Today was a day of reconciliation. A day to come together, not move further apart. And I would do all I could to help that happen.

'Good heavens,' Mrs Gibson said, looking from one face to the other. 'You look like you rose from the grave. Fergus is furious, and this lovely girl here is about to cry. Merry Christmas to us. Oh, by the way, my contribution, Doctor.' She took out of her bag a battered box of Mr Kipling's mince pies.

'Thank you, Mrs Gibson.'

'You're welcome. They were half-price. They went out of date a couple of days ago, but I'm sure they're fine.'

'Oh well, if they're off, we have a doctor in the house,' Lorna said, approaching us in that sunny, fluffy way of hers, determined as always to see the silver lining. Our eyes met, and we understood each other in a flash. She would help me keep everyone's spirits up.

We stepped inside to the lovely smell of cooking turkey and a dressed-up table, and I made a beeline for the oven. All good, thankfully; no cremated birds in sight. We girls began to put the lunch together – Mrs Gibson sipping a pre-lunch sherry – while Fergus and Matthew went for a walk.

'You okay?' I whispered to Susie. She shrugged, arranging tiny vanilla candles in front of each place setting. 'Look, I know things are complicated between you guys, but . . . Hey, I'll tell you what. Come with me.' I took her hand and led her upstairs to my bedroom, Hyde following us. I'd noticed the cat seemed to have a crush on Susie, because he turned from a predator into a purring, rub-my-tummy mess every time she was around.

Solemnly I opened the wardrobe and took out a large box wrapped in shiny red paper. 'I got this for you. I was supposed to give it to you after – I have gifts for everyone – but maybe this is the right moment.'

It was heavy, and she slipped her arms around it to help me carry it. 'Oh my God! It's enormous! What is it?' Her eyes were shining and she had the excited smile of a little girl. I mentally blessed every shop that delivered to the island, including Thimble and Thread, the Edinburgh craft outlet. She slipped down onto the floor to open it and unwrapped it at the speed of light. For a moment she was silent, contemplating the many-drawered craft cabinet in front of her.

'This is *amazing*.'

'Wait, open the drawers.'

She did, and oohed and aahed as the cabinet revealed its treasures: jewellery materials, paper and envelopes, a selection of pens and scrapbook materials, felting wool and needles, even tiny pewter hearts and stars. 'I'm in heaven!' she sighed.

'I'm so glad you like it, Susie,' I said, drinking in my moment of glory.

'*Like* doesn't quite describe it, Grace! You're the best,' she said, and gave me a vanilla-scented hug. 'I have something for you too.' Out of her pocket she took a small parcel wrapped in tissue paper. Inside, there was an exquisite little bracelet made with beads, silver wire and a tiny shell. 'I found the shell on the beach, just down there . . .' She gestured towards the beach. 'I thought you'd like something from here, you know . . .'

'It's beautiful. You're a real artist, Susie,' I said, and clasped it around my wrist. 'So, what are you going to do with . . .' I began, but when I looked up, her expression was haunted. 'Oh Susie, are you sure you're okay?'

'Sorry, I'm so happy with my present, I really am!' She smiled a brave smile. 'It's just that . . . I tried to speak to him. Dad. Because it's Christmas, you know. He said some strange things again, things I didn't understand . . . I didn't know what he was talking about. Mum said nothing about that.'

'About what?'

'About him being accused of things, I—'

'We're back!' We heard Fergus's voice from downstairs. I laid my hand on Susie's.

'We'll sort it. No more mysteries, Susie, I promise you. We'll unravel your dad today. You and me.'

She was silent for a moment. 'You must have spent a fortune,' she said eventually.

'Well, when you're a famous artist I'll sell your stuff on eBay and recoup my investment,' I said seriously.

'Susie, you have such a nice voice, you know. I heard you over all the old drones at the concert,' Mrs Gibson said in between mouthfuls. She was a tiny woman with the appetite of a wolf.

Fergus smiled. 'She does, yes. I remember you singing as a wee girl . . .' He stopped suddenly. Susie was looking at him in a way that I could only describe as *starving.* She was starving for her dad's words, for his affection, for his memories of her.

'What do you remember?' I asked gently.

'Nothing. Nothing, it doesn't matter.'

'Of course it doesn't.' Susie's voice had a steely edge. She was angry, and I couldn't blame her. 'Nothing about me matters!'

'Susie . . .' I knew they needed to let it all out, but not at the Christmas table. 'Please, let's not do this now.' Matthew was white and mute, Lorna wore a fixed smile, and Fergus . . . Fergus had a strange look in his eyes. I felt a storm coming, and it hit faster than I'd imagined possible.

'It's funny, you know. You act the victim when the only victim here is me. You and your mother destroyed me, Susie. You did.'

Both Susie and I looked at him open-mouthed. They'd clearly had a dram or two at Matthew's place when they'd gone for a walk earlier, and it had loosened Fergus's tongue; but what he was saying made no sense. How could Susie have destroyed him?

'Aren't these vanilla candles lovely?' Lorna said in a brittle voice.

'Look, Susie. This must be very upsetting for you, and for you, Fergus . . . but you need time and space to talk it out. Not around the table on Christmas Day.'

Matthew had reverted to being a social worker all of a sudden, and his words actually seemed to hit home.

'I'm sorry. Sorry, Grace,' Susie said. Her eyes were brimming.

I put a hand on her arm. 'It's fine, sweetheart. Let's just eat now.'

Fergus got up, staggering a bit on his bad leg, and Matthew rose quickly to help him. 'I'm sorry too. I'm sorry, Grace. And I'm sorry, Susie. I'm so sorry. For everything.'

He disentangled himself from Matthew's grip and wrenched open the front door, letting in a blast of freezing salty December wind. I heard Matthew murmuring soothing words, words of reconciliation as they stood on the doorstep, but Fergus left anyway. My heart sank – did he not understand how much we needed him?

Susie sat with her head bowed, and to my surprise, Mrs Gibson took her hand. 'It's okay, my love,' she said. 'You're a lovely girl and he's an old fool. Always has been, since he was this tall; five years old he was, and he fell head first into a cask when his dad was looking the other way. He smelled like the inside of a pint glass for two days. I thought, nothing good will come of this boy. But something good did come. You.'

That was the most astonishing bit of my Christmas morning, and it'd been crazy enough already.

'Can you pass me the chipolatas?' Mrs Gibson continued. Now that was more like her.

I stayed seated, tried to keep things normal, but I couldn't. I was too worried for Fergus. I had to go to him; I had to speak to him. I had to finally make him tell me what was going on. As old and festering as his wounds were, I had to at least try to heal them.

'I'm . . . I'm going to see if Fergus is okay,' I said, and left the Christmas table and all my preparations behind, feeling so guilty about the people who'd come to my house as a refuge, a place of celebration, and were now faced with this. But I couldn't leave Fergus alone, not now.

'It's okay, you go, we'll be all right,' Lorna said, always the trouper.

The cold, white afternoon had already turned into twilight, lilac sky and grey waters, a palette of shades of purple that made everything melt into one. Black branches against the sky, the evening star rising over the dunes, the distant sound of Corrywreckan. Fergus's car wasn't there; I prayed he'd gone home or to the distillery, otherwise I'd simply not know where to find him, and the idea of him upset, half drunk, unsteady on his legs was a frightening one. I drove up to the distillery first, but there were no lights in the office. I don't know why, but something told me to keep looking. I walked around, calling his name, and my voice seemed almost a sacrilege in the magical light and quiet of the place.

'Grace! I'm here!'

My heart missed a beat, and I followed his voice to

the warehouse. For a moment I couldn't make out anything, as I went from the gloom to the warm yellow lights inside; then I thought maybe I was seeing things. It couldn't be.

Fergus was up on a tall ladder, inspecting a row of casks. His head nearly touched the ceiling of the warehouse. I felt sick. The ladder looked unsteady enough, but his legs even more so.

'Fergus!' I shouted before I could even think. He turned towards me . . . and then it was as if he'd folded in on himself, as if his legs simply couldn't sustain him any more.

The thud as he hit the ground was sickening. It took me a moment to realise what had happened – it had all been so quick. Fergus lay broken on the ground, unconscious, his legs bent behind him in an unnatural way.

26

Grace

'Will he be all right?' I asked, knowing as a doctor that it was an absurd question.

'I can't say, Grace,' Dr Woerner replied in his faint German accent. We were lucky that he'd agreed to have Fergus at St Fintan's, instead of transporting him to the mainland by helicopter. It wasn't the first time I'd thanked our lucky stars that they'd chosen Seal to build the hospital. 'I just don't know yet. You're a doctor, I can tell you straight. He took a blow to the head; we need to see how it goes. If he wakes up . . .'

'If?' The world spun around me.

I have so many things to tell you.

I had so many things to tell you.

Why didn't I, when I still could?

Why did I think there would always be tomorrow?

For a moment, I lost myself in the blue and white pattern of the linoleum, my pain and worry attempting to transport me somewhere else. No. I blinked. I had to be rational, I had to be clear-headed. For

Fergus. For Susie. 'And when he does wake up?' I said in the steadiest voice I could muster.

'If he regains consciousness, well, he has a few broken bones – to put it mildly – and I don't know what the long-term consequences will be.'

'I see. I see.'

Oh Fergus, why? Why were you so foolish, so completely reckless? Did you not know how much your daughter needs you?

Did you not know how much I *need you?*

My mind raced with thoughts and regrets and questions that couldn't find a voice. I had to keep it together.

'How did it happen?' Dr Woerner asked. 'You said he fell from high up.'

'Yes. He was on a ladder. Someone who works with him – Matthew Shearer – said they'd had problems with some casks. He was having a look at them.'

'On Christmas Day?'

'Long story. Fergus has a condition – an orthopaedic condition. His hips are not properly formed, and . . . well, I'll get the specialist on the mainland to email you his records.'

'I saw it from the X-rays. He shouldn't have been on a ladder. In fact, he shouldn't have been on his feet at all really. This is the kind of thing you can ignore at twenty, but at fifty, it impairs you. At sixty, you're in a wheelchair.'

'I know.' I took a breath. I did know, but it was shocking to hear that one day Fergus would not be able to walk.

If he lived.

'I told him a million times to watch himself,' I whispered. 'Can I see him?'

'Come with me.'

To my embarrassment, tears rolled down my face as I scrubbed my hands before entering the ward. The memories of the harsh words I'd thrown at him and the regret about what I should have told him tortured me. In all my years of practice I'd seen every manner of human weakness and mistake and always shown compassion to my patients. I didn't judge, I was all too aware of the complications of life, of how hard it was to stay true to yourself, to do the right thing. But when it had come to my friend, someone so close to my heart . . . more than a friend, I had to admit it at last. Enough lying to myself, coward that I was . . . When it came to him, I'd made no effort to understand – or not enough effort anyway. I'd been too busy judging him, mothering Susie instead of trying harder to inch them closer in any way I could.

I walked down the spotless corridor until I reached Dr Woerner, who was standing by the door to Fergus's room. He led me in with a hand on my back. I tried to control myself, but a small, almost inaudible lament came out of me as I saw Fergus lying in that bed, white, helpless, sunk in an ailing sleep.

Why did I not try harder to understand you?

Why did I not let myself . . .

I struggled to even think those words, but it was

time I came clean with myself. What I wanted to say was: *Why did I not let myself love you?*

'Come and stay with me tonight. You can't be there all on your own, sweetheart.' Susie had asked over and over to go and see Fergus, but Dr Woerner and I agreed it was better for her not to. I didn't want her to see her dad like that. Now she was at my table, picking at the macaroni cheese I'd made for her. Lorna was with us, like a benevolent angel, keeping our spirits up with endless cups of tea and kind words. Dr Woerner had promised to ring if there was any change, and every single muscle and nerve in my body was taut, all my senses painfully alert, waiting for the call that could spell salvation or disaster.

'Thanks. I just need to get a few things from home, if that's okay,' she said softly.

'Of course, I'll drive you. Susie, as you're going home . . . they gave me this at the hospital . . .' I walked over to my jacket, hanging in the hall, and took out a transparent bag with the things that had been in Fergus's pockets. I placed it gently on the table, and Susie's lips trembled. She opened the bag and took out a watch, a set of keys, a tiny parcel wrapped in silver paper.

'This is for you,' she said, and handed it to me.

'For me?' I took the parcel from her hand and looked at it for a moment, then sat down and leaned back on the chair.

A Christmas present for me. Carefully wrapped, with a little label. *Grace*, it said in black biro, with a sketched Santa hat beside it. I smiled, but I felt the tears gathering behind my eyes, and steadied myself. I couldn't make Susie any more upset than she was already.

'Open it,' she said softly.

I unwrapped the silver paper, revealing a blue velvet box. I lifted the lid; resting on a bed of silk was a pendant with my initial, G, and a tiny heart charm. I couldn't help it. My eyes filled with tears.

'Oh Grace. He'll be fine. He'll be fine, I promise,' Susie tried to console me.

'It should be me comforting you,' I said, and took her hand.

'It's gorgeous,' Lorna said from behind me. She squeezed my shoulder, and for a moment we were a little trinity of mutual support and affection.

'Can I?' Susie said, taking the pendant from its box. She stood and clasped it around my neck.

'Thank you.'

She ducked her head. 'It goes with my bracelet. All silver,' she said, in an attempt to be upbeat. But her eyes betrayed her. 'Grace, how long will Dad stay in hospital? I mean, you're a doctor, you must know . . .'

'A long time, I think. It will take a while for him to be allowed home.' *If he survives.* But I wouldn't tell her that.

'And what will I do?'

I shook my head. I wasn't sure what to say. I wanted her to come and stay with me, but I couldn't ask Fergus, of course. I would have to check with Susie's mum, as much as I was desperate to just assume that Fergus would want her to stay with me.

Susie looked away. 'I was hoping you'd say . . .'

'Sweetheart, listen. What you're hoping I'll say is what I hope I'll be able to say. I would love to have you here as long as you want. But we need to make sure your mum and dad agree. Your mum, as things stand.'

'Good luck with that.'

'Maybe you should have some faith in her,' I said, without quite believing in my own words.

'In the woman who threw me out of the house because she was getting married?'

'Yes. I see what you mean. Come on, no time like the present. Let's make that call and get it over and done with.'

'She won't speak to you. She doesn't even speak to me.'

'She will. I can assure you.' Thinking of Fergus broken and unconscious in hospital gave me strength.

It took me over half an hour to get to Lin. I had to explain the whole thing to her assistant, then the assistant passed me on to her secretary – yes, she had one of each, the famous actress. The secretary said they'd call me back. I wasn't holding my breath, but eventually the phone rang.

'Hello . . . Yes, I'm Grace Chatto, the island doctor.'

'Island?'

'Seal Island. Where your daughter lives.'

'Oh God, of course. Sorry, I'm preparing for a part. When I *prepare*, I can't think of anything else.' Not even your own child, I thought. 'And why am I talking to you?'

'Because Fergus is in no fit state to speak. He had an accident; he's in hospital. It's serious, I'm afraid. I'm looking after Susie at the moment, and I phoned to ask you if you were okay with it. If Susie could stay with me. I can write a formal letter, of course . . .'

'Wait. Is she coming to California?'

'No. Well, she doesn't want to, no.'

'Is she going to that school, then? Because she spoke to Marion only a short while ago – that's my assistant, you know . . .'

'No,' I said with all the patience I could muster. 'She would like to stay with me, Miss Kruja.'

'Mrs Guzman.'

'Sorry. Mrs Guzman. She would like to stay on the island with me.'

'But why are you calling me?'

'Because, like I said, Fergus is in hospital, and I couldn't just keep your daughter without telling you.'

'Okay then. If that's what Susie wants. Just let me know if you need any money.'

'I think we'll be okay, thank you,' I said, slightly bewildered, nodding towards Susie. She exhaled and smiled.

'Dr Chatto? Grace?'

'Yes?'

'Tell her . . . that I'll be thinking of her. Quite a lot, actually.'

'I'll tell her. Bye then . . .' But Lin had put the phone down.

Only then did I realise that I'd told her twice that Fergus was in hospital, and she'd never asked what had happened, or how he was.

'That was about a million times easier than I thought it would be,' I said. 'I'll prepare your room, sweetheart, and then maybe we'll ask Lorna if she can drive you over to your dad's house so I can man the phone. Don't you just wish mobiles worked up here?' I gave a weak laugh.

'Yeah, okay. Thanks.'

'I'll make your bed, then.'

'Grace. Don't worry. Everything will be okay,' Susie said in that serious way she had sometimes, switching between child and almost-adult in the blink of an eye.

"Susie . . ."

"Yes?"

"Your mum asked me to tell you she'll be thinking about you."

Susie gave me an even gaze. She didn't reply. Right at that moment, in the silence of the house, the phone rang.

Somehow I knew who it was, even before seeing Dr Woerner's number on the display. My hand was shaking as I brought the phone to my ear, and even more when I put it down.

I opened my mouth to speak, but on seeing my expression, Susie burst into tears. She could guess what had been said.

'Sweetheart, listen. I need to drive down to the hospital, okay?' I said in a too-calm voice. 'You wait here with Lorna, and try not to worry.'

'He's dead, isn't he? He's dead?' she almost screamed.

'No, no, baby, of course not. He's just not recuperating as quickly and as well as they hoped, so I'm going down to keep him company.'

'To say goodbye if he dies,' she sobbed.

'Oh Susie . . .'

'I want to come with you.'

'Darling, seeing your dad like that . . .'

'I have things to tell him. Things I should have told him before all this. Maybe he'll hear me.'

I enveloped her in my arms. I wanted to take her pain away, take it all on myself, make everything fine for her. 'I hope so. I have things to tell him too,' I murmured, and through the kitchen window I saw that soft, fat white snowflakes had started falling from the black sky.

27

Matthew

Molly and I were sitting on the floor together in front of the living room windows. I'd switched the light on outside, so I could see the snow falling, falling.

A white Christmas after all.

It struck me that in another life, another universe, I would have spent the day at a table with Mia and our families . . . But all that was locked somewhere in my mind. I couldn't go there. Also, there was too much rubble between me and those memories, days where events had followed one another in a rhythm so frantic it was almost cruel.

Hannah's tears on my shoulder, Mia's photograph cradled by the sea; the sense that I could live again.

Selena disappearing in front of my eyes, along with the promise of the message she had for me, whatever it might have been, wherever it had come from.

Fergus lying in hospital, between life and death.

Fergus. A man who'd welcomed me with such easy generosity, who had trusted me in spite of my past. I wished I could do something. I wished I could give him some of my strength.

Molly moved closer to me. For a moment she sat still, then she looked up and sniffed at my hand. I crouched down to stroke her, then sank my face into her fur, breathing in that dog smell of comfort and absolute loyalty. Thousands of years ago, on a night infested by predators and made endless by fear and cold, a man just like me must have done the same thing, feeling a dog's fur for comfort, falling asleep together like one pack.

Selena had gone, I didn't know where. I'd seen something impossible happening before my eyes, a human being disappearing like mist, like vapour.

I'd seen a ghost.

After you've seen the impossible, where do you go from there?

When Mia came to visit me, I was lying in a hospital bed, delirious with pain, traumatised and full of drugs. A hallucination, of course. But now there was nothing wrong with me. At least not that I knew of. I'd been lucid as I ran along the beach, trying to get to Grace as quickly as I could; I'd been lucid as Selena began to disappear. What I had seen was no vision; what I had seen was real.

When I had seen her skin paling and becoming transparent, so that I could make out the outline of pebbles and shells through her body; when I couldn't feel the weight of her head on my arm any more as I knelt over her, and the fingers I was holding had dissolved so that my palm had curled up into itself – I was well, I was sober and in my right mind.

Was I?

Because if you're not in your right mind, then you don't *know* you aren't. Oh God. Maybe I was losing my mind. If you were hallucinating, you wouldn't be able to tell reality from madness, you'd believe your hallucinations were real.

But I held Selena, I touched her skin.

She'd mentioned Mia's name, she'd said she had a message for me.

Had it been a message from Mia?

Oh God. I really had gone crazy. I held my face in my hands, Molly yelping softly beside me. I'd just remembered something.

When I'd asked Fergus about Selena, about the girl who'd come and met me at the distillery every night for five nights, standing in front of the small grove, he'd said he'd seen *nobody.* On impulse, I grabbed Mia's camera and switched it on. Selena had been in the pictures I'd taken on Seal – if you're in a photograph, you exist, don't you? Now I wished I'd showed them to somebody.

Red light on, pictures sliding on the screen – but she wasn't there any more. She should be there, standing on that rock – she wasn't. Her silhouette had been etched against the sky in this one, her profile and flowing hair in this one; her face, close up, had been in this frame with Corrywreckan in the distance. She wasn't there any more.

People didn't just disappear from photographs.

There was only one explanation: that she'd never been there in the first place.

Grace

We held his hand, we whispered in his ear, we sat upright on the plastic chairs until Susie couldn't take any more and they set her up in a small room nearby, on a fold-down bed. I allowed myself a moment in front of the window to watch the snowflakes falling, so perfect, so fragile; then I kissed her on the forehead, tucked the blanket to her chin and returned to Fergus.

His skin looked so fragile with the line in the back of his hand, the bruising, the paleness that almost showed the veins underneath. Infection had set in from somewhere, invading him, making him burn with a fever they couldn't control. *Drip, drip, drip,* the antibiotics went in, together with the painkillers, and he fought, he fought.

I fought with him, so hard that I could almost feel his fractures in my own body, the infection in my blood. I wanted to be with him every step of the way, to give him all my energy, all I had.

I don't know how it happened – I must have been truly bone-weary, because I fell asleep with my head on the windowsill, and I didn't even awake when nurses and doctors came in to check him. After a couple of hours, I opened my eyes. A ray of light shone on the floor, illuminating the dust particles inside it. Dawn. The night was over.

I sat up and took his hand, my heart in my throat. He was warm, but not boiling. I touched his forehead. The fever had gone down. His breathing was regular, not that terrible panting he had done in the middle of the night.

I placed a light kiss on his forehead, and in a voice so soft that nobody could hear it but him, I whispered three words in his ear, the words I should have told him long ago.

28

Grace

I stood with my fingers curled around Fergus's pendant, a smile on my face. I could have dropped with tiredness, but I was too happy to care about small things like not having slept more than four hours in two days.

Susie had come to see her dad. She'd stepped into the room hesitantly, nearly on tiptoes, holding a small bouquet of fabric flowers she'd made herself. I was a bit apprehensive, but when I saw the expression on his face as he spotted her, my anxiety disappeared.

'Susie,' he said feebly.

'Dad! Dad!' she burst out and ran to him, stopping just short of hugging him, for fear of causing him hurt. Instead, she leaned her face on his chest, and he slowly raised an arm to touch her hair.

'These are for you. I made them.'

'They're beautiful, Susie. Thank you.'

'I was so scared. I'm so glad you're okay.'

'I'm sorry. So sorry, Susie. For everything,' Fergus croaked. I clasped my hand over my mouth.

'It doesn't matter, Dad. It's all finished now.'

'You were just a child . . . I should have forgiven you . . .'

Forgiven her? The smile on my face faded and I tensed up. I knew there was a difficult conversation ahead, and although Fergus was so weak, I could hardly stop it from happening.

Susie frowned and dried her tears with the back of her hand. 'Forgiven me for what? What have I done?' she said calmly, without anger.

'You . . . you don't remember? You don't remember the video? When your mum left me, the video you made . . .'

'Which one? Mum shot hundreds of them. She had this idea that I would be an actress, like her; obviously I didn't have the slightest intention, but she just wouldn't give up . . .'

Fergus tried to sit up, but I stopped him, laying my hands on his shoulders. 'How can you not remember? I know you were a small child, but surely you would remember something like that?'

'You're scaring me, Dad.'

'Fergus, she clearly doesn't know what you're talking about.'

'When your mum and I broke up, she sent me a video where you said . . . you spoke about all the things I was doing to you. But it wasn't true, none of it was true.'

'What things? Dad, are you sure you're okay? Grace,

I don't know what he's talking about!' Susie was distraught.

'Take your time, Fergus. What do you want to say? I'll help you . . .'

Fergus took a breath and grimaced a little. I could see he was in pain, but at least the two of them were talking, finally. I couldn't bring myself to break the spell, even if what he was saying was bizarre.

'I didn't want to leave you with her. I knew she didn't care about you. I wanted to take you with me to Scotland. I fought for you. We were so close, remember? You and your mum . . . not so much. She never showed a lot of interest in you, apart from trying to make you a mini-me. She wanted you just to spite me. I'm sorry, darling, I don't want to hurt you, but it's true.'

'I know. I know my mum by now.'

'She got full custody. I was devastated, so I decided not to move back to Seal, to stay in London and see you as often as I could. But she said a clean break was better for you, that I shouldn't see you at all. She said if I tried to fight it, she would get the best lawyers and destroy me. I said I didn't care . . .' He moaned, a low moan of pain.

'Fergus . . .' I began, but he waved me silent. He wanted to let it all out.

'So she said it was *you*. That you never wanted to see me again. That you'd said . . . you'd said I'd hit you.'

'Oh my God,' Susie whispered.

'I was devastated. I didn't understand how you could have—'

'But I didn't, Dad! I never said that!'

'I didn't believe her at first. But then she showed me the video. I'll never forget it. You said you never wanted to see me again, that you were better off without me, that I'd done all sorts of things to you. That I should leave you alone with your mum. She gave it to her lawyer. Social services got involved . . . they said I was an abusive father. I couldn't go anywhere near you.'

Susie sobbed. 'I never shot that video! I never said those things!'

I held my hand over my mouth.

'She must have forced you, or deceived you, I can see it now. Of course it couldn't have been you . . . you were only seven. What an idiot I was to think you could have said those things.'

Susie was sobbing.

'Please believe me, Susie. I never touched you. I never laid a hand on you.'

'I know, Dad, I know. I swear, I have no memory of that video . . . but I shot so many, Mum sent them to agencies, remember? I know the way you were with me when I was a child. You were wonderful. I was heartbroken when you left. Mum said you didn't want anything to do with me. You never wrote to me, never phoned . . . but I see why, now; you must have been so angry.'

'Not just that. I wasn't allowed to make any contact.

And also you said . . . Lin made you say that you were scared of me.'

I could hear my heart in the silence. A door opened and closed in the distance; a car came and went under our window. Everything was heightened, unreal.

'Then why did she let me come here?'

'She was finished with you, I suppose. Like she'd been finished with me. She didn't care any more. And anyway, she knew that it was all lies, that you would come to no harm with me. I'm so sorry, Susie. So sorry. I shouldn't have believed your mother. I should have known . . . But I was in pieces . . .'

Silently Susie laid a hand on his cheek and dried his tears.

'It's all forgotten,' she said, with that generous heart of hers.

That night, I was woken by cries and sobs. They came from Susie's room. I dashed across the hall, switched the light on and ran to her. 'Susie! Susie, it's a nightmare. Wake up. You're fine. You're safe . . .'

She opened her eyes, still flailing, and for a moment it looked like she didn't know where she was. I sat beside her on the bed and touched her cheek, her shoulder, her arm. 'Susie!'

'Grace?'

'Yes. I'm here. You're okay.'

'Where's Dad?' She was confused. I checked her forehead, but it was cool. She was simply half asleep.

'In the hospital, doing very well. He'll be home soon. And he loves you very much. Remember? He told you.'

She kept looking at me for a moment, then she leaned back on her pillow and sighed. Her blue-black fringe was damp with sweat.

'Sorry. I woke you up.'

'It's no problem. I'm a woman of leisure for a while; I don't need to go to work in the morning.' I'd been given a period of carer's leave, so a young doctor from Glasgow was looking after the islanders in my place.

'I don't understand.'

'What do you not understand?' No wonder she was confused by everything that had happened to her. Her selfish, deranged mother had put those accusations in her mouth, destroying Fergus's life, his name, his reputation.

'I can't remember that video.'

'Well, it was made, clearly, so your mum must have forced you, or tricked you.'

'She made me do so many. No agency ever called back, not even for her. I was a crappy little actress.' She laughed, and then was serious again. 'I can't believe what she did. I lost all illusions I had about her when I was very young, but I never thought . . .'

'You need to put it behind you now. You and your dad have so many things to say to each other . . . so much to catch up with.'

'Yes. I can't believe that . . .' I was quiet for a moment

and waited for her to finish. 'I can't believe that something so bad – breaking his legs that way – has brought on something so good.'

'Sometimes it works out that way, doesn't it? You think you're falling, and instead you're rising . . .'

'Yes. Oh Grace.' She sighed, a deep sigh. 'It was a horrible nightmare. Really horrible. I was alone, nobody wanted me . . .'

'Oh, sweetheart, that is not true.'

'I didn't want to leave you. In my dreams you were calling me. You were saying, "Gureisu, Gureisu, come back!" '

I froze.

'What? What was that name . . . the name you called yourself?'

'Oh, you mean my real name? Susie is just a nickname. You see, my mum is half English, half Japanese . . . her real name is Lin Hiragi. Can you not see it from my eyes?' She smiled. Yes, I could see it now, though I'd never noticed before – the almond-shaped eyes, and that straight, silky black hair . . .

'I see. And . . . what was it?' I wanted to hear it once again, in case I'd misheard.

'Gureisu. Grace,' she said, smiling, and wiping away a rogue tear. 'We have the same name really.'

Gureisu.

Make a wish.

29

Matthew

I carried a box of chocolates and a couple of books under my arm. I was desperate to tell Fergus that everything was fine at the distillery, everything was under control. That we were holding the fort for him. That he'd given me a chance when I needed one, and I would not let him down now. The distillery had given me a reason to get up in the morning, to keep it all together for my friend to come back and take charge again.

I was on my way towards the turreted grey stone building that hosted the main part of the hospital when something stopped me.

A few notes, a memory. A melody.

Debussy: 'Rêverie'.

The sweet sound of a piano coming from somewhere, playing Selena's music.

I don't know why I followed it inside that other building, the modern one, when I knew it wasn't there that Fergus was. The silent building, the place Mike Casey had spoken about when I first arrived.

Except it wasn't silent, because music filled it, and suddenly I remembered: when I'd walked all around the island looking for Selena, there had been music then too, coming out of an open window.

I walked on slowly, following the soft, beautiful notes. The music didn't manage to change the atmosphere, sterile, forbidding and impossibly sad. Like a prison, where all sentences lasted forever. I was desperate to get out of there, and yet I couldn't – the music was calling me. A nurse passed me in the corridor and didn't say anything, though clearly I wasn't supposed to be there, with my books and chocolates, in a place where nobody could read or eat chocolates or anything else. I walked along a corridor that stretched into the distance. Some doors were open, and I could catch glimpses of what was inside. Now I knew why Sergeant Casey had been so spooked by the silent building. I passed a room where a man lay immobile, unknowing, his eyes open, posters and pictures on the ceiling so he could see them. An older woman, a machine breathing for her, another elderly lady sitting on a chair beside her and looking outside with melancholy eyes. A splash of pink and yellow, tulips on her windowsill . . .

Slowly I walked on, feeling vaguely guilty as I looked through the open doors, seeing what I wasn't supposed to see. It was like I was spying on people who were at their most vulnerable, their most exposed. I should turn back, find Fergus and reassure him that the distillery was all right. But the music continued, and I had to follow it. It was a memory. It was a question. A question I needed the answer to.

I turned a corner, and there in front of me stood a man with his face in his hands. Beside him, a small woman, bones like a bird, was crying silently.

'Ann, please. A little bit longer.'

'Please don't. Don't ask me that. I can't see her suffering any more,' the woman said. Her face was as white as the walls.

'If you need more time . . .' said a man in a white coat – a doctor, I realised. He had a German accent and a kind manner, resting his hand on the tall man's back. A nurse wearing a compassionate expression was bent beside the woman.

The man shook his head. His face was drenched with tears. It was horrible to see such an imposing man crying like a small child. I had to leave these people, I had to let them play out their domestic drama in private. It wasn't fair to stand there watching.

'Believe me, Dr Woerner,' he said, 'I don't think for a moment that this thing she's got, this infection, is your fault . . . We brought her here, to Seal, because we knew she'd have the best chance, and she did, she really did . . .'

'Thom. She went the day of the accident. Don't you understand? She was gone then. We made her linger on . . .' The woman shook her head. 'I want her to go listening to music, her favourite music . . .'

'Excuse me? Are you looking for someone?'

The doctor was talking to me. And yes, I was looking for someone, but he wasn't here, and I didn't really know what I was doing.

'I'm sorry,' I said, and stepped forward. The doctor's eyes widened. He'd been expecting me to step back, not forward. And then it hit me.

The antiseptic smell.

That was Selena's scent: rose and something else, something pungent. Disinfectant. A hospital smell.

'Who are you? What are you doing?' the big man said, and I felt his sorrow turning to anger, but I couldn't stop. I had to follow the music, I had to get into that room.

'I'm sorry,' I heard the words coming out of my mouth, but I wasn't really aware of having said them.

I step inside, and there is a hand on my arm, words of protest; the hand gets firmer, it hurts, I don't care. I look at the white bed in the middle of the room. A girl, long brown hair in a braid held together by a red ribbon, bedcovers to her waist to reveal a white nightgown, lace at the neck and sleeves, still white hands by her sides. And then I call her, and they hold me back. I free myself; someone shouts but I don't care, I have to speak to her, I have to touch her. I fall and kneel beside her bed, and hold her hand. More shouting; people pull me away, and I have to let go, I can't hold on to her hand because I'm scared I'll hurt her, but I call her by the name I gave her, and all of a sudden the hands that held me back let me fall, and everyone runs to her.

Somewhere behind me, I hear a man's voice, the big man who was crying before.

'It's him! It's Matthew Shearer. I know his face, I know his face. He's the man who did this!'

But the horror and astonishment of his words slips over me and can't get a grip, because her small white fingers hold mine, because her eyes are open, her grey-green eyes, and she's looking straight at me. *Selena, Selena, Selena.* I keep calling her over the dancing music, and I can't stop.

30

Grace

I sat beside Fergus with a sigh, in our hands cups of steaming coffee, the sweet air of early spring all around us. My garden was coming back to life, and the scent of new greenery that rose from the land was perceptible even over the omnipresent scent of sea and salt. Fergus's rehabilitation was proving long and hard, and he still had to spend most of his time in a wheelchair, but we were getting there. He was as stubborn as they came, and it had become a personal challenge to gain victory over his own battered bones. The hospital physio rooms had become his battlefield. He leaned on the side bars as he took hesitant steps on a mat, he closed his eyes and raised his legs a few inches, once, twice, three times, and sweat poured down his face. Slowly but surely.

As we sat there in silent bliss, we heard light footsteps behind us.

'Hey, guys! Hi, Dad.' Susie placed a kiss on Fergus's cheek.

Things hadn't all fallen into place for them in one

go after Fergus's revelations. It had taken hours of conversation, of trying to translate gossamer feelings and sensations into words, of finding a way to heal so many years of misunderstanding, of mutual distrust. Susie had sworn that she would never speak to her mum again, and even if that was what she wanted to do, even if her mum had caused her so much pain, it had been a difficult decision to make; hard for her to see her mum for who she really was.

Susie had grown up a lot over the last four months; a little bit stronger, an inch taller, her short hair styled into a bob and the blue streak gone. She looked less and less like a child and more and more like a woman.

'Hi! How's Ewen?' I said.

'We don't want to know,' Fergus growled in mock severity.

Susie laughed. 'He's good. How are you feeling?'

'Like I could get up and run a mile,' Fergus said, and he looked like the cat who had got the cream. It was unmistakable that something had happened. To my shame, at age fifty-one, I blushed.

Susie looked from her dad to me and back, and for a moment her mouth fell slightly open.

'Seriously?' she gasped.

'Had you not guessed?' Fergus laughed.

'No! I mean yes! But I didn't think . . . You're actually together?'

'Yes. She's all mine.'

I blushed even deeper and joined in the laughter.

'Honestly, Susie! Your observational skills are second to none!'

'I thought you were friends!'

'We are. Very good friends,' Fergus said with a mischievous look. Susie rolled her eyes. 'Oh Dad!'

'Is it a problem, Susie?' I said softly.

Susie shrugged. 'Nah. It's the best thing ever.' She sat beside me and leaned her head on my shoulder in a moment that was childlike and meaningful at the same time – she still hadn't learnt to hide the tenderness she felt, like adults do. I stroked her silky black hair and wondered at my good luck in finding her.

Fergus's hand sought mine, and I held it tight. And so I sat between the two people I loved most in the world, a gentle wind smelling of flowers and machair and sunny waters blowing on the three of us.

Rose

So much of my recovery has been about remembering, following the red thread of my life. The strange journey with Matthew has brought me back to myself until I can see it all – like a bird flying up, up into the sky I can take in the whole scene rather than just little bits. I can see the happy years and Jacob's love for me, his kindness. The way he protected me from everything, from the whole world. I chose Peter over him and condemned him to despair. A million times he told me that I was never to leave him. I knew what it was going to do to him, and I blamed myself more than I can ever say. But I couldn't help myself – I couldn't live like that any more, caged like an animal, always beside Jacob, always with him. I had to set myself free.

And now I remember. I remember what happened the day of the accident, and I remember the message Mia gave me. I'd been dead for three minutes, they told me, when I flew to the stars and saw her.

As Jacob drove, there was only the sound of the rain tapping on the car windows, splashes whenever we passed through a puddle, and the soft noise of the engine – but in my ears there was a din, and the deafening noise spoke of guilt, of broken pieces. Pieces of my family. Pieces of me. And then Jacob made it even worse.

'Look. I'm sorry. About the whole Peter thing. About having driven Mum and Dad away.'

What had brought this on? After our lovely day, after the good news about his job? I gazed at his face in profile against the droplet-covered car window.

'Hey. You're going to lead that project, you're going to find a girlfriend – I don't think you'll have any trouble there! You're going to be all that you can be. You're amazing, Jacob, it's just that you can't see it.'

'This morning, I didn't go back to see my boss. I went to London. I had someone to see.'

'Who? A girl?' I smiled.

'My family. My real family.'

My heart sank. That was the reason for his tight, dark face as he'd spoken on the phone. 'Oh Jacob, no . . .'

He snorted. 'Yep, you got it right. The word to sum it all up is *no.* I shouldn't have,' he said with a mock cheerfulness that chilled me.

'Then why did you?' I murmured.

'Because I wanted to know the truth.'

'They were addicts, Jacob; they beat you, they locked you out of the house . . . Why, why did you have to go and relive all that? Tell me why!' My eyes were full of tears. My brother, my beloved brother. I couldn't bear to see him hurt again, I just couldn't.

'No, they weren't.' He shook his head.

'What do you mean?'

'They weren't addicts. In fact, they were perfectly normal people. He's an accountant, she runs a bookshop. They never had any children after me, obviously. They gave me away because they didn't know how to handle me. The things they did, leaving me outside, giving me sleeping pills, were because I was unmanageable. I hit them, I never slept. I was put in an institution, then fostered out.'

'What? It can't be . . .'

'Oh, it is.'

'Jacob, listen. You just admitted that they left you to sleep outside, they gave you sleeping pills. Now that makes me think they were the mad people, not you!'

'Apparently not. I was locked up in a mental institution for children. Though they wouldn't put it like that, of course.'

'Oh Jacob . . . What reason could they have to do such a thing, such a horrible thing?'

'I scared them.'

'But . . . why?'

'Same reason why I scared Mum.'

I felt cold. The suburban sprawl passed before my eyes as I tried to digest what I was hearing. For a moment, I thought I would have to ask him to stop the car and let me be sick by the side of the road.

It was too much, too much.

I had to revert to the here and now, to what we knew, what we were. What we had, together or apart.

'You know, Jacob . . .'

He looked at me briefly and then turned his eyes to the road again.

'My dream . . . my dream is to have you over for dinner at our place. I mean, Peter's and mine, in Aberdeen. I'll cook you your favourite: Thai green curry with lots of prawns – you love them. Yes?'

'Of course,' he said, but something in his voice had a strange chime, and I felt the hair at the back of my neck rise up.

'I had such a great time,' I said. 'I mean, I know you had a terrible experience, but it was so good, to spend time together . . .'

'Yes. It was a good way to end.'

'End? Oh Jacob, I'm just moving down the road really.' I tried to laugh.

'Rose, I have to thank you for being my family. It was . . . amazing. Amazing. While it lasted. But you know what? I can't take it again.' He smiled, and I realised his cheeks were wet. I felt sick.

'Jacob?'

'I can't take someone leaving me again.'

I opened my mouth to comfort him, to say *I'm not leaving you, I'm never leaving you*, but I was too scared, because the knuckles on the steering wheel were white, and the look in his eyes was spaced out, far away. Like he was already gone.

At that moment, I knew what he was about to do, and all my muscles froze in terror. He swerved suddenly, and I can't remember very clearly, but I think I screamed as we kept going in the wrong lane, so, so fast, and then another car appeared and it was too late, too late for anything.

While I lay in the hospital bed, drifting in and out of consciousness before losing my fight and slipping into a coma, I heard someone saying that a woman in the other car had died.

And now I know who he was, the man my spirit went to while I was asleep. The man who has believed himself guilty all this time.

And I have remembered the message I was to give him, the message from Mia, the floating spirit I met during those long, long instants I was dead. As he kneels beside me, holding my hand, I look him in the eye, and I say: *I remember now.*

He says nothing, just keeps looking at me, voices in the background, running footsteps. I have to hurry and make the words in my head come out of my dry, parched throat. And I do, my voice barely a croaky whisper, almost inaudible.

'It wasn't your fault. The man in the other car, he wanted to die. Whether you read that text message or not, it wouldn't have made a difference. This is what the star . . . this is what Mia wanted me to tell you: that *it wasn't your fault.*'

Epilogue

Matthew

'I'm going to try,' she said, leaving no room for discussion. I tensed up, half frightened, half proud, as she pushed against her hands, against the armrests of her wheelchair.

'I'm here, Rose. You can do it. You can do it . . .' I whispered in her ear as I stood close to her, ready to catch her if she fell.

'Oh.' She let out a breath and closed her eyes for a moment as she stood, the sea in front of her, the wind on her face, her hair blowing gently behind her. Molly was watching her, intent, as if cheering her on. Then she opened her eyes and smiled. 'Next I'll be dancing.'

'Yes. You'll be dancing for me.'

Rose turned around to smile at her mum, who was waiting for us on the asphalt road, while we'd ventured down onto the sand. Her mother had been at her side since Rose had woken up. She'd taken a room at the Seal Inn, and would not go back to her life in Aberdeen until the rehabilitation was finished. Rose's dad visited every week, while Peter – well, he came to see her once. Rose had written him a letter, which I didn't read, and he never came back.

I watched her profile, sweet, determined, as she stood and breathed in the sea air. And then her strength left her and I was there to catch her and hold her up against me.

'It's just a matter of time. We'll get there, Selena.'

Selena was our secret name, the name she'd wanted me to call her. And here we were, two twenty-somethings in love, battling every day for Rose's health. In between physiotherapy and medication, our days were made up of silly magazines that we laughed over, and Debussy, and a Mexican soap opera we'd discovered by chance and followed religiously every night from Rose's hospital bed. We'd recruited a few other patients, and every night, we would all sit and watch the adventures of Maricruz and Ramon in sun-drenched, drama-filled Mexico.

We tallied up Rose's progress in a notebook I'd bought in the Design Gallery, from *I sat up!* to *Rose held fork and spoon today!*

Wheelchair expedition all the way to the hospital coffee shop.

Mary is the best physio on this planet, leg raises x 10 today.

Saw pics of Balletnorth show and cried, then more exercise. Will do it!

OUTSIDE AT LAST!

On and on our notes went, some hers, some mine, some little notes from Rose's mum and dad: a chronicle of everyday success and backwards steps and fighting on.

But beyond this ordinary existence was the mystery of how Rose had come to me as Selena while her body lay in a hospital bed. Of how she'd met Mia when Mia was already gone, and was entrusted with delivering Mia's message, the message that would set me free. This girl, this beautiful, broken dancer whose body was asleep, had come looking for me to release me from my guilt.

And it had been Mia who had sent her. Mia who'd seen Rose in a dream before all this happened. Was this always meant to be? Were Rose and I supposed to be together; was this the final act of a plan we were unaware of – four people held together by a red thread, tying us to each other, killing two of us and throwing the other two together, creating a love unexpected?

Often I lay on Rose's bed and just watched her sleeping, willing her wasted muscles to get stronger, her thin frame to fill. I touched her hair as delicately as I'd touch butterfly wings; I looked into her green, green eyes. I laid my hand on her hip and felt like I'd known her forever. The girl lying in this bed, the dancing girl in the photographs. The girl sent to me so we could breathe life into each other once again.

Grace

I stood in my garden in the sun, with my brother's letter in my hand.

Dear Grace,

I'm sorry we couldn't meet up for Christmas last year. I'm so looking forward to seeing you in the summer. We're all well over here and I hope everything is well with you. I'm writing because I got a letter from Japan!

Do you remember little Tetsuko? Not so little any more. She must be about fifty or so. Here's a picture of her in her kimono. She's a priestess in a Shintoist temple, can you believe it? The same little girl who played hide-and-seek with us.

Charlie has been in touch with the family on and off, but they lost touch at some point. Anyway, Tetsuko says in her letter that she met someone from Seal there, at her temple . . . what are the chances? There must only be three hundred souls in that island of yours. She knew you were living there because Charlie told her. She said she gave this person a gift for you. Did you ever get it? Anyway. Off to the airport to get Liam home from uni. Take care.

James x

The world spun before my eyes. Tetsuko. The little girl with half-moon eyes and her hair in bunches. The priestess at the Shintoist temple.

Gureisu, grace. The *omamori* really was for me, just as Catriona had guessed in that mysterious way of hers. And for the other little *gureisu*, Susie, who'd come to me on an autumn morning to show me that motherhood had many forms. My cheeky, sweet, funny Susie, the grace of my heart; and Fergus, who'd knocked at my door once before until finally I'd had the courage to let him in.

I wasn't surprised when I realised the *omamori* was gone from my bedside table. I did look for it, but part of me knew I would not find it. It had done its job – and then some.

Because that night, the night of the talisman hanging from the tree and the strange warm wind, I'd sent my wish up to the sky.

And now here it was, my wish come true.

My little family, come to me to tell me:

That it's never too late.

Acknowledgements

My heartfelt thank you to:

Ariella Feiner and Molly Jamieson, Sherise Hobbs and Emily Gowers, everyone at United Agents and Headline, Ivana Fornera, Francesca Meinardi, Irene Zaino, Simona Sanfilippo, Doris Oancea, Romina Rinaudo, Angela and Cinzia Tarditi (with endless gratitude) and the people of Caravino. And of course, as ever, to Ross, Sorley and Luca Walker, for everything.

Special thanks to my little Luca, for your music and the joy it brought to our household! You make me a very proud Mum and your accordion is the best soundtrack I could have.

Read on for an enchanting extract from the first Seal novel . . .

Keep Me Safe

Available now from Headline Review

1

Snow in March

Anna

When Ava started inside me, sudden and surprising like snow in March, I didn't have time to ask myself the reasons for such a miracle. I was working too hard, worrying too hard. With all the practical problems and the morning sickness and trying to stay awake during my night shifts, I didn't have much time left to consider what was happening: a human being had taken up residence in my belly, and was growing, growing. Somebody with eyes and ears and hands and legs and a heart. And more; she was more than a body and its parts. A soul lived inside this body-in-the-making, a consciousness, a set of feelings and emotions and thoughts like sparks inside her tiny brain.

I fretted about how I'd look after a baby, with my shifts and little money and no family at hand to help, while the man who did this to me in the first place was lost in one crazy project or another. He was forever wheeling and dealing somewhere while I threw up and cried and surveyed the wards full of new mums, their babies beside them in plastic cots, not quite believing I would be one of them soon. I couldn't sleep, and when I did, I had strange dreams, dreams of water and the sea and grey waves swallowing me. And then Toby would caress my barely-there bump and promise me the world, promise our baby the world – I didn't believe him any more, of course, but I didn't want my child to grow up without a father, like me.

I knew she was a girl. And not just any girl – she was *Ava.* I loved her with an intensity that blew me away. Somehow, in the lottery of procreation, one I witnessed every day in my job, this baby, *this* baby and no other, among the millions of possible genetic combinations, had been given to me. An old rhyme came into my mind, one my Scottish grandmother used to sing:

Of all the babies who swam in the sea
Ava was the one for me . . .

While I was making beds, or fetching nappies for the midwives, or cleaning up mess, I was aware of her, like a constant song in the back of my mind. My belly grew, the fears grew, my love for her grew. In this city of eight million people, I thought as I contemplated the London skyline out of the staffroom window, there was now one more.

Months went by as my secret came into the light, my bump too big to hide. Ava talked to me in every way but words. *I know you, baby – I've known you forever,* I thought as I chose curtains for her nursery, and a Moses basket, and I dreamt of the day I'd hold her in my arms. *I love you, I've loved you forever*, I whispered to her as we lay in bed in the middle of the day, waiting for another exhausting night shift.

I lay half naked with a little thing breaking me from the inside, my body clamping onto itself over and over again. When she finally came out, after what seemed like days, I looked into her eyes, semi-blind and alien black, and I had the strangest thought: that I had fooled myself believing I knew her, this little soul that had sat inside me waiting, this creature I'd been a vessel for.

I didn't know her at all. I had no idea who she was.

I never told anyone about what came into my mind the moment she was born – about the way I didn't recognise her like I thought I would, and how that feeling of *of course, it was you all along* never happened for me. A sense of knowing the creature that has been inside you for nine months and finally getting to meet her – it wasn't like that. I didn't know her, I never had known her. She was somebody other from the little life I had imagined.

It would have been impossible to explain such a weird sensation. People don't talk about these things anyway, and your head is all over the place after you've given birth. You're bound to have strange thoughts.

I soon forgot all about it as Ava grew into herself and I grew into my new life, a life where it was Ava and Anna, our little family.

My daughter's eyes have lost their alienness and now she's fully here, fully herself. Now, I do know her. Ava Elizabeth Hart, six years old, happy and chatty and lively and fearless like I never was, so different from me and yet so much mine, a part of Toby and me and yet herself.

But when it all began, when Ava told me about a life she had without me, with people I didn't know – that day I thought again of the moment she was born. I thought of the moment they placed her gently in my arms, wrapped in a white blanket, my blood still encrusted in her hair, and she opened those otherworldly eyes and the first thing I thought was *I love you*, and the second was *Where were you before?*

2

All that remains

Anna

I always knew it would happen one day. I always knew Toby would leave us; I was even surprised he'd waited so long. Despite all my efforts, I had failed to keep this lopsided little family together.

I dreaded the day he'd go, not because of me – all my feelings for him had ebbed away a long time ago – but for Ava. She was so close to him, even if he kept letting her down in one way or another. She adored her father; whether or not he actually deserved to be adored was of no concern to a little child.

One winter afternoon, my child-minder, Sharon, phoned me at work to say that Toby had been to the house, stuffed some of his things in a suitcase, and left. I stood there with the phone against my ear, frozen. I could only imagine how it must have felt for Ava, sitting in tears and terror while her dad rushed around packing clothes. It was like a bolt from the blue for her; as for me, I'd played the scenario so many times in my head, I nearly had a sense of déjà vu.

Sharon told me that he'd left behind a note addressed

to me, and a distressed little girl sobbing her heart out. She said that before stepping out of the door he'd spoken to Ava, that he'd told her he was very sorry, but he was going somewhere far, far away, that we'd be better off without him; that he was a loser, that he'd tried but nothing had worked out for him.

He said all that *to his six-year-old daughter.*

Anger burnt scarlet through me as I put the phone down and ran to the ward sister to tell her I had to go home at once. I was a new nurse – I had gained my qualification at last, after years of menial jobs and studying at night while Ava slept – and I was working for an agency.

I hurried out into the freezing evening air; I jumped on a train, and then another, in a daze, tears not of regret but of fury swelling in my eyes. He'd hurt Ava. He'd done the one thing I could not forgive him for. After all the years I'd forced myself to be with him, so we could give Ava a family . . .

When I barged into the flat, Ava was on the sofa watching CBeebies, clutching Camilla, her favourite doll. Her eyes were puffy and red, but she wasn't crying any more. She was sucking her thumb, which was something I had been trying to help her grow out of. She looked very small and very lost.

'Ava, sweetheart . . .' I said as I sat beside her.

She didn't look at me, she didn't move.

'Ava . . .'

'She's been like this for over an hour. She hasn't said a word,' Sharon whispered, her kindly coffee-coloured face shadowed with worry. I felt my heart quickening and my hands tingling; the familiar signs of panic.

I wrapped my arms around my daughter. She let me hold her close, and leaned her head on my chest, still sucking her thumb. I stroked her long black hair and her face – milky skin and almond-shaped black eyes, maybe the heritage of an Asian ancestor we knew nothing about.

'Everything's fine. Mummy is here . . . Where's the note?' I asked Sharon in a low voice, not wanting to disentangle myself from Ava. Sharon seized a piece of paper, roughly folded in four, and handed it to me.

Dear Anna,

I'm so sorry. I've been nothing but bad news in your life. I'm off to Melbourne to stay with a mate for a bit, and then hopefully get a working visa. I explained everything to Ava, so she wouldn't get too upset . . .

I'm going to kill him, I thought.

. . . you deserve somebody to look after you properly. Ava deserves a proper father . . .

You're right on that one.

You and Ava are better off without me. Please remind Ava how much I love her.

Toby

And here's where you're wrong, Toby, I said to myself. Very, very wrong. *I* am better off without you; *Ava* isn't. You stupid, irresponsible, selfish man who couldn't hold down a job, who would spend thousands of pounds on a fancy car and then have no money left to buy food, who would feed Ava ice cream for lunch and dinner and then be aghast if she threw up, who was always too busy for the nursery run but found time for a daily catch-up with his friends – your daughter needs you. Not just someone to look after us, but her father.

But you left anyway.

'It'll be okay, baby,' I said into Ava's hair, squeezing her dimpled hand. I felt her letting out a small sigh, full of the grief and loss she didn't know how to express.

It was dark outside, and Ava still hadn't spoken. Dinnertime had come and gone, and she was sitting at the table with an array of untouched plates in front of her. Fish fingers and mash, a ham sandwich, a bowl of tomato soup. Nothing tempted her.

'Let's order pizza!' I said, trying to sound cheery, or even just normal. I was getting desperate.

'What do you say? Pizza?' I repeated, exhaustion squeezing the sides of my head until I felt nauseous. No reply. 'Please, Ava. You haven't eaten anything since breakfast.'

She just sat there looking at me with a blank expression, not saying a word.

*

I phoned the hospital and then the agency, and told them that my daughter was sick and I had to take a few days off. They weren't happy, but they grudgingly accepted my unexpected leave. Then I called Sharon and said I wouldn't need her for a while, but I would keep up with her wages, of course. Finally I phoned Toby's mother. I don't know why. It wasn't like I would get any sympathy or help. Whatever her son did – rack up thousands of pounds of debt, leave yet another job, get beaten up by someone he owed money to – she just found excuses for him, and cried, and said he was such an affectionate boy and it wasn't his fault if he was *a bit immature*.

'Did you know about this?'

'About Australia? Yes. He told me not to tell you until he was ready . . .'

'Well he told Ava. *Before telling me*. He told her he was going away and she was better off without him. Ava is six years old, for God's sake!'

'He's confused. He's just a confused boy with nobody to advise him properly,' she pleaded.

'He's not a boy, Gillian.'

Oh, all the things Gillian didn't know. Toby was very much a man, a man who ranted at me whenever things didn't go his way, who slammed doors, who always knew the right thing to say to make me feel I was worth nothing. But his mother didn't know any of this. She was never to know. It would break her heart, and one heart broken was more than enough.

'You know the way it is. They are always little boys to their mothers!' She laughed a foolish laugh. There wasn't even any point in being angry with her.

'Good to know that my daughter has a boy for a father,' I hissed.

A little silence, and then came her favourite mantra, her excuse for so much of what Toby did. 'He wasn't ready to be a father.'

As if it had been my fault. As if I'd planned it. I closed my eyes briefly, cursing the day I'd been taken in by his charm, his endless optimism. I was young, and I was alone and starved of affection after a cold, loveless childhood; I'd fallen for his promises.

'If he phones, Gillian, tell him we never want to see him again.'

'What? You can't stop him seeing his daughter!' she whined in a tremulous, how-can-you-be-so-heartless voice.

I put the phone down.

'Please, sweetheart. Maybe a cookie?' I tried again.

I'd made chocolate chip cookies, hoping that baking would channel my confusion a bit, and that they would tempt Ava into eating something.

Still no answer. She just looked at me with those dark eyes of hers, two pools of silent sadness in her white face.

I was ready for a long, long cry, but I couldn't do that in front of Ava. I gently led her into the bathroom and gave her a warm bath with bubbles, chatting to her in a low voice, though she never replied. Then I took her to her room, where I slipped her Little Miss Sunshine PJs on, dried her hair, and tucked her, Camilla and myself into her bed. We lay together, hypnotised by her magic lantern turning and turning, until we both fell asleep.

She didn't speak for three days.

Dawn rose on the fourth day of Ava's silence. I was lying on a mattress in her room, after another white night. Later I would take her to the doctor; I couldn't deny any more that something was terribly, terribly wrong. That something had broken inside her.

I propped myself up, resting my head on my hand. She slept on her back, her chest slowly rising and falling. Little Briar Rose, trapped in an evil spell. She was so beautiful, my daughter, and so small, so vulnerable. It broke my heart that I couldn't protect her from everything, anything that could harm or upset her. That I couldn't save her from this heartache, like I hadn't been protected or saved when I was a child. That I hadn't given her a better father, or, it turned out, a father at all – she would be fatherless, like I had been. Maybe I shouldn't have worked so hard all those years . . . Maybe all the nights I spent on my course books and all the times I was too exhausted to even speak had slowly corroded our family life. But I'd had no chance of an education, no chance to do anything for myself – I *had* to get my qualification. I had spent too many years watching the nurses doing their amazing job while I was stuck cleaning floors. I knew there was more in me; I knew I had more to give. And I did it for Ava too, to give her a better future. To give her the chances I'd never had.

Tears threatened to flood out of me again, and again I stopped them. During those three ghastly days, I had only cried once, when I was sure Ava was in deep sleep; I couldn't bear the idea of her seeing me crying, and alarming her even more than she had been already.

All of a sudden, she stirred. She jerked her head towards the wall and back again. A small whimper escaped her lips, and then another, as she tossed and turned. I sat on her bed and took her little body in my arms. She began to cry, harder and harder, and her sobs rose to the sky and wrecked my heart. And the worst thing was that she was crying with her eyes closed, like all that pain was coming from the depths of her, unbounded and unchecked, exploding after four days of silence and stillness.

'Shhhhh . . . Mummy's here . . .' Tears were falling down my cheeks too. I couldn't bear it. I couldn't bear to see my daughter in so much pain.

'Mummy!' she cried, and again those dreadful, dreadful sobs – the cries of someone abandoned, all alone in the world. I could feel what she was saying with those sobs – *I've been abandoned, I'm lost* – and I held her tight.

'I'm here, baby, I'm here with you,' I whispered in her ear.

Suddenly her whole body became tense and tight; she was rigid in my arms, just like she used to get as a toddler when she was throwing a tantrum. My heart bled. Then, at last, she relaxed. Her eyelashes, damp with sleep and tears, fluttered some more.

'Ava. Ava!' I called.

Finally she opened her eyes.

'Mummy,' she said in a whisper.

My heart soared. She was speaking again.

'Ava . . .'

'Mummy,' she repeated.

'I'm here . . .'

She blinked over and over again, studying my face. Then she looked straight at me as if she didn't recognise me, and I'll never forget the words that came out of her mouth. I'll never forget the moment when, as I held her in my arms, my face so close to hers that our noses nearly touched, she asked calmly and quietly: 'Where's my mum?'

Keep in touch with me

Daniela SACERDOTI

Sign up for my newsletter
www.danielasacerdoti.com

Become a fan on Facebook
OfficialDanielaSacerdoti

Follow me on Twitter
DaniSacerdoti

Con amore,
Daniela x

'Will satisfy even the most hopeless romantics. Her descriptions of the idyllic, wild isle are evocative and vivid'
Daily Express

'I was hooked from the beginning'
Alice Peterson

'The supernatural element gives the novel its edge'
Sunday Express S magazine

'I fell in love with this book'
Prima magazine

'Heartwarming and intriguing'
Dani Atkins